P9-CKA-403

GAINING GROUND

GAINING GROUND

The Renewal of America's Small Farms

J. TEVERE MacFADYEN

Holt, Rinehart and Winston • New York

Published by Holt, Rinehart and Winston,
383 Madison Avenue, New York, New York 10017.
Published simultaneously in Canada by Holt, Rinehart
and Winston of Canada, Limited.

Library of Congress Cataloging in Publication Data
MacFadyen, J. Tevere.
Gaining ground.
1. Farms, Small—United States. I. Title.
HD1476.U5M32 1984 338.1'0973 83-13003
ISBN 0-03-069563-5

First Edition
Designer: Helene Berinsky
Printed in the United States of America
1 3 5 7 9 10 8 6 4 2

Portions of this book have appeared in different
form in *Horticulture, Country Journal,* and
Orion Nature Quarterly.

ISBN 0-03-069563-5

To J.H.M. and M.E.E.M.

CONTENTS

ACKNOWLEDGMENTS

This is a book about people. Three years ago, when I set out to explore the changing condition of America's small family farms, I had thought it would be a book about politics, economics, and technology—a book about agriculture, in other words, in which people played supporting roles. I've learned a lot since then, and chief among my lessons has been the realization that the story of American agriculture is first and foremost a story of people.

Agriculture, I see now, is the most human profession. It exists in the relationship between people and the land, and the quality of that relationship is manifest in the character of our agriculture. In agriculture, as nowhere else, the effects of man on the environment, malignant or benign, are directly expressed. A reckless farmer armed with the latest agricultural technologies can swiftly lay waste to vast territories. A responsible farmer, on the other hand, equipped with simple tools and working on a small scale, can eventually restore even the most badly abused land to productivity. American agriculture since World War Two has tended to favor recklessness over responsibility. Laying waste, it turns out, requires very few people, and perhaps the most revealing and destructive feature of modern large-scale industrialized agriculture has been its emphasis on removing farmers from farms. Restoration, by contrast, requires people above all else—dedicated people committed to the arduous pursuit of incremental, sometimes almost imperceptible change. The future of American agriculture—the future of America, really—depends on such people, and in this book I have tried to tell a few of their stories.

I undertook this project secure in my belief that modern industrialized agriculture could not long survive, that its reliance on dwindling supplies of inexpensive capital and natural resources and its wanton destruction of the environment guaranteed its eventual extinction. I was confident, moreover, that cracks in the agribusiness façade already opened by shifting cultural and economic priorities would favor the development of smaller-scale, decentralized, more labor-intensive and regionally responsive agricultures. I still believe these things, but I am not so sanguine anymore about the prospects for positive change. There is a formidable momentum propelling modern conventional agriculture into the future, even as evidence of its failings accumulates. The odds against turning this tide often seem impossibly high. Anyone looking at the future of American agriculture will find ample cause for pessimism. The cause for optimism, such as it is, lies with the men and women who are the subjects of this book, and who are its heroes as well—the people who have devoted themselves to bringing about the necessary change.

I did not know when I began how long it would take me to collect their stories, nor how widely I would have to travel to find them, nor how difficult it would be to render for anyone who did not travel with me my impressions of what I saw and heard. I didn't know much of anything, in fact, and to the extent that my readers now are more enlightened than I was then, the credit must go to a host of generous people: Rob Aiken; Nancy Bailey; Lee Bellinghausen; Marty Bender; Barry Benepe; Wendell and Tanya Berry; Hank and Cecilia Bissell; Wesley Buchele; Paul Campbell; Jim and Carmine Cincotta; Martin Culik; Dick and Judy Dye; Ralph, Rita, Tom, Steve, and Pat Engelken; John Fleming; Julia Freedgood; Jennie Gerard; Philip Gerard; Dennis and Louise Gregg; Ralph Grossi; Dick Harwood; Caroline Herter; Randy Hoover-Dempsey; Wes, Dana, Scott, Laura, and Sarah Jackson; Lindsay Jones; Samuel Kaymen; Bud Kerr; Judy Krones; Ron Krupicka; Karen Lehman; Wm. Levine; Chuck Little; Gene and Carol Logsdon; Patrick Madden; Paul Maxwell; Bill Norris; Larry Orman; Walter Pickett; Don and Nita Polly; Bob Rodale; Marcy Roth; Elizabeth St. John; Gus Schumacher; Sam and Elizabeth Smith; Marty Strange; Bill and Ellen Straus; Bob and Anne Van Houten; George and Tammy Walker; Jane Weissman; Barry Werner; Edgar Weubben; and Gary Young. I owe an enormous debt to each of them, and to others I'm sure I've neglected to mention, for their time and expertise unselfishly dispensed, and in many cases as well for my care and comfort while I was on the road.

I am grateful, too, for the patience of my close friends, especially Jay Vogt and Gary Hirshberg, who time and again listened at length to my convoluted ideas and reliably set me straight. Mike Congdon, my agent, kept track of my comings and goings and saw to it that I earned my keep. Jack Macrae, my editor, lent the manuscript perspective, clarity, and order—qualities that would have been in sorrowfully short supply without his close attention.

Finally, and most fondly, were it not for my family, who seemed confident even when I was not, and for Julie Salestrom, whose unflagging care and counsel more than once restored the confidence I'd lost, this book would surely never have been written.

J. Tevere MacFadyen
Brooklyn, New York
Summer 1983

GAINING GROUND

PREFACE: TO MARKET

It is four hours before dawn on a weekday December morning. The Triborough Bridge is deserted. We have the Brooklyn-Queens Expressway mostly to ourselves. To westward, Manhattan's midtown cordillera of high-rise offices blazes bright as noon, but the city is as close to dormant now as it's ever going to get. An on-again, off-again freezing drizzle is temporarily off again, and at the corner of Coster Street and Lafayette Avenue in the Hunts Point section of the Bronx a dozen self-employed professional women emerge from darkened doorways to transact business in the pale pooled incandescence of streetlamps. Business tonight seems less than brisk. One or two half-heartedly approach our van, then turn away. "They're out there in every kind of weather," Carmine says as we wait for the light to go green. The women are attired in the standard seasonal uniform of the trade: spike heels and full-length fake fur coats. Under their furs they wear very little. During the summer, Carmine reports, they sometimes dispense with the coats. In a curious sense we're all here for the same reason. We've come on business. They're here to offer an assortment of personal services to the long-haul truckers who deliver trailer loads of fruits and vegetables to the New York City Terminal Market, three blocks east at the junction of Hunts Point and East Bay Avenues, whence most of the city's supply of fresh produce is distributed. Carmine is my greengrocer. We're here to go to market.

Carmine likes to get to market early, before midnight, as the action is just beginning. He makes this trip twice weekly, oftener some weeks, leaving his Brooklyn apartment at around ten to exchange his tiny Fiat for a blue Ford van, driving twenty minutes or so north to the Bronx, spending perhaps three hours at the market. Then he returns to the store, transfers his purchases into the walk-in cooler there, retrieves his car, and continues home. If everything goes smoothly, Carmine can expect to be in bed by three. At three o'clock in the morning the New York City Terminal Market (Hunts Point) is still accelerating. Between three and six is when the bulk of the deliveries come in, big straight trailers and pigs—trailers that for some portion of their journey have ridden piggyback on railroad flatcars—packed to the gills with perishables. The market then is dizzy with backing and filling. The docks swarm with lumpers, contract laborers who off-load the trucks and play bumper-cars with their forklifts. Drivers do not generally shut off their rigs while the trailers are being emptied, so there is an incessant bass-baritone chorus of idling engines. The atmosphere is redolent of diesel fuel and decomposing vegetables.

The Hunts Point terminal market comprises an archipelago of broad low islands populated by commission merchants, the middlemen—and very few women—who buy produce from packers and shippers and sell it to retailers, who sell it again to me and you. The islands' interiors are given over to cavernous temperature-controlled storage facilities. Most of the trading takes place outside on the platforms, under cover but open to the elements, where salesmen set up towering pyramids of produce, insult one another, and cut deals with a steady stream of buyers. For a vegetable, Hunts Point initiates the last leg of a long voyage that begins in the field and ends at the dinner table. It is a greengrocery of nearly inconceivable proportions, and yet it is also strangely ephemeral, a kind of performance art. Everything here tonight will be gone two nights hence. The market is not so much a place as an experience. At Hunts Point you can glean information on the weather three thousand miles away, the availability of illegal migrant labor, the value of the dollar overseas, what will be on special next week. Watching what happens here in the dead of night yields some insight into the vulnerability and the incredible complexity of something we routinely take for granted: our food system. Coming to market can teach you a bit about how that system works—not much perhaps, but enough to send you away convinced that the fact that it works at all is close to miraculous.

The store where I buy most of my groceries is slightly smaller than the detergent display at a typical suburban shopping mall. It is sandwiched between a drycleaner's and a bodega in a part of town where until recently there was more Italian spoken than English. It's called Jim & Andy's. Carmine is Jim's son. Jim perpetually threatens to retire, but that isn't a probability I'd bet much on. (Andy, who worked for Jim when the store first opened, has long since succeeded to his own establishment, a salumeria highly regarded by local savants. His name lingers, as it will undoubtedly linger forever.) When Carmine was a boy his father wheeled a pushcart through the streets of south Brooklyn, peddling fresh fruits and vegetables. Eventually he staked out a particularly profitable claim, and when a nearby storefront became available he took the plunge and rented permanent quarters. By eventually I mean something on the order of decades. "That was a big step," Carmine says. "Moving indoors. My father still talks about how he can go back out on the street again and peddle if things ever get too tough."

Jim sent his kids to college, and all save Carmine drifted away from the family business. Jim & Andy's is a greengrocery of the old-fashioned sort that's fast becoming a rarity in America. Fruit and produce, the sign says, and fruit and produce is what it sells. The store is a thriving throwback to a time in the not too distant past when bread came from the bakery, meat and poultry from the butcher, fish from the fishmonger, and butter and eggs from the creamery. The small grocery, like the small farm, has been disenfranchised by contemporary technologies and economics and caught in a crossfire of rapidly changing lifestyles and aspirations. Its demands are many and its rewards chiefly nonmonetary. The children of grocers today are far more likely to become electrical engineers than they are to inherit their fathers' aprons.

Upon graduating from the City College of New York, Carmine took a job as a junior executive at a Park Avenue corporation. There he acquired a fondness for Lacoste shirts and Brooks Brothers oxford-cloth boxer shorts, but he chafed at the bureaucratic etiquette and he was incurably bored. He bailed out before long to join forces with his father, and he has subsequently found that he likes the life of a greengrocer. He enjoys the freedom, the absence of routine, and he relishes his stock in trade. "I'm interested in food," he told me one night on our way to Hunts Point, "professionally, of course. I eat out a lot. I've been to most of the best restaurants in the city, to Lutece, Pavillon, Four Seasons." With his four-star meals this grocer from Brooklyn drinks vintage wines, and he savors fine cigars afterward. Every year in September when the store closes for a week's vacation Carmine retreats to a cabin on Mount Desert Island off the coast of Maine, where he consorts with the local fishermen and eats his fill of lobster. Whenever Jim finally does decide to step down, Carmine will be ready and waiting. He has already begun negotiating to buy the building that houses his store.

Carmine's shopping list tonight is fairly typical. He wants some staples: several varieties of apples, navel oranges, avocados, iceberg lettuce, yellow squash and zucchini, cauliflower, head broccoli. For his traditional clientele he hopes to find rapini, the loose Italian broccoli, Bosc pears, sweet red peppers, and reasonably priced artichokes. For food-conscious young WASPs like myself who have begun to infiltrate the neighborhood he will buy Boston and red leaf lettuces, shallots, honeydew melons. For a customer who is a commercial caterer he will track down expensive exotica: arrugula, witloof, *mâche*, radicchio, albino asparagus. Indulging himself, he will pay astronomical prices for fresh-cut herbs: oregano, basil, tarragon—"I can't charge enough to make any money on them, but I just like knowing they're in the store." He'll keep his eyes open, too, for loss leaders: mushrooms he can hawk off the hood of his father's car at three dollars for a three-pound basket, carrots he can afford to let go at three pounds for a dollar. He is not immune to impulse shopping. If he sees something he likes he'll buy it.

We insert the van between two trucks parked at the loading dock outside Country Wide Produce, our customary first stop. The commission merchants at the market are known as houses, and Country Wide is Carmine's favored house. He will fill half his order there. For the balance he will visit a half dozen other houses. Every house is different. Some, like Country Wide, offer a full line of produce. Some specialize, in bananas, for instance, or brussels sprouts, garlic, or nuts. Some houses deal solely with food service purveyors who serve institutional kitchens: hospitals, hotels, schools. Some supply primarily people like Carmine—proprietors of small independent groceries. New York is unusual for the number of such enterprises it supports, and thus for the relative health of its terminal markets. The neighborhood grocery is a convention that never really expired in this city, and it has lately been resuscitated by a wave of Korean immigrants who, like the Italians before them, come equipped with large families willing to work endless hours at the store. Italians have long been New York's greengrocers, but nowadays when an Italian grocery closes, a Korean market will nine times out of ten appear in its stead. There are three already within a few blocks of Jim & Andy's. If Carmine admitted to having any competition at all it would come not from supermarkets but from the Koreans.

In many middle-sized American cities, however, the retail marketing of food is increasingly dominated by outlets of a single supermarket chain. The larger and more powerful chains buy direct from packers, or even direct from growers. They do their own warehousing and distribution, eliminating any need for a commission house. In these communities the terminal markets gradually atrophy. Competition among wholesale suppliers slackens. The number of commission merchants declines. Small independent grocers, who rely on the terminal markets, no longer enjoy the same breadth of cost or quality as they once did. They find themselves having to pay more for what they buy and charge less for what they sell, so as to match the discount pricing of the chain stores. The chains can discount because they buy and sell in huge quantities, leading them to deal more and more exclusively with the few high-volume growers and packers who can guarantee big deliveries of crops grown on contract for a predetermined price. Small farmers and local growers lose a local market for their produce, and control of the food system concentrates into fewer and fewer hands.

The implications of this concentration are not foremost among Carmine's immediate concerns. At the moment he's more interested in the price of *mâche* (or corn salad), a leafy green cultivated in and exported from Belgium, which he considers exorbitant. It's the last crate in the house, slightly lassitudinous, and Carmine anticipates a bargain. A bargain does not seem to be forthcoming.

"C'mon," Carmine protests. "You can't charge me that much for this! Look at it! You know I won't pay that."

"You will if you want to leave with it." We are at the house of H. Schnell & Co., whose sales staff consists of elderly Jewish gentlemen in faded brown smocks.

"Look at it!"

The *mâche* looks not too bad, maybe a bit limp, maybe yellower than it ought to. To me Carmine confides whispered strategy. "It's okay, nothing great but not shit. I want him to think I think it's shit, though."

"There's nothing wrong with that *mâche*. It's perfect stuff." The salesman is scrupulously polite but inflexible. "D'ya want it or not?"

"Not at that price I don't."

"D'ya want it?"

"C'mon!"

In the end Carmine ekes out a slim saving, saving face more than anything else. We leave with the *mâche*, and with a Styrofoam carton of white asparagus as well. The asparagus originated in Chile. It came to New York aboard a jet freighter belonging to the Chilean national airline. The *mâche* flew KLM. By the time it reached Hunts Point the asparagus had accumulated a value of better than five dollars a pound, wholesale. We abstain from fresh Greek figs and burlap bags full of Italian chestnuts, but Carmine wavers and then succumbs to the temptation of a flat of New Zealand raspberries. Three dollars the half-pint. At houses where he does a lot of business Carmine has established credit, but for the most part he pays as he goes. He carries in his pants pocket a wad of bills thicker than a pack of cigarettes. Along Bruckner Boulevard, by which he must traverse a stretch of the south Bronx en route to Hunts Point, armed men not infrequently relieve the drivers of trucks waiting at traffic signals of substantial sums in cash. Carmine does not stop for a lot of lights.

We proceed along the platform in search of Anjou pears—Bartletts, Carmine complains, slip too swiftly from unripe to rotten—red peppers, and cauliflower. Carmine prefers cello flower, California-grown and shipped already wrapped. (Once, earlier in the fall, I watched him scour the market for cello flower when the docks were stacked with wirebound boxes of locally grown cauliflower from Long Island. "Local flower is shit," Carmine ruled. It wasn't. It was in fact very nice. It was also half the price. Carmine left with local flower.) Now he says he's ready to give up his hunt for inexpensive artichokes. There are plenty of chokes in the market, but their price is high and holding. Carmine believes it will drop, so he wants to wait before buying. He consults his list as we move down the dock, noting prices asked and paid. At each house where we pause we enter into the same exchange. Carmine reflects discourteously on the salesman's parentage. The salesman laments Carmine's prematurely arrested cognitive development. Carmine defames the salesman's reputation as a judge of good produce; the salesman defames Carmine's. Money is discussed. Should a deal eventually be consummated the salesman writes up an order card and gives it to a stock boy to be filled. Small orders we take with us or fetch when we've finished shopping. Larger quantities are delivered by a forklift to the van.

Loading the van is my responsibility. If everything is to fit inside, it will have to be stowed Bristol fashion, packed in tight and solid to prevent the cargo from shifting in transit. The weight of the load must be evenly distributed, so that the overburdened vehicle will not wander about the roadway of its own volition. Citrus cartons, reliably rectangular, are admirably suited to successful loading; tall and narrow-bottomed baskets of Florida green beans somewhat less so. Certain items, owing to their tender nature, obviously want to perch atop the heap. The intercontinental raspberries will ride up front with us, guarded against possible mishap on my lap. Loading the van is a precise skill. I am a rank amateur. I bring to my assignment common sense and a desire to please, which taken together do not apparently equal skilled precision. Carmine goes off to settle accounts and leaves me in charge of loading. When he returns I obediently remove from the van the greater part of what I've just finished putting in, and then he instructs me on how to do the job correctly. This has happened more times than I care to remember.

Driving back to Brooklyn, Carmine discourses on the meteoric rise of the Korean greengrocery. The Koreans, he says, push up the price of produce at market by their disinclination to haggle. "Don't buy it then," salesmen have been heard to tell Carmine. "I'll sell it to a Korean." Carmine haggles because he knows he will be haggled with in turn by his customers, especially those customers who are Italian, black-clad and grandmaternal. He haggles, too, for the love of haggling. It's a point of honor. The Koreans who come to market seldom haggle. They pay the going rate, then tack on a percentage at retail for their profit. They can get away with this, Carmine avers, because they draw a different clientele. In a neighborhood caught in the throes of gentrification, the Koreans attract the gentry: young professionals pressed for time, hurrying home late. These newcomers unflinchingly pay such steep tabs in part at least because they have no choice. At that hour the Koreans operate the only game in town. Korean groceries never seem to be closed. It's also true, as Carmine points out, that even exorbitant prices do not add up to outrage if you're buying only a little. The gentry eat scanty. They buy for one, maybe for two. They want an onion and a dozen mushrooms. Italians, on the other hand, particularly Italian families, like to eat hearty. They'll close the store early before they'd miss a meal. By the time the attenuated gentry pass Jim & Andy's shuttered storefront on their way to patronize the Koreans, Jim is already digesting his dinner. One of the things that initially endeared me to Carmine and his father was my manifestly healthy appetite. "Unlike some of the people who come in here now," says Carmine. Not for me one lonely lettuce and an Idaho potato. When I go to Jim & Andy's I carry a capacious canvas bag. I depart with it filled.

The mechanism by which I eat as well as I do is wondrous and delicate. When the van has been unloaded and the walk-in re-stocked Carmine awards me an honorable discharge and sends me home carrying a shallow tray of fragile fruit picked three days earlier and eight time zones away. The wonder of this ought to be self-evident, but what may be more remarkable is the fact that ripe raspberries in December no longer seem especially noteworthy. Along with the passing of the neighborhood butcher and greengrocer we have taken in stride the passing of seasonal foods. As the production and distribution of food shifted from a regional to a national and then an international arena, questions of season lost a lot of their relevance. Everything is always in season somewhere.

Granted, midwinter raspberries may be a luxury too rich for most people's blood, but we hardly think twice anymore about oranges, which for our grandparents were a special Christmas treat enhanced by months of anticipation. In the span of not quite two generations we have come to assume a year-round abundance of fresh produce as almost a part of our birthright. Taken alone, this presumption would probably have no great significance, but it is indicative of something much larger. Our diets, once dictated largely by climate, are constrained now mainly by the limits to our disposable incomes. Over the past half-century the American food system has been fundamentally transformed. That we have derived innumerable benefits from this transformation is plentifully apparent, but the transformation's costs, inconspicuous at first, are becoming more and more obvious. What would once have been unimaginable—polishing off a bowl of New Zealand raspberries for breakfast in Brooklyn, for example, or draining a tumbler of Wisconsin milk at the counter of an Arizona diner—has quickly become commonplace. At the same time, though, what had been decentralized and inherently resilient has evolved into something monolithic and dangerously brittle.

The character of the change that's overtaken our agriculture, and some of its consequences, can be captured in part in a carrot: a faintly bitter-tasting, average-sized carrot, hard and dry and colored an anemic yellow-orange. A thoroughly representative supermarket carrot, in other words, that I brought home with me one early summer morning from Jim & Andy's in a plastic bag with six others just like it. They did not promise to be surpassingly tasty. I bought them because they were the only carrots in the store.

I had moved back to New York the previous winter after living awhile in the country, in a part of New England blessed by a lucky confluence of culture, climate, and topography with a still flourishing profusion of small family farms. The farmers were mostly Polish, first- or second-generation immigrants, and they were mostly well along in years. They raised some things in quantity for wholesale to the Boston terminal market—onions and potatoes, winter squash and cabbages—but they grew truck crops as well, and provided an assortment of fresh vegetables for local consumption. Every farm had a roadside stand, or so it seemed, manned more often than not by someone too old or infirm to work in the fields. I got into the habit of going from one to another, buying something from each, as much for the pleasure of their softly accented conversation as because Kostek had the better broccoli or Syznal the best corn. In this manner I was taught to distinguish a good carrot from a merely passable one, and I learned enough to know as I forked over my money at Jim and Andy's that carrots far superior to the ones I held in my hand would be harvested soon not an hour's drive from where I stood. I felt sufficiently secure in this limited expertise to remark, with the smug air of an insider, "Won't be long before we get decent carrots again. Locally grown."

Carmine never even looked up.

"Nah," he replied. "Can't get local carrots anymore. Carrots all come from California."

No local carrots? Where was I going to get a decent carrot? More to the point, I wondered as I pocketed my change how long I would be able to afford these pale bi-coastal facsimiles. Living among farms had altered my perspective. I'd become accustomed to paying for vegetables without having to subsidize their travel expenses as well. It costs more today to ship a carrot from California to New York than it does to grow it in the first place. New Yorkers pay fifteen cents on the pound for vegetable transportation alone, and New York, with the rest of the Northeast, currently imports fully three-quarters of what it eats. Most of the fruits and vegetables consumed here are produced thousands of miles away, in Florida or California or the southwest. They are the products of an extraordinary new agriculture: grown on boundless expanses of flat arid land, tended by fleets of huge machines, picked by armies of laborers, packed and shipped before they ripen. This is an agriculture that has made possible an unprecedented centralization of production. It is the agriculture that has rendered scattered small farms like Kostek's and Syznal's more or less obsolete. It is as well, or was until recently, an agriculture capable of producing extraordinary profits. But the future of that profitability—and in a larger sense the continued viability of what has come to be thought of as conventional American agriculture as a whole—is very much in doubt. Because while it is an agriculture whose productivity has often seemed almost magical, the trick turns on an increasingly costly, difficult, and destructive petrochemical sleight-of-hand.

Not long afterward I began shopping at Greenmarket, the urban equivalent of a roadside stand. Greenmarket is a triumphant anomaly: a rural farmers' market come to town. Begun in 1976 with seven farmers assembled on a vacant midtown lot, it had grown in six years into a network of markets throughout New York, operating six days a week at sixteen sites distributed from the foot of the World Trade Center north to Harlem and on into suburban Westchester County. At the biggest of the markets, held on Saturdays in lower Manhattan's Union Square, four dozen farmers work hand over fist to dispense some forty thousand dollars' worth of locally grown produce in the course of a ten-hour day to more than twelve thousand regular customers. Twice weekly from June to December the growers drive their trucks into the city from farms in the surrounding countryside to occupy Union Square's western flank, and drifts of fresh vegetables temporarily displace dozing junkies. At Greenmarket I found satisfactory carrots, exceptional carrots in fact. I found oak leaf lettuce and six varieties of sweet corn, burgundy beans and white icicle radishes, kohlrabi and purple kale and bushel baskets of fragrant mushrooms. On Saturdays in Union Square I found wildflower honey, homemade cheeses and smoked meats, twin-yoked eggs and fresh-killed chickens, and if I arrived early enough, bright bouquets of cut flowers.

I suffered an addiction. I let my work slide. I regretted weekend invitations in deference to my ritual Saturday pilgrimage. At Greenmarket I found something strongly reminiscent of the farms I'd known in Massachusetts. I found myself lingering longer each week, and as I did I was struck by the contrast between this sort of agriculture and the agriculture exemplified by Hunts Point. The farmers at Greenmarket were precisely the kind who were supposed to have been passed by by the parade of agricultural progress, and yet here they were plainly thriving, while the agriculture that had been heralded as their replacement—the miraculous new agriculture responsible for Carmine's carrots—is by all accounts in desperate straits.

Cause and effect in contemporary agriculture have gotten strangely braided. Is the damage inflicted by insects newly immune to the latest insecticides the cause for intensive pesticide applications, or in a sense their effect? Densely compacted soils, the legacy of heavy and powerful farm equipment, demand the use of heavier and more powerful equipment, which further compacts the soil. Chronic overproduction of major feed grains depresses grain prices, causing farmers to increase production so as to sell enough to break even. American agriculture, seen from afar, might seem to be the very model of Jeffersonian democratic capitalism: a farmer buys seed and plants a crop; the crop grows; the farmer harvests what's grown, then takes it to market and sells it. This is the essence of free enterprise, supply and demand in action.

Close up, with the romantic veneer peeled back, things look considerably more complicated. Ask a farmer why he doesn't plant a winter cover crop to hold precious topsoil on his hilly land and you'll receive in return a dissertation on the economics of production and international trade. Wonder aloud about the strained relationship between the price of pig feed and the price of pork, and you can anticipate a lengthy discussion of tax policy and vertical integration in the meat industry. What actually takes place down on the modern-day farm is less an archetype of free enterprise than an object lesson in how far a fellow can stray from the path of righteousness and still be thought a faithful parishioner.

The modern farmer buys seed (corn, let's say, more often than not from a seed company that is the wholly owned subsidiary of a multinational conglomerate) and plants a crop (the extent of which will be determined by his participation in any one of a bewildering array of government subsidy and set-aside programs); the crop grows (or doesn't grow, depending on whether or not the farmer can afford to irrigate his land, on how much he's willing or able to spend on chemical fertilizers and pesticides, and of course on the weather); the farmer harvests his crop (with the assistance of a large and exceedingly expensive piece of equipment designed solely for that purpose and trundled out of the tractor shed for two weeks of every year, an investment whose cost can only be justified by its use on vast tracts of land and its not inconsiderable merits as a tax write-off), then takes it to market (or more likely to a local grain elevator, where his corn will be stored for a fee while he waits to see what transpires on the floor of the Chicago Board of Trade) and sells it (sells it, that is, only if the market price should happen to surpass the floor price set by government subsidies; otherwise he'll release his corn to the government and accept the subsidy price instead).

If this claustrophobic scenario does not sound appropriately bucolic, consider for a moment the complaint of one Cy Carpenter, president of the Minnesota Farmers Union, who testified in 1982 before a regional hearing of the House Committee on Banking and Finance in Minneapolis. "The farmer has been pushed into a place where his biggest single cost today isn't labor," Carpenter informed the Congressmen. "It's capital: the cost of getting money." If what Mr. Carpenter says is true—and there is every indication that it is—it suggests that the venerable self-reliant Jeffersonian ideal has been so altered over the years as to have become practically unrecognizable.

The effects of this change are especially acute in the Middle West. New England, where the myth of the family farm is probably most deeply ingrained, was long ago left in the wake of what the poet and agricultural critic Wendell Berry calls "a curious set of assumptions . . . about 'progress.' If you could get into a profession, it was assumed, then of course you must not be a farmer. If you could farm more profitably in the Corn Belt than on the mountainsides of New England, then the mountainsides of New England must not be farmed."

As the focus of agricultural attention shifted west, agriculture became peripheral rather than central to New England's economy. The farms that remained have stayed relatively small, partly in deference to topographical reality and partly because there has been no significant pressure on them not to. The firestorm of agricultural modernization and expansion that has swept across the Farm Belt struck the northeast only a glancing blow. In the southwest, by contrast, large-scale agriculture prevails. Big farms are consistent with a heritage harking back at least as far as the Spanish colonial latifundios.The landscape of the region, being infinitely flat and arid, is not only more accommodating to agricultural high technology than the patchwork sidehills of New England but to some extent demands it, in the form of sophisticated irrigation systems. If the Northeast in its studied recalcitrance has proved a poor client for the agribusiness formula of capitalization, mechanization, and purported efficiency, the Southwest has become its standard-bearer.

So the battle has been waged mostly over the middle ground, especially the fecund and well-watered Corn Belt, ranging west from western Pennsylvania through Ohio, Indiana, Illinois, Missouri, and Iowa, into eastern Nebraska and Kansas. These are the states that farmers built, cultivated, as their residents are fond of saying, from fencerow to fencerow, where agriculture is now and ever has been the economic mainstay, and where the small family farm is a tradition increasingly challenged by an ascendant new order. That part of the United States which folks from the East and West Coasts tend to diminish with the rubric "Midwestern" is unarguably the premier assemblage of agricultural real estate in the world. When the pioneers abandoned the rocky northeast and pushed west into the prairies and plains they found no reason to regret their decision. The terrain they settled is unafflicted by mountains or deserts. The rain falls often enough to keep things moist and the sun can generally be counted on to put in regular appearances. The soil is almost sinfully rich. Three-quarters of the region's cropland is overspread with what the United States Department of Agriculture (U.S.D.A.) classifies as soil "suitable for continuous cultivation." Of America's "prime farmland"—that select acreage deemed best when slope, soil type, and prevailing weather patterns are weighed against one another—the five Corn Belt states claim fully twenty percent. A little of such land goes a long way, and so has a lot, providing prosperity as its principal crop. Americans are as well fed as they are thanks in no small measure to geographical good fortune. If Iowa, Illinois, and Nebraska had been plunked down in Albania instead, we would not be selling grain to the Russians; they would be selling it to us.

It is lovely country, more scenic and more varied than its coastal detractors will admit. Much of the Corn Belt is more or less flat, it's true, but quite a lot of the land is gathered in soft rolls and folds. If travelers passing through on an interstate highway can't tell one place from another, residents can, and they are just as capable of regional chauvinism as people from anywhere else. I met a woman in central Kansas, where the word "flat" begins to achieve real resonance, who complained of the homesickness she'd felt while attending college in eastern Iowa. Her malaise came on strongest at dawn or dusk, when her view of the sun on its way up or down was obscured by gently upthrust hills. "I like it here where you can *see*," she said. "You can't really see anything there." What is most striking about the Midwestern landscape is the degree to which it has been domesticated. It is the environmental equivalent of a Holstein cow. There are woods in the Corn Belt, but no forests—there is no room for forests between the fields. One estimate has it that ninety-five percent of Iowa is under cultivation.

The Farm Belt does not look at all like a battlefield, but there is a war under way there. It is a war like the one fought in Vietnam, not merely for territory but for the hearts and minds of a people. What is being contested is the future of American agriculture, and some of the crucial battles are being fought on fertile fields handed down from parents and grandparents, on farms bought for two hundred dollars an acre and put up for sale at two thousand. It is in the Midwest that modern agriculture must succeed or fail, where the old image of decentralized, locally responsive small farms must make its stand against the new vision of corporate agribusiness. No matter what happens anywhere else, if the small family farm cannot survive in the Farm Belt, it cannot be said to have survived.

WHAT WENT WRONG

The transformation of the American food system developed during an era of cheap and abundant energy, and it was propelled by ample reserves of inexpensive capital. Farming and food processing have been hit especially hard by the advent of tight money and high petrochemical bills. One of the new agriculture's central premises has always been that bigger is not only better but cheaper, that mechanization costs less than labor, and that the larger an operation grows the greater that advantage will become. Events of the 1970s disproved this equation. It was assumed all along, for instance, that the savings realized from large-scale centralized production would more than outweigh the added transportation costs that centralization entailed. But the cost of transportation has soared past anyone's wildest estimates. So have the costs of pesticides and fertilizers and the whole chemical gamut demanded by modern monoculture farming, even as the share of all farm inputs claimed by agricultural chemicals has escalated in twenty-five years from three to sixteen percent. The price of fuel for farm equipment has risen only slightly faster than the price of ever larger and more powerful implements needed to till the densely compacted soil of county-sized fields. Since 1967 the amount of fuel used on a typical American farm and the average horsepower of a tractor have both doubled. Over the same period there has been a fourfold hike in the price of diesel fuel. With the cost of everything going up so fast around him, the poor farmer—or more accurately, the poor agribusinessman—has had to dip deep into the treacherous realm of rented cash, and the cost which for farmers has seemed to be rising fastest is the cost of borrowing. Interest rates for agricultural loans in 1980 were six times what they'd been fifteen years earlier. Agricultural indebtedness, meanwhile, now runs to ten times earnings. It has tripled in the past decade. Total United States farm debt has left the $200 billion mark far behind, and the curve of its continuing climb is very nearly vertical.

The economics alone are dismal enough, but what's markedly more worrisome is a swelling biological deficit. A second assumption on which the new agriculture has been predicated is that any and all potential environmental impediments to either its implementation or its sustainability could be technologically overcome. If growing a crop too many years in a row depleted a field's fertility, supplemental nutrients could be provided with chemical fertilizers. If planting the same varieties year after year paved the way for occupying armies of noxious weeds or infestations of omnivorous bugs, their advance could be halted with herbicides or insecticides. If plants or animals proved inconveniently maladapted to innovative production techniques, they could be genetically redesigned. Dry lands could be irrigated and wet ones drained. Vegetables picked green for easier shipping could be artificially ripened on their way to market. The new agriculture is founded on arrogance: a belief that biological problems must inevitably have technological solutions.

This has turned out not to be true. Increased soil salinity, to cite just one example, is heavy irrigation's bitter revenge. Large sections of southwestern cropland have already had to be taken out of production because horticultural researchers have found nothing commercially useful that will grow in saline sand. And even when it works, all this technology costs a lot of money. Cash production expenses as a percentage of farm income have expanded apace with the technological revolution in agriculture. On the largest and most up-to-date operations, purchased inputs now skim nearly ninety cents from every dollar earned. This too has had biological consequences. Just to keep up the payments, farmers have had to push land and livestock up to and beyond their biological limits, with predictably devastating results. Fifty years after the Dust Bowl, topsoil erosion is now worse than it has ever been. On particularly susceptible soils, such as some in the hills of eastern Washington's wheat belt, annual losses of one hundred fifty tons per acre are not uncommon. The Soil Conservation Service defines as "tolerable" topsoil erosion of no more than five tons per acre per year. Agricultural chemicals poured on to spur production are prime contributors to rural water pollution. In much of the West there is irrefutable evidence that finite underground aquifers are rapidly being sucked dry by nonstop irrigation. Worst of all, the magical talent of agricultural science for producing perpetually higher yields through technological intervention seems finally to have been exhausted. In real terms the fabled productivity of American agriculture has peaked, and it may actually have begun to decline.

The rise and imminent fall of modern American agriculture are separated by an astoundingly brief interval. When Carmine's father first began peddling produce from his south Brooklyn pushcart, a considerable portion of what he sold was still grown on comparatively small family-owned and -operated farms located within a few hours of the city. His carrots then most likely came from Orange County, New York, where growers of root crops are graced with fine, permeable, silty black mucklands perfectly matched to a carrot's preferences, or from south-central New Jersey, which not for nothing was nicknamed the Garden State. They were grown on farms very much like those represented at Greenmarket: old-style truck farms which at that time still supplied nearly all the fresh produce for markets in nearby cities and towns. They were raised by diversified farmers who, while they made most of their money from vegetables, probably padded that seasonal income with earnings from a small dairy herd or a flock of broilers or laying hens.

Jim's carrots were the products of what for lack of a better term might be called the old agriculture: conserving, labor intensive, locally responsive, flexible by design and of necessity thrifty. These were the dominant qualities of American agriculture until well after the close of World War Two. Taken together they form the conceptual outlines of a model after which the typical farm of the day was almost without exception fashioned. The specific crop and enterprise mix was subject to regional interpretation, of course. Milk might contribute the bulk of a Vermonter's income, for example, while cattle or hogs served as the mainstay in Iowa, or cotton and peanuts in Georgia, but two ruling principles inevitably obtained: the farms were relatively small, at least by inflated contemporary standards, and they were structurally heterogeneous. A farm, practically by definition, had to be compact enough to be intimately attended and effectively managed by a single farmer, and to be kept free of an undue dependence on hired help. Limits to its growth were likewise imposed by the physical characteristics of the land to be farmed and the technology available for farming it, and by the peculiarities of the market being served. There was only so much of any one commodity that a geographically limited population could absorb, so variety took the place of volume, and self-reliance substituted for scarce cash. Bigness being out of the question, farmers instead pursued a sort of broadness. They sought stability through diversity. The highest aspiration of such farmers was an elusive steady state in which the foreseeable but unpredictable vicissitudes of weather and market would offset one another to yield a measure of security. Not many farms ever entered this privileged preserve, but those that did established a benchmark for all agriculture. The best examples of the old agriculture—and any that remain in business today must be counted among that elect—are finely tooled and well-balanced operations. Their various enterprises function together in smooth synchrony, like the lubricated mechanism of an expensive watch. They manage the same kind of trompe l'oeil as a symphony orchestra: making something incredibly complicated seem simple.

Carmine's carrots are by contrast exemplary products of the new agriculture. They come from California—some from Arizona and Texas too, a few perhaps from Michigan or Canada, and despite his denials he might now and again stock a New York-grown carrot, but the majority by far are natives of The Golden State: "Mr. California" and "Chef Carote," "Mark O Merit" and "Look Mom!," "Peter Rabbit," "Bugs Bunny," "Bunny Munch" and "Bunny Luv." Most of the carrots Carmine sells—

along with forty percent of all the fresh produce and more than half of the carrots grown commercially in the United States today—hail from somewhere in California's great Central Valley. It's an extended chain of valleys, really, strung end to end along the state's mountain spine. The Central Valley extends eight hundred miles from the Mexican border toward Oregon on an axis tilted just west of due north, bounded on one edge by the Sierra Nevada and by the Coast Ranges on the other, fifty to a hundred miles across.

The Central Valley is essentially a desert, but still it has quite a lot to say for itself agriculturally. Its landscape is unvaryingly level and flat, nicely meeting the requirements of enormous planting and harvesting machines that lend themselves very little to turning around and even less to stopping. The Valley's climate is dependably uniform, with year-round temperatures ranging upward from warm to hot, facilitating the continuous and seasonless production to which we consumers have become so accustomed. Its soil is reasonably fertile and unencumbered by rocks or impenetrable layers of clay. Even the Valley's most conspicuous liability—an average rainfall of less than ten inches annually—actually works in its favor. Since virtually all the moisture for growing crops must be supplied through irrigation, the amount of water delivered and the locations to which it flows can be strictly controlled. Control is what the Central Valley is all about. Above all else the Valley is predictable, a guaranteed sure thing, which is precisely what makes it so attractive to practitioners of the new agriculture.

Central Valley vegetable production may be the quintessential expression of modern agriculture's methods and goals. Until fairly recently vegetables were considered the small farmer's specialty, because smaller operations seemed inherently better equipped to respond flexibly to the fluctuating demands of sensitive, high-value row crops. Less temperamental field crops like corn and wheat, it was traditionally thought, lent themselves more easily to large-scale production. What transpired in the Central Valley during the decades following World War Two effectively turned these assumptions upside down. In the Valley, carrots became a field crop. So did iceberg lettuce, broccoli, and most notoriously, tomatoes. The personal attention that had once been supplied by legions of small farmers was obviated by the development of new and improved vegetable varieties more amenable to intensive mechanization. The farmers themselves were determined to be superfluous. Small farms were rapidly incorporated into much larger outfits. By 1978, fewer than ten percent of the farms in California worked less than a thousand acres. The single biggest agricultural landowner in the Central Valley, Tenneco West Incorporated, lists total holdings of more than a million acres. What had been a skilled craft was converted by massive infusions of research, capital, and technology into an essentially industrial process.

In *Three Farms*, his book on the transformation of American agriculture, the journalist Mark Kramer recalls watching a Central Valley carrot harvest. "In the world of large-scale corporate agriculture in California," Kramer writes,

> it turns out that all harvests look about the same. The shape of the machine varies; the sparseness of human labor varies slightly. The form is the same. Eighteen-wheelers gather in a staging area next to the flatness currently being worked. Oddly constructed harvest equipment does something special. In the case of carrots, the awkwardness of the machine includes protuberant wings, and a little platform on the back where someone sits, aiming some mechanized rooting about. The result of these manipulations (not to mention those of ag engineers, steel fabricators, extension researchers, bankers and the like) is that two rows of harvested carrots, dug from a forty-inch-wide carrot bed that proceeds toward the horizon in parallel with thousands of others, wind up in a big hopper. The hopper winds up in the assembly yard, and thence behind a truck that lugs it off somewhere to a processing plant where the carrots are cooled, washed, topped, and packaged, all automatically.

There's more to the difference between Jim's carrots and Carmine's than simply taste and quality. They are divided as well by a philosophical chasm containing two contrasting definitions of productivity. The new agriculture has been incessantly applauded for its purported productivity, and a procession of statistics is trotted out to support that assertion: how many fewer Americans remain enslaved by the supposed drudgery of farmwork; how much more food today's farmer can produce than his father ever could; the amount by which this year's record harvest eclipses last year's bumper crop. But productivity is an unhandily slippery concept. If the old agriculture was somewhat less productive than the new, it was also a lot cheaper. The old ideal of productivity involved doing the most with the least, while the new, far from shunning expensive investment, has embraced it as the swiftest route to increased production. In fact, most of the measurements intended to underline the new agriculture's increased productivity don't measure productivity at all—they measure total production. Total production, even total production per worker, is not the same thing as productivity. Productivity is calculated by subtracting from total production the real costs of all the inputs required to produce that total. Figured this way, the new agriculture doesn't stack up so well.

In the old agriculture a farmer improved his productivity mostly by adding labor, usually his own. If he could come up with a few extra hours at planting time he'd put in a half-acre of potatoes for market. If his daughter could be persuaded to take on a greater responsibility, the chicken house might be made to accommodate another hundred birds. His cash outlay was minimal. His total production increased a bit, and with luck so did his income. In the event that receipts from the new enterprise failed to reflect his additional investment of time and labor, he could easily enough cut back.

The new agriculture increases total production by adding purchased inputs: land, equipment, chemicals, and so forth, incurring considerable overhead in the form of debt service and higher operating expenses—overhead that will still have to be paid even if the expansion proves financially disappointing. This will not come as news to American farmers, as many as half of whom are flirting with bankruptcy. It's noteworthy that the farmers with the least to worry about today are those who resisted the new agriculture's sweet entreaties—farmers who chose not to expand or expanded only slowly, who kept up mixed production and avoided the export grain market, who instinctively shied away from excessive borrowing—farmers who were called foolish by their fellows. It looks now as if the fools may ride out the storm that threatens to sink their fellows. The new agriculture can't afford to be flexible. The old agriculture couldn't afford not to be.

From a public relations standpoint, the masterstroke of modern agriculture has been its success at substituting total production for real productivity as the standard by which its performance is judged. Total production has indeed increased, but what has been achieved in the process is not productivity so much as the illusion of productivity—an illusion which can last only so long as the biological and financial expenses of increased production don't catch up with its benefits. The key to the Central Valley's bountiful harvests, for example, is irrigation: irrigation funded in large part by the taxpayers through extensive state and federal reclamation projects. The amount of irrigated cropland in the United States has tripled since 1940. Leaving aside for the moment the environmental question of whether entire rivers ought to be diverted to make deserts bloom, or for that matter the political issue of who exactly should benefit from such diversions, the prevalence of subsidized irrigation has the troubling effect of lulling us into a false sense of security. It creates the impression of abundance, but it is no more than an impression. Two thousand gallons of subsidized water currently go into the production of a dollar's worth of Central Valley grapes. The real cost of that water is twenty or thirty times what the Valley's farmers are paying for it. If the subsidies were suddenly to disappear, it's a safe bet that the grapes would soon be gone as well. Similarly, the deep-welled center-pivot irrigation systems that have made arable millions of acres of high plains rangeland draw groundwater up from the depths using pumps powered by electricity or, more often, natural gas. Prices for both of these energy sources are tightly controlled, providing a de facto subsidy. If the price of fully deregulated natural gas were to quadruple, as some experts predict it will, so will the cost of irrigation.

The myth of modern agricultural productivity withers under close scrutiny. It's constructed of myopic assumptions and half-truths. As small farmers make a forced exit from farming, the fewer, bigger operations that remain are made to seem more productive. Chemical pesticides and fertilizers inflate yields for the short term while masking the long-term biological implications of rampant waste and destruction. The reality is that the two factors that have contributed most to the whirlwind rise of the new agriculture have been artificially undervalued. As the costs of capital and energy stabilize at levels more closely approximating their actual worth, the so-called productivity of modern agriculture starts to taper off, sometimes precipitously, and its built-in biological liabilities become more apparent. In point of fact, the very small-scale garden-type agricultures of Europe and Japan can claim a better rate of real productivity than our technologically sophisticated large-scale farms. They, moreover, can look forward to maintaining their productivity indefinitely. We unfortunately cannot.

It is tempting to view mainstream agriculture's immediate difficulties in purely financial terms, as they have tended to be portrayed in the press, and to imagine therefore that they might have purely financial solutions. At best, this is wishful thinking. Not that there aren't financial difficulties: farm expenses have risen steadily since the boom years of the mid 1970s, while farm income has simultaneously declined in the face of weak markets and mounting surpluses. Commodity prices have all but collapsed: corn that brought $3.50 a bushel in the fall of 1980 was selling for less than $2.00 a year later, well below the cost of production. The depressed farm economy has dampened if not eliminated demand for agricultural land, and the land that was used to secure the loans that financed the new agriculture's hectic expansion has plummeted in value. Prime Midwestern cropland, snapped up a few years ago for prices upward of $3,000 an acre, goes begging now at $1,500. For farmers with shrinking equity, operating credit is harder and harder to come by. Without credit these farmers can't put in a crop. Without a crop they can't repay their loans. The Farmers Home Administration reports a delinquency rate of 25 percent, and knowledgeable observers estimate that another 30 to 40 percent have escaped insolvency only by temporarily refinancing their debt. Foreclosure looms. The cure for all this, conventional analysts contend, is money. If petrochemical prices eased slightly and the worldwide recession lifted, international markets would eagerly consume our stockpiled crops, commodity prices would rise, lending rates would decline as new capital became available, and everything would be hunky-dory.

The tragedy of such facile analyses lies in their deliberate shortsightedness. Their appeal is understandable, but the hope they hold out is false and pernicious. Their implicit message is that the conditions that have led to American agriculture's present malaise are wholly external. It isn't the new agriculture itself that needs reforming, we are assured, so much as the economic environment in which it operates. The system is portrayed as essentially healthy, requiring at most minor adjustments.

What these comfortable fantasies refuse to acknowledge is that the system is fundamentally flawed, ill-equipped for survival under circumstances that, far from being transitory, in fact represent a new norm. Tinkering with the system won't solve its basic structural problems any more than treating symptoms cures disease. Even if the current economic pressures can somehow be alleviated, the impending biological crisis will only be exacerbated as farmers expand their production in a rush to cash in. If, for example, some means could be found to levy a tax on topsoil erosion commensurate with the nearly incalculable cost of replacing what's being lost, then the illusion of modern American agriculture's productivity—to say nothing of its sustainability—would fade in a heartbeat. Without such a tax the reckoning may take a bit longer to arrive, but it will nevertheless come. The new agriculture is the spendthrift heir of postwar prosperity, living in luxury on unearned income. We are spending our capital, biologically and economically both, and as Andrew Carnegie understood only too well, we can't keep that up forever.

Harvard government professor Robert B. Reich, in *The Next American Frontier*, suggests that the trouble we find ourselves in is neither temporary nor accidental. Rather, he says, the plight of American industry in the 1980s is a logical outgrowth of the industrial system designed and implemented after World War Two. At its apex in the late 1960s that system seemed spectacularly successful, but since then it has fallen on tougher times, and nowadays it's a crippling burden. "The central problem of

America's economic future," Reich writes, "is that the nation is not moving quickly enough out of high-volume, standardized production. The extraordinary success of the half-century of the management era has left the United States a legacy of economic inflexibility. Thus our institutional heritage now imperils our future." Reich's subject is industry, but he might as well be describing American agriculture.

What has to happen next, says Reich, is a profound restructuring of American industry into a less hierarchical, more responsive form. "Flexible-system production is rooted in discovering and solving new problems; high-volume, standardized production basically involves routinizing the solutions to old problems. Flexible-system production requires an organization designed for change and adaptability; high-volume, standardized production requires an organization geared to stability." Industries left clinging to high-volume, standardized production, Reich warns, are easily toppled by fluctuations in the marketplace, while "because flexible-system production is premised on ever-changing markets and conditions, it is less vulnerable than high-volume production to shifts in demand."

For farmers fighting a losing battle with the payments due on land and machinery they bought in order to produce as large a quantity of commodities as possible, which nobody now seems much interested in buying, that last comment must have a certain poignance. The new agriculture took its cue from industry, forsaking the flexible-system production that provided Jim's carrots for the high-volume standardized production that supplies Carmine's. For farmers as surely as for automobile manufacturers, the era of high-volume, standardized production is swiftly drawing to a close. The new agriculture, which worked so spectacularly well for a while, no longer works well at all. The time has come to transform American agriculture again, not into a quaint approximation of the old agriculture's forms but into a new realization of the old agriculture's values: conserving, labor intensive, locally responsive, flexible by design and of necessity thrifty. What we need now is something that works.

2

SOMETHING THAT WORKS

Most people, asked to describe their image of an organic farm, will conjure up misty visions of Vermont or northern California—scenes peopled with wraithlike young women in peasant blouses tending rows of medicinal plants, and hirsute, philosophically inclined novice farmers wandering out to milk the goats—visions that would have to be considerably enlarged before they could include Ralph Engelken. As organic farmers go, Ralph Engelken would seem to deviate markedly from the stereotype. He is a spruce, sixtyish father of eleven who farms five hundred prime Corn Belt acres just north of the village of Greeley, in northeastern Iowa. Far from having the haphazard aspect of an outfit operated by earnest amateurs, Ralph and Rita Engelken's Barrington Hall Farm is all business. The barns are experienced but well maintained, and they have been supplemented of late with a new machine shed—a single-story, pastel-colored corrugated steel building of the variety very much in favor these days on up-to-date Midwestern farms. Inside, there is a full complement of modern middle-sized farm equipment, some of it nearly new. The nearby farmhouse is a low-slung contemporary affair, sheathed in beige fakestone and rimmed with weedless flower beds. There are late-model American-made cars and trucks parked in the drive.

A cursory inspection of Barrington Hall Farm reveals nothing to differentiate it from countless other farms dispersed over the rolling landscape for hundreds of miles in every direction. Indeed, what dominates Ralph Engelken's barnyard is not some obscure organic icon but a genuine Farm Belt status symbol: a row of four towering Harvestore silos, each twenty feet in diameter and sixty or seventy feet tall, painted a distinctive midnight blue. "Come on through town and out the other side," Rita Engelken had told me. "We're easy to find. Just look for the Harvestores." Harvestores are upright, airtight, glass-lined silos manufactured by the A. O. Smith Corporation, and of the various means for making and storing silage—legumes, grasses or grains chopped green and partially fermented under cover, greatly prized as a livestock feed because a sizable proportion of the crop's nutrients are preserved—Harvestores are undoubtedly the most expensive. Their proponents call them "the Cadillac of silos." Detractors refer to the tall, dark blue cylinders as Thermos bottles. Depending on your perspective, the farmer who invests in Harvestores is either a savvy operator who understands the wisdom of spending a bit more to get the very best, or else a free-spending sucker seduced by a showy image. In either event the presence of a new Harvestore alongside the barn serves as public testimony to its owner's financial well-being. At Barrington Hall Farm, as if to underscore the point, the family mailbox has been mounted atop a cast-off propane tank painted Harvestore blue.

The standard portrayal of an organic farm would have to stretch a little too, to accommodate the annual Delaware County 4-H Beef Banquet, under way this evening in the two-tone institutional green meeting hall of the county extension service office in Manchester, the county seat, ten miles southwest of Greeley. This is a celebration of some prominence on the local social calendar, at which the final outcome of this year's 4-H beef cattle competition will be announced. The banquet comes a month or so after the county fair and culminates a full year's effort on the part of the teenagers it honors. Scrubbed and laundered, they line up behind their parents for plates heaped with Salisbury steak, mashed potatoes, green beans, and dinner rolls, exchanging polite greetings with the adults ("Hello Steven, how're you tonight?" "Hello Mr. Robinson. Fine thank you, sir") and jittery gibes for their peers. At the long rectangular table the generations diverge, youth gravitating en masse toward one end, elders gathering convivially at the other. The kids drink milk. The grownups prefer coffee, black.

What's happening here is more than an awards ceremony. It is part of an initiation. Every one of the contestants already plays an important role in the operation of the family farm—which, it's safe to say, couldn't manage without them—but this is their moment of glory, an acknowledgment of their maturing abilities as farmers in their own right. This is the next generation's chance to step into the spotlight, but at the same time it's a kind of agricultural Little League: there's quite a lot of parental prestige riding on the results.

The process these youngsters are at last completing is by design an accurate miniature of full-scale farming. To participate is to take instruction in the principles of an agrarian catechism. The course of study began many months ago, when each contestant sought out and purchased a likely-looking calf to raise, selected from among animals available on their home farm, at neighboring farms, or at livestock auctions. The calves were bought with their own money, often borrowed against anticipated earnings from the eventual sale of the animals, a lesson in the workings of agricultural credit. The contestants fed and looked after their charges in addition to doing their regular chores. At the county fair, entrants assembled their animals for a review and ranking, known as a live grading. Then the cattle were hauled to a packing house, slaughtered and butchered and graded again—this time according to carcass quality and yield—and sold, mostly to area markets. This evening's banquet is the grand finale. When all the coffee cups have been refilled and the limp paper plates cleared from the table, the presentation will begin. Each animal's ranking after slaughter will be contrasted to its placement in the live grading, the particulars of its case detailed and discussed in a kind of post mortem, and finally the checks will be handed out.

The Engelken clan eagerly anticipates this reckoning. The banquet's master of ceremonies is the same honorable gentleman who conducted the live grading of animals at the fair. While he's setting up his slide projector Ralph observes that discrepancies between the live grading and the carcass ranking can tend to be embarrassing for the grader—live grading being inherently subjective. Ralph's two youngest sons, Tom and Steve—who with their younger sister Pat are the last of the Engelken kids left at home—have animals under consideration. Tom's steer was left out of the top ten altogether on the live grading scorecard. Steve's was ranked tenth. Ralph expects both to do better in the carcass placing.

Feeding beef calves is Ralph Engelken's forte. Barrington Hall Farm fills a specific niche in the cycle of modern beef production. Ralph specializes in something called backgrounding. He buys young cattle just past weaning, when they weigh less than five hundred pounds, and holds on to them for perhaps six months. Then, after three meals a day of his hay and oats, corn and sweet silage have added another two or three hundred pounds to their bulk, they're sold to feedlot operators who serve an unvarying menu of ground corn to bring them up to a market weight of approximately twelve hundred pounds.

This is an arrangement ideally suited to the Engelkens' circumstances. As an organic grower, Ralph sustains the fertility of his soils by keeping better than half of his 410 tillable but hilly acres in legume hay at all times. Typically, he'll have a field in oats for a year, hay for three years, and corn for two, then back to oats again. The oats are undemanding and prosper in the shadow of nutrient-hungry corn. Three years of deep-rooted sod aerates and restores the soil structure, while the rhizobium bacteria associated with the roots of leguminous plants transfer atmospheric nitrogen from the air into the earth, enriching the soil in preparation for another couple of seasons of corn. Happily, cattle in their adolescence do especially well on a diet rich in legumes—at Barrington Hall Farm it's mostly alfalfa, either as hay or in its ensiled state as haylage—but for their final fattening they demand more corn than Ralph can produce from his own land without chemical fertilizers. Backgrounding enables him to feed exclusively homegrown rations, and simultaneously provides him with an ample supply of the principal fertilizer he needs to grow them: manure, removed from his stockyards and composted before being distributed copiously over his fields.

Making a profit at backgrounding, Ralph contends, hinges on the same fundamentals that should give his sons an advantage in the 4-H competition: a commitment to growing and feeding only the highest-quality feeds, and an ability—part instinct, part experience—to select the best animals for feeding.

When the lights go out there are two projectors trained on a screen at the rear of the room. One, an overhead, displays the entry's vital statistics: the name of its owner; the number on its ear tag; the animal's live weight and the weight of its dressed carcass; the dimensions of its loin eye (an indicant of its meat-to-bone balance); the thickness of its back fat and the percentage of its internal fat, or marbling; its U.S.D.A. quality grade (Prime, Choice, Good, Standard, or the ignominious Commercial and Utility) and yield grade (the ratio of carcass weight to live weight); and, of course, its live placing and carcass placing. The second projector offers for each entry a revealing sequence of three photographs. The first slide portrays owner and animal together, alive, in the show ring at the fair. The next is more stark: a cut-away view of the animal after slaughter, or rather of half the animal, dangling from a hook at the packing house. Last comes a close-up of the butchered animal's loin eye.

As the slide show proceeds the grader keeps up a running commentary. "He doesn't have a lot of natural thickness to him, you see," he says of one animal, then clicks the carousel forward for a closer inspection, "and his loin eye's not too awfully big anyway." Of another entrant he notes, "This steer is cleaner in his underline than the one before, but he's not really an extremely big steer either. He's almost a little thin. I wonder if he didn't gain a little slower than he should have." Most of the animals involved in the competition, including both the Engelken entries, are of indistinct ancestry: some Hereford here, a bit of Angus there, Charolais infused with a hint of Brahman. Purebred cattle, Ralph has told me, are reserved mostly for use as breeding stock and cost too much to raise for meat. Barrington Hall Farm takes its name from a purebred Black Angus herd that Ralph once owned at a time when he was in the business of raising registered bulls. For backgrounding he sticks with mixed breeds. "I do like the colored cattle," he admits, casting his dubious eye on the pale milky coat of a Simmental cross—a recent in-migrant from Switzerland—shown now at the right of the screen. The grader seems to agree. "A lot of these exotic cattle now," he is saying, "they're just a little thick around the shoulder."

Tonight's lecture offers a cross between anatomy and art history, with a smattering of culinary arts. To hear Ralph interpret it, the bulk of the talk has been given over to the grader's unsuccessful attempts to justify his earlier judgments. Among the sources of the grader's unease is the fact that the animal he'd rated highest on the hoof ranked only sixth in the carcass placing, while cattle he'd snubbed at the fair turned up high on the carcass chart. "This steer was extremely thick from behind," he defends, "and he's a little inverted in the tail head. To be honest, I'm a bit surprised at those numbers." The numbers may be found on the final ranking chart, on which, as forecast, the Engelkens are fully vindicated. Tom's previously unseeded steer comes out second in the carcass placing. Steve's animal captures fourth. His father, beaming, confides that his youngest son is a natural judge of good cattle. "I love taking him to the sales barn with me," Ralph says. "He's just got a fantastic eye." The boys' checks disappear into their shirt pockets, and we pile into the car for the ride home.

In the somewhat circumscribed cosmos of organic agriculture, Barrington Hall Farm is a brightly shining star. Eight years ago, when researchers led by Barry Commoner and William Lockeretz of Washington University's Center for the Biology of Natural Systems undertook to compare the operations of fourteen conventional Corn Belt grain and livestock farms with fourteen of their organic counterparts, they included Barrington Hall Farm among their subjects. More recently, the U.S.D.A.'s study team for organic farming paused at length in Greeley on its way toward formulating the Department's own *Report and Recommendations.* A regular traffic of visitors finds its way to the prominent blue Harvestores, and the silos' owners do quite a bit of traveling themselves.They appear often at organic farming conferences and conventions, disseminating their very personal version of the case for non-chemical farming, and they have even gone so far as to write and self-publish a book, *The Art of Natural Farming and Gardening*, which details the ingredients of their recipe.

Ralph and Rita Engelken make unlikely luminaries. Rita's a compact, rectangular, gently graying woman in her middle fifties, a grandmother several times over. On the morning when I arrived she was freezing cauliflower in her kitchen. She held out her hand in greeting. Shaking it was like inserting my fingers into a soaking wet steel trap. Her husband, two years her senior, is equally small of stature. His skin is wind-weathered and dark. Crow's-feet spread from his eyes and the corners of his grin like fissures across a plaster ceiling. He has a sharp, beaked nose, and his elfin protruding ears usually support a ventilated duck-billed seed-company cap. Ralph Engelken's seed cap only rarely comes off, and when it does his scalp is revealed as innocent of insulation. His concession to vanity in the face of speaking engagements and photographers is a chestnut-brown toupee. He wore it the night of the 4-H Beef Banquet, and when he emerged from his bedroom thus coiffed I hardly recognized him.

Ralph and Rita were raised within a few miles of each other on family farms in Delaware County. They come from German Catholic stock in a part of the country where the towns have names like New Vienna, Osterdock, Guttenberg, and Farmersburg. Ralph's mother died when he was nine. He was farming full-time by the time he was thirteen, when he assumed from his ailing father complete responsibility for the family's diversified 80-acre farm. At twenty-one he married Rita, and they began farming on shares—keeping part of their harvest for themselves and paying the landowner with the rest—on an 80-acre parcel in Colesburg, just down the road from the Engelken home place. Later they paid cash rent for a while on a different 80 acres, in adjacent Petersburg. When that land was sold out from under them they moved next door, farming on shares again, with 240 acres in crops, a 100-cow dairy and a flock of 500 chickens. In 1958 they bought the first of two contiguous parcels they now own in Greeley. There, at one time or another, they have raised pigs for market, bred registered Black Angus bulls, and produced slaughter-ready fat cattle from their own herd, before settling finally on backgrounding.

Ralph Engelken's formal education came to an abrupt halt after the eighth grade when he took over for his father on the farm. Like most farmers at the time, he learned farming on the job, and from the peripatetic county extension agents who made their rounds from farm to farm dispensing the best that the land-grant system had to offer. The agricultural methodology Ralph absorbed while growing up was perforce organic. The farms of Delaware County then were uniformly small, mixed output operations in which most of the grain or hay grown on the farm was fed to livestock. The livestock made manure. The manure went back onto the fields. That was how farming worked, how it had always worked. But soon Ralph began hearing of a new and ostensibly better way to farm. "I was the first one in town to farm with chemicals," he recalls. "When we were in Petersburg we were chemical farmers," Rita says, "and boy did we pour it on. We started with all the bad ones, DDT and 2,4-D and the rest, all the ones that are banned now in this country, because that's what we were told was best." Ralph approached the new technology with characteristic gusto. In the early 1950s he invested in large-scale spray equipment and became a custom applicator, mixing and spraying pesticides on thousands of acres of other farmers' crops. It was a profitable sideline and he kept at it for five years. He had no reservations about what he was doing. As he remembers that period, he considered himself farsighted, astutely ahead of the times.

It is commonplace in the annals of organic farming to come upon testimony from converts that relates their rejection of chemical farming and their subsequent embrace of organics. Patrick Madden, an agricultural economist at Penn State, tells of a California rice farmer who changed allegiances in the mid-1960s: "He said that fifteen years ago he was walking across his fields when he had a disgusted, depressed feeling. He'd been in the Navy years before, assigned to a tiny cubicle without windows, and he'd had such claustrophobia that he swore if he ever got out alive he'd take up an occupation where he could be in contact with nature. That's what led him into farming in the first place. 'So here I was,' he told me, 'out on my own farm, and I felt as if everything around me was dead. There was a terrible smell of chemicals coming out of the soil. I couldn't hear any birds singing. I couldn't see any butterflies. I felt just like I was walking in a sepulchre. I decided right then that I was going to phase out my use of chemicals and get started on a more natural system.' " Nearer at hand, in central Iowa, a once conventional Corn Belt farmer named Richard Thompson, who now farms organically, experienced a similar awakening. "I was out washing hog pens one day when I got the word," Thompson told a reporter. "That's a dirty job, and a funny place to learn something that will change your life. But I heard a voice as clear as daylight, and it said to me, 'Get along, don't go along. Get out of the rat race.' "

The Engelkens' revelation came by a more circuitous route. Upon moving to Greeley in 1958, Ralph and Rita called on the local parish priest to come out and bless their new home. It had seemed to Rita for some time that her kids' colds were taking longer than they should to clear up. The children had developed mysterious fluid build-ups in their joints, odd swellings, rashes, and lesions. Rita herself had painful open sores that refused to heal. Ralph complained of constant itching. The family had gone from one doctor to another without receiving a satisfactory diagnosis, much less any relief. By the time they got to Greeley they were, by their own admission, becoming slightly desperate.

The plain-collared, heavyset, cigar-chewing fellow who met them on their doorstep was a most unorthodox clergyman. Father Louis White was in the habit of sermonizing from his Sunday pulpit against the environmental sins of conventional agriculture. In northeastern Iowa in the late 1950s this was enough to prompt some irate parishioners to establish an alternative congregation, but Father White preached on regardless. When the Engelkens hit town he took one look and issued an inflexible dictum. Your problem, he declaimed, is chemicals. He ordered them to cut out the pesticides and synthetic fertilizers and dispense with their adulterated diet. It wasn't long before he had the family eating whole wheat flour and sunflower seeds and

drinking long draughts of well water spiked with
and honey, and he steered Ralph firmly in the d
ganic agriculture. The Engelkens were good Cath
did as they were told. Ralph quit using chemicals
spring. He relied on frequent cultivation to comba
results were less than spectacular. The land on his new farm was close to worn out—corned to death, in the argot of the region—and eliminating its accustomed chemical supplements quite nearly eliminated the harvest as well. The family's health did seem to be improving, though, and Ralph was encouraged by incremental gains in each season's yields, so he hung on. What finally made the whole thing jell, he says, was his belated discovery of compost.

"More than any other factor, I believe composting has helped our farming operation swing into high gear," Ralph Engelken writes in *The Art of Natural Farming and Gardening*. "My only regret is that we did not start doing it earlier." The supremacy of compost is one of the ruling postulates of organic agriculture, but the actual nutrient value of the stuff is a little tough to pin down. Ever since the introduction of synthetic fertilizers the usual measure of a fertilizer's strength has been a three-digit code, the N-P-K formula, indicating the relative concentration of three key constituents of plant growth: nitrogen (N), phosphorus (P), and potassium (K). The "10-10-10," for example, stenciled across the top of a fifty-pound sack at your neighborhood Agway reveals its contents to be ten percent nitrogen, ten percent phosphorus, and ten percent potassium, with the balance in sand and lime. What corn likes best is the nitrogen. In the Corn Belt the fertilizer of choice is anhydrous ammonia, a stable gas created when atmospheric nitrogen is flared under pressure with methane. Anhydrous, as farmers refer to it, is kept in pressurized tanks and injected into the soil through rake-like knives drawn behind tractors. The N-P-K formula of anhydrous ammonia is for all practical purposes 100-0-0, which greatly facilitates the favored Corn Belt crop rotation of corn, corn, and corn (or in farm writer Gene Logsdon's variation on the theme: corn, soybeans, and Miami).

The numbers for compost don't look so impressive. They're

harder to figure, of course, because the quality of compost fluctuates wildly depending on what it's made from and how it's made, but it's safe to hazard that the world's richest compost—the triple cream Camembert of composts—won't contain more than four percent each of N, P, and K, and probably much less. Skeptics assert that compost's only real utility is as a soil conditioner. As a fertilizer, they say, it's practically worthless. Believers counter that while nitrogen, phosphorus, and potassium are plainly important to plant growth, any analysis that limits itself to that triumvirate misses the mark. Compost, they claim, is crammed full of micronutrients, trace elements like molybdenum, manganese, boron, cobalt, and zinc, which, because they are bound up in a loamy organic humus, won't leach out after the first rain. This is precisely what seems to be happening with synthetic fertilizers: nitrate levels of more than one hundred parts per million, more than double the quantity thought to represent the upper limit of potability, are not uncommon in groundwater samples taken from heavily fertilized Farm Belt areas. Irrigating with such water would accomplish much the same result as applying bagged N at eighty pounds to the acre. At the same time, the farm pond that once beckoned families for a summer evening swim has increasingly been reduced to a foul-smelling algal stew by the accumulation of phosphates in the run-off from nearby fields. Adherents of composting further note that compost enhances soil life, fostering the work of earthworms and microorganisms, as opposed to anhydrous, for instance, which is essentially a toxic fumigant. Compost-enriched soils do a superior job of retaining rainfall, thanks to their larger proportion of organic matter, giving crops grown on them an edge during dry spells. Aficionados sometimes imply that the provision of N, P, and K is only the least of compost's countless attributes.

Be all that as it may, the thing compost does best for Ralph Engelken is make excellent use of manure. And manure is something Ralph has quite a lot of. A healthy young steer, eating well, will generate perhaps twenty thousand pounds of manure over a twelve-month period. At any given moment there might be as many as eight hundred healthy young cattle eating well in the yards at Barrington Hall Farm. It follows that something must be done with all their manure. What Ralph does is turn it into compost, reducing its bulk by half. Manure spread raw on fields is a good deal less valuable as a fertilizer than manure that has first been composted: piled, mixed with other organic refuse (spoiled hay, bedding straw, cornstalks, that sort of thing), aged awhile, and churned to imbue the pile with oxygen and instigate its aerobic decomposition. When Ralph talks about making compost he does not have in mind a cute little pile at the end of the garden path. Ralph makes two thousand tons of compost a year. He applies four or five tons of it annually to every acre of his cropland. To collect raw manure from his yards he enlists a front-end loader, and a high-capacity tractor-driven manure spreader deposits the dung in windrows ten feet across, four feet tall, and hundreds of yards long. The requisite aeration is accomplished with a 105-horsepower International Harvester 856 tractor towing behind it a huge and ungainly implement that straddles the windrow and flails away like an oversized side-mounted eggbeater. If you want one of these it will set you back about $7,000. If you want one anywhere in the vicinity of Greeley, Iowa, you will have to buy it from Ralph Engelken, since he is his state's franchised dealer of Wildcat Easy Over Compost Turners.

Former Secretary of Agriculture Earl Butz, a champion of the new agriculture, once declared in response to a television newsman's inquiry that before America's farmers could convert en masse to organics, it would first be necessary to decide which fifty million people should be allowed to starve. This is the commonest criticism of organic farming: that it inevitably leads to a decline in yields. The example of Barrington Hall Farm suggests otherwise. Ralph Engelken's 200 acres of hay, cut three times over the course of a season, yield an average of 12 tons to the acre. A yield of 8 tons would be satisfactory, 10 quite respectable. His cornfields reliably produce harvests in the range of 150 bushels to the acre, matching or exceeding the Delaware County average. On one 30-acre patch beside his barn he has grown corn every year for the past fifteen years. Continuous cropping of corn is theoretically impossible without chemicals, since soil nitrogen supplies in an organic system are customarily maintained by including a nitrogen-fixing legume in the crop rotation. Ralph's yield from that field last year worked out to 168 bushels per acre. On his best corn ground he did better than that by 40 bushels or more—and the Engelkens' best land is nothing fancy. The terrain is hilly, its soil cover comparatively thin. Ralph can't grow soybeans, for example—or more accurately, he won't—because of the erosion they'd cause on his hillsides. He's not about to complain, mind you. He knows his land would inspire envy in the eyes of farmers stuck with the precipitous sidehills of New Hampshire or Vermont. He merely means to suggest that his creditable yields cannot be attributed solely to the indigenous fertility of his soil. What's more, he says he not only grows more corn and hay than many of his neighbors, he grows better.

Rita descends to the basement and returns with a battered brown valise, from which she extracts, a few at a time, a tightly capped collection of jars. The first pair I'm shown are one-gallon canning jars identically labeled NOVEMBER 20, 1981. Inside each, poking up against its lid, is a single ear of field corn. One of them, from the Engelkens' land, is thick as a stevedore's wrist and shingled with yolk-yellow, dented kernels. The other, from a chemically farmed field nearby, is invisible beneath a layer of cottony white fungus. "They keep saying they want proof," Rita declares. "Well, here's their proof!"

She now produces two Gerber baby-food jars dated 1964, one holding perfectly preserved whole corn kernels and the other only dust. Rita and Ralph hosted a slide show one evening, featuring comparative views of the Engelken farm and a mercifully unnamed neighbor's. Here was Ralph's hay shortly after first cutting: dark green and luxuriant. His neighbor's: patchy and pale, sparsely germinated at the ends of the field where the herbicide applicator had reversed directions while spraying the prior year's corn. Ralph's corn in June: knee high and exuberantly leafy. His neighbor's: anemic and struggling to get started. Ralph's topsoil: light and loamy, the color of coffee grounds, the texture of a successful soufflé. His neighbor's: dry and gray, like medium sandy gravel. The show climaxes with a photograph of the root mass attached to a mature corn plant yanked from the continuously cropped field beside the Engelkens' barn. Ralph's corn has a stalk two inches across and an anchor of tightly woven, hairlike roots the size of a man's head. His neighbor's: no roots at all to speak of. "Why, you could pull that thing up with two fingers!" Ralph exclaims. "You couldn't get ours out of the ground tugging with both hands."

In 1980, at the Natural Organic Farmers Association's annual midsummer gathering in New Hampshire, a writer and researcher named Daniel Zwerdling delivered an address entitled "Long Term Strategies for Organic Agriculture." The Department of Agriculture's *Report and Recommendations on Organic Farming* was newly released that year—in fact it made its debut at the conference—and Zwerdling had just spent a year studying the commercial prospects for organic farmers as part of the U.S.D.A.'s larger investigation.

When he'd first begun going round to farms telling farmers he was interested in organic agriculture, Zwerdling recalled, responses typically tended to be curt. He was shown to the door of more than one farm house. After a while he determined that the cause of his troubles was semantic, and he abandoned the word *organic*. "Every time I'd ask a farmer what organic agriculture was," he remembered, "I'd get a different definition. Nobody could say exactly what it meant." When he asked instead about increasing yields and reducing the demand for petrochemicals, his reception perceptibly warmed. Farmers were eager to step off the treadmill that brought them to the bank in an ever escalating quest for more operating capital, more fertilizers, more pesticides, and bigger and more powerful equipment. But they were also instinctively leery of terms like *organic* and *natural*. "Every organic farmer I interviewed, except one, was organic for purely economic reasons," Zwerdling recounted. One grower who'd switched from conventional to mostly organic methods took him aside and swore him to secrecy. Organic farming wasn't terribly well thought of thereabouts, he explained, and if word were to get out that he'd gone "natural" it could hurt his credit rating.

"Which brings me to why I am opposed to organic agriculture," Dan Zwerdling bravely announced to a roomful of Natural Organic Farmers. "Personally, and I know many of you will disagree, I think the single most effective thing you could do at this conference would be to change the name of your organization from the Natural Organic Farmers Association to the Association for Sustainable Agriculture. That would go a long way towards communicating with the people you really need to communicate with, the farmers." At the N.O.F.A. conference I ran into Mark Kramer, author of *Three Farms* and a keen observer of the agricultural scene. He looked a little shell-shocked. "There's lots of different coots here," he allowed. "The fringes are well represented. Trying to understand American agriculture by starting here would be like trying to understand baseball by interviewing an eighty-year-old, blind, crippled batboy who's never left the clubhouse."

But if the conference menu included such novelties as "Understanding the Goddess: How She Relates to Agriculture, to the Earth, and to Ourselves," there were also "Strategies for Preserving Agricultural Lands," "Farmscale Composting," "Economics of Commercial Organic Vegetable Production," "Technologies for Direct Marketing," and "Soil Amendments for Biological Agriculture." If there was a lot of long hair and loose clothing, and bare feet padding along the hallways, there were plenty of filled notebooks and well-used clipboards. The N.O.F.A. conference, in all its slightly schizophrenic multiplicity, provides a fair profile of the organic agriculture movement. There exists a deep philosophical chasm not only between organic and chemical farmers but between the fanatic orthodoxy of a gardener who will plant and harvest only in harmony with cosmic cycles, and the hard-headed pragmatism of the vegetable farmer who when faced with the decimation of his cash crop may retaliate with a little judiciously applied spray here and there. In the demilitarization of this conflict lies the best hope for the movement's future, and quite possibly for the future of American agriculture. It is encouraging that the perpetual argument over fine points of organic doctrine has lately made room for a burgeoning concern with cost-price ratios, marketing strategies, and farm business planning.

The U.S.D.A.'s *Report and Recommendations on Organic Farming* was everywhere in evidence at the conference: a pale green paperback perused in the shade of a tree, spread open on lunch tables, peeking out from a registrant's thick sheath of notes and handouts. The report was a cautious document, skimming the surface of its subject and falling back often on a call for further research. "Contrary to popular belief," the authors observe, "most organic farmers have not regressed to agriculture as it was practiced in the 1930s. While they attempt to avoid or restrict the use of chemical fertilizers and pesticides, organic farmers still use modern farm machinery, recommended crop varieties, certified seed, sound methods of organic waste management, and recommended soil and water practices." More importantly, "There are detrimental aspects of conventional production, such as soil erosion and sedimentation, depleted nutrient reserves, water pollution from run-off of fertilizers and pesticides, and possible decline of soil productivity. If these factors are considered, then cost comparisons between conventional (that is, chemical intensive) crop production and organic systems may be somewhat different in areas where these problems occur."

What this adds up to is a tentative acknowledgment by the government of claims long featured in organic rhetoric. "The study team found that many of the current methods of soil and crop management practiced by organic farmers are also those which have been cited as the best management practices for controlling soil erosion, minimizing water pollution, and conserving energy. . . . Moreover, many organic farmers have developed unique and innovative methods of organic recycling and pest control in their crop production sequences. Because of these and other reasons . . . the team feels strongly that research and education programs should be developed to address the needs and problems of organic farmers." Which may not be bold enough to satisfy hard-liners but constitutes a considerable concession coming from the agency often viewed as the devil incarnate by backers of organic agriculture.

On the other hand, the report warned, organics are no panacea. Organic agriculture is comparatively energy-efficient but in the event of a broad-based shift to organics the energy savings realized from a reduced demand for petrochemical fertilizers and pesticides would be at least partially offset by greater fuel usage, since much of the work conventionally performed by chemicals must be done mechanically in an organic system. The price, according to the report, would likely be sharply curtailed agricultural exports and, perhaps, higher domestic food prices. Large-scale cash grain farms could probably not survive without chemical supplements.

The long-term biological viability of an organic farm depends on returning to the soil as many nutrients as the harvests remove from it. In practice this is accomplished by some combination of crop rotation and animal manures or organic wastes, neither of which fit neatly into the picture of agriculture painted in the past half-century. Much of a farmer's land, much of the time, must be planted to a soil-improving crop (alfalfa hay, for example, which fixes nitrogen in the soil) whose income potential can seldom match that of soil-depleting crops (wheat or corn or other cash grains). Similarly, the application of manure is time-consuming and laborious, especially on large acreages, and requires an ample supply of manure—something absent from most big grain farms. One of the U.S.D.A. report's more intriguing suppositions is that the United States may not produce enough organic wastes to sustain, under an organic system, high levels of agricultural production.

Even granting that many of the most vexing problems of conventional agriculture might be ameliorated, if not solved outright, by a general adherence to organic principles, there remains a formidable public relations handicap. Mainstream agriculture simply refuses to take organics seriously, U.S.D.A. report or no U.S.D.A. report. The recognition on the part of the movement's boosters that this liability is to some degree self-inflicted has been slow in coming, but it surfaced as a sub-theme at the N.O.F.A. conference. The movement's tendency to get sandbagged by trivial particulars was ridiculed by the avowed pragmatists present. The purists' rebuttals castigated pragmatists for selling out and forsaking their roots. One leading activist, Eliot Coleman, framed the debate in an article entitled "Setting the Furrow Straight": "A controversy exists in agriculture. . . . New schools are disputing the soundness of accepted farming practices. The two camps line up and take pot shots at one another with harsh words but few facts. Little is gained in the process. Although many peripheral concerns may be represented, when speaking specifically of agriculture, 'organic' and 'chemical' are the standards most often borne by clashing ideologies. In my opinion, the 'organic-chemical' controversy is pointless and counterproductive." Coleman goes on to say that times are tough for all farmers, however they farm, and notes that the primary harvest of divisiveness is inertia. His assessment is remarkably candid: "Most of the responsibility for this must be borne by the organic movement itself. Its arguments have usually been presented in such a naïve and sectarian way that misunderstandings have effectively blocked communication between organic and conventional farmers."

Toward the end of the three-day affair, during a panel discussion on "The Economics of Commercial Organic Vegetable Production," a veteran organic vegetable farmer named Howard Prussock delivered a dose of sober advice. After bemoaning the inequities of having to compete with part-time farmers for a share of the summer fresh vegetable market ("It's a racket; they'll undercut you every time") and admitting that enormous labor costs and an unreliable pool of workers had prompted him to invest in mechanization just as fast as he could raise the capital, Howie Prussock had this to say: "If you've come here for the truth and the light, you've come to the wrong place, because you won't get that from me. They don't give farmers medals for being organic. If you go broke and close down, they won't come round with a plaque that says: THIS FARMER TRIED LIKE HELL FOR EIGHT YEARS AND FAILED.

"The first requirement for organic farming is obsession, and how well you do depends on how obsessed you are. If you are not sufficiently obsessed, I'd suggest saving your money, investing in stocks and real estate, and staying away from farming."

If obsession is the measure of an organic farmer's success, then Ralph Engelken must surely be obsessed. After twenty-five years as a card-carrying organic farmer he is a demonstrably prosperous man. He seems no more obsessed, however, than any other farmer beset with a fortnight of intermittent rain at haying time. I've come to Barrington Hall Farm to help with the haying. It's late July; the second cutting is about half done.

This morning's first task is to unload a couple of hay wagons filled too late last evening to be put up before supper. The entire interior of the farm's biggest barn serves as a haymow. It's warm inside, sweet and dark. The gables are open at each end, and swallows fly in one and out the other, performing aerial acrobatics between. Bales are stacked in trellised tiers toward the rafters. From the hayracks parked beside the doorway Ralph muscles bales onto a hay elevator, a kind of upwardly inclined conveyor belt that transports them into the mow. There are four of us up here, forming a steeply diagonal bucket brigade. At the top of the elevator stands Francis, the hired man, Ralph's sole full-time employee. Francis pulls bales off the elevator and tosses them to Tom, stationed two tiers above him. Tom forwards the bales to Steve, a bale higher still, who throws them to me. In deference to my perceived frailty I have been assigned the uppermost—and easiest—position. I have only to distribute the bales around me; I've been spared having to yank them up over my head in a full bench press. For this I am properly grateful. The hay is new and green. The bales—the buckets passed along by our brigade—weigh upward of fifty pounds apiece.

The majority of the farm's hay would normally be made into haylage—harvested with the big self-propelled Field Queen forage chopper and pumped into the Harvestores. This year, though, the population of Ralph's cattle yards is unusually low. The problem of a weak beef market has been exacerbated by the high price and scarcity of good feeder calves, a situation brought on by abundant rainfall in the Western plains that has allowed ranchers to leave young stock on the range longer than they otherwise could. Having fewer cattle to feed, Ralph requires less silage, and he's hoping to sell baled hay this winter to compensate for lost income. Unfortunately, the same rain that's keeping the plains verdant plays hell with the haying in Iowa. It has rained every other day for weeks, and it rained again last night. When we've emptied the two racks Ralph commandeers Steve's dirt bike and rides into the fields to see if they might be dry enough by afternoon to make a little hay. I watch him from the house, bobbing in and out of view, a red seed cap perched atop a yellow motorcycle, tacking across a variegated green sea.

In the meantime we do odd jobs. Francis drives off in the Field Queen to salvage some wet hay. Tom attends to minor adjustments and repairs on the haybine, another self-propelled implement, used to cut standing hay before it is raked and baled. In the intervals between days of decent haying weather Ralph has been renovating one of his cattle sheds, and he dispatches me in that direction with an armload of sheet-metal scraps to patch holes in the siding. Ralph Engelken is a wealthy man, and with cash flow from Barrington Hall Farm's various enterprises approaching two million dollars a year, he is a successful farmer by anyone's standards. Some insight into how he got that way may be gleaned from a coffee can full of nails I've been issued for fastening patches to the shed's exterior. All the nails in the can have been used once or twice, pulled and pounded straight. To guard against rust they've been liberally doused with oil. Used oil, drained during periodic engine maintenance and reserved for just such purposes.

Ralph announces at lunch that he intends to spend the afternoon buying cattle and invites me to come along. We drive twenty minutes north to the town of Edgewood, where weekly cattle auctions are held at a small sales barn. Ralph tells me he prefers another larger auction, further north in Waukon, but this one's handier. As we wend our way through the maze of holding pens it becomes apparent that today's activities will be largely recreational. The selection is disappointing. There aren't many animals that meet Ralph's specifications. Having familiarized himself with what's available, he makes his way past the sales ring and takes a seat. The gray-painted bleachers are quite full. On a rainy day, a lot of farmers drop by just to pass the time.

The auctioneer is thin and sallow. He wears a cowboy hat and speaks into a microphone, conducting the proceedings from a sawdusted apron under a boldly lettered disclaimer. NOTICE: GUARANTEE ON ALL LIVESTOCK IS BETWEEN BUYER AND SELLER. WE

ACT AS AGENTS ONLY. He seems a skilled ventriloquist, barely moving his lips yet uttering a steady barrage of pinched, nasal, nearly unintelligible talk. "Here's a heifer for you boys just freshened Sunday boys tits and bag okay boys the man says. Here's a real milkwagon for you boys she'll do a good job for the money boys." The animal under consideration, a first-calf Holstein heifer, gazes dolefully out at the audience. After her comes a smallish Brown Swiss who looks as if she might make a nice family milker. There are heifers and steers, presented singly and in groups, newly weaned calves and matronly old dowagers—plenty of cows and dairy crosses but not many beef cattle. "We're just selling the heifers in this lot boys. Any of them calf you don't own the calves." Ralph has been taking notes in a small spiral-bound memo pad. A trio of young Hereford steers exits stage left. I lean over to ask if he's planning to buy any cattle. "I just bought those three," he replies. Oh. He's interested in the next lot too, heifer mates of the three he now owns, but he won't bid high enough to get them. "Sometimes I just can't tell where the price differences come from." In the end he purchases a total of five animals ("They're average. They'll do all right") before he tires of the sale and goes to the cashier's to settle up. That done, he escorts me down the street to a crowded tavern where we kill the afternoon drinking boilermakers and indulging his buddy LeRoy. LeRoy introduces himself as the chairman of the Foreign Trade Committee of the Delaware County Cattlemen's Association, and he's more than a little exercised about European protectionism and Japanese exploitation of American markets. The Japanese, it seems, have taken to shopping at Iowa livestock auctions for first-class animals with which to upgrade their herds back home. Like the Korean greengrocers at Hunts Point, they smilingly pay top dollar, oftentimes pushing up prices for the very best stock past what locals can afford. It's this, Ralph explains, that has so inflamed LeRoy's ire—that and the boilermakers.

The next day breaks bright and hot, ideal for haymaking. We can't really get going until yesterday's rain has burned off the fields, but by mid-morning the action begins in earnest. Tom takes the haybine over the far ridge to start cutting. Ralph, with one of the farm's several smaller tractors, rakes cut hay into windrows. He's double-raking on the last pass, combining two windrows into one, so that the baling will go faster. Not far behind trails the big International, captained by married daughter Linda, home on what passes for a vacation. The 856 pulls a boxy red New Holland baler. The baler is hitched in its turn to a hayrack. Operating yet another tractor, Steve ferries loaded racks from the field down across a muddy gully and up the other side to a corrugated steel shed on a hilltop some distance from the barnyard, an auxiliary hay storage facility that will soon be filled to bursting. He pauses there just long enough to assist Rita and Pat with the unloading, then rushes back to return the empty rack and pick up another full one.

I work with Francis on the hayracks. Francis has been in Ralph Engelken's employ for seven years now. He lives in a house trailer on Engelken land, and as is the custom takes morning and noon meals with the family. He was a long-haul trucker, he offers, but gave it up. He doesn't say why. Francis is of indeterminate middle age. He is solid. He does not appear to enjoy shaving. He has fewer than a full complement of teeth, and he grins often. Rita has told me that once a year, when Francis goes fishing on his week's vacation, she performs radical housecleaning on his bachelor quarters.

The baler labors and rattles, chugging, stuttering, punching out fastidiously wrapped packages of alfalfa and mixed grasses: timothy, brome, orchard. It operates with maddening punctuality. The bales come up fast and furious from the double-raked rows. In the bottoms where the hay grows thickest it's not easy to keep up, even with Linda driving dead slow. Once around the field fills a rack. Eighty bales. Two tons of hay. Francis sinks an iron cant hook into a bale as it crests the top of the chute, jerks it onto the wagon bed, and positions it just so. I imitate Francis. When I've placed a bale Francis waits politely for me to turn my back before repositioning it the way he wants it. I think of Frost's description of Silas, the hired man:

He bundles every forkful in its place,
And tags and numbers it for future reference,
So he can find and easily dislodge it
In the unloading. Silas does that well.
He takes it out in bunches like big birds' nests.
You never see him standing on the hay
He's trying to lift, straining to lift himself.

After a while I conclude that Francis might be better off without me, and accept a ride with Steve to join Pat and Rita in the shed. They are less discriminating, happy to have any help they can get. That the hay crop thus far has exceeded all expectations is at once gratifying and problematical. Most of the first cutting was chopped for haylage, filling three and a half of the farm's four Harvestores. In a normal year the second cutting would be baled, and with a full complement of cattle in the yards enough silage would be consumed before the third cutting came around that a good deal of that hay too could go into the silos. This year the silos are emptying more slowly. With seventy acres yet to cut the mow is already three-quarters full, and in several weeks the whole two hundred acres will be coming on again for a third time. Ralph would very much like to sell most of that hay standing in the field—provided he can get his asking price for it, sixty-five dollars a ton—in part at least because he's rapidly running out of places to put more bales. To curb the burgeoning surplus he will turn his brood cows out into the field we're now haying, consigning the crop to pasture rather than letting it grow up for a third cutting.

Steve pushes bales off the racks into the south-facing mouth of the shed. Pat, Rita, and I wrestle them back toward the rear wall, tumping them tight into an interlocking pattern like paving stones in a Tuscan piazza. My presence frees Steve to accelerate his delivery schedule, and loaded hayracks soon arrive with alarming frequency. Pat is fifteen, pretty and slim. She cannot possibly weigh more than 120. Three bales on the high end of a fulcrum would send her into orbit. She bucks bales two at a time, grabbing their twine waistbands and bulling them into place. Rita hefts bales to chest height and propels them fifteen feet through the air toward their prospective destinations. The tin roof of the shed is griddle hot. There is not even a memory of wind. Long pants and gloves are de rigueur bale-bucking attire, a bale of alfalfa being roughly analogous to a fifty-pound steel wool scour-pad. So should be long sleeves, but I can't stand it. After a few hours my bare forearms are finely minced and sauced with a profoundly pruritic solution of hay dust, pollen, and sweat.

Steve departs to collect another load. Rita mutinies, on the pretext of showing the visitor the ruined foundation of the farm's first farmhouse. We escape to a shaded glen where a perpetual spring has been fenced to keep the cows out of it. There is a lilac gone wild beside a soft, vaguely rectangular depression in the ground. The remains of a root cellar can be seen in the embankment nearby, still solid and dry inside, a neat stone arch intact at its entrance. Rita points out a row of fifteen black walnut trees, fully grown and laden with fruit. I lower my face to the shallow pool at the head of the spring and discover a fine crop of watercress growing in the tiny freshet that flows there. For the next ten minutes I graze happily, washing down my peppery fodder with gallons of icy spring water, then trudge up the hill again to confront our leguminous nemesis.

At eight in the evening the baler's counter indicates that we've made 977 bales, and Ralph decides to call it a day. He doesn't want to cut any more until he feels surer of the weather. Ralph hums as he works—no tune, just a melodic counterpoint—and he stops humming when he's done. "Another day, another dollar," he remarks. In fact, he's made a good deal more than that. Late last winter the price of sweet legume hay in this part of Iowa peaked at nearly $3 a bale. Ralph seeds his hayfields once in three, four, or even five years, at a cost (excluding fuel and machine time) of perhaps $25 an acre. From then until he plows it down, his expenses consist solely of whatever it costs him to harvest the approximately 36 tons of hay—slightly more than 1,400 bales—which that acre can reasonably be expected to produce before it is succeeded in his rotation by corn. "Where I really make my money is with the low input costs," Ralph explained to me one night at a sleepy little bar (the Eighth Inning

Inn, with a view of the American Legion league softball diamond) in Colesburg, near where he and Rita rented their first farm together. "On my hay ground I figure I'm paying out about eleven dollars an acre, all told. I don't tell people that very often, because they won't believe me anyway, so why bother?" Ralph contemplated the foamy head on his beer, then risked a maxim. "The best thing for the farmer," he said, "and I think the best thing for America too, is to get to where your input costs are as low as you can get them, then let nature do its work."

Our little flotilla of farm equipment sails for the barn. We bring along the baler, as it has taken to leaving some of its knots untied and wants adjusting before tomorrow. Rita, Pat, and Linda left an hour ago to get supper ready. Steve departs in the pickup to fetch Tom, so he won't have to drive the haybine all the way down and back. We once again leave the last two racks filled to be put up the following morning. Francis tows one of them with the 856 and Ralph pulls the other behind an ancient and unmuffled Deere. He has Linda's little boy Otto with him, pretending to drive, and as he backs the rack into the equipment shed where it will spend the night he bends his head close to whisper in his grandson's ear.

Before leaving Barrington Hall Farm I climb to the top of one of the seventy-foot Harvestores. It is a beautiful early morning: clear, calm, still cool. The atmosphere changes as I go up. Close to the ground there's a strong smell of manure and new hay; the air is heavy and damp from last night's brief rain. At seventy feet it's thinner, somehow fresher. There is a breeze up there that was not present down below.

I watch Francis jockey the front-end loader around the dugout pit silo, scooping out corn silage to feed the cattle milling about in the lot directly beneath me. To the east, beside a newly cut hay piece, Ralph's Easy Over Compost Turner is parked near a compost windrow that stands out from the field like a long scar. The oats ripening behind the house and garden are nearly ready for harvesting, and the Engelkens' earliest corn—far off at the perimeter of their property—is already in tassel. There's more corn to the west and north of the barn, and farther north still

I can make out the hayfields we baled this week, then a patch of deep woods, then the hillside where Tom's been cutting, with the red haybine parked in the middle of it, trailing a concentric tail, as if it were the secret hidden at the center of a maze.

I spent part of an afternoon up there with him, riding shotgun, feeling like a passenger on somebody's fancy power boat. The haybine is the size and shape of a Levittown one-bedroom but Tom navigates with nonchalant elan, overlapping his last pass just enough to ensure that he leaves no uncut tufts in his wake. He is eighteen years old—built like a fireplug, sprouting a moustache—and admits he's eager to get started on his own. Next year, in addition to working for his father, he plans to farm 160 acres on shares, cash-cropping corn and soybeans in an attempt to save some money. He'd like to milk cows, he thinks, and says hopefully that one of his older brothers might help stake him to a 30-cow dairy. Rita has mentioned this possibility as well—half torn, it seems, between wanting to see her son make something of himself and wishing he'd stay on the farm.

Round and round the field we go, our circles contracting with each circuit, following the topographic contours into protected little coves that dip into the woods off the main field, where the hay stands waist tall. Round and round, lulled by the throbbing engine and the heat of the sun, the rhythmic revolving of the rakes, the serrated cutter blades shuttling open and closed as a frothing green wave curls into the machine's gaping maw: clover and alfalfa, pink clover blossoms and purple alfalfa flowers, or chard grass, timothy, and an occasional weed, while ahead of us an evanescent cloud of yellow and white butterflies ascends from the field.

3

OUTGROWING THE GARDEN

At the Natural Organic Farmers Association (N.O.F.A.) conference in New Hampshire in 1980, where I first met him, Sam Smith had lured an overflow crowd into a steamy, airless classroom for a slide presentation and discussion of his small organic truck farm. He had been in business for only five years, on a farm so small (two acres under cultivation) as to be virtually imperceptible on the map of American agriculture. But he was said to have developed a system for farming those two acres that differed significantly from most of the existing models: an efficient and biologically conservative scheme founded on the principles of organic gardening but applicable to much larger operations. He was also said to be doing pretty well at it.

Sam Smith is a head-scratcher, an affable fellow whose bemused and self-deprecating manner mask massive determination. He is a thinking man's farmer, an officer of the International Federation of Organic Agriculture Movements capable of seemingly effortless segues from striped cucumber beetle control to global cropland deficits, and he quickly disabused his listeners of unrealistic expectations. "I would argue that a small system like mine *is* sustainable," he said, but he also spoke frankly of failure: the drainage tiling that didn't quite drain, the greenhouse that he hadn't known enough to insulate properly, the new vegetable varieties that looked so good in the seed catalogue but wouldn't move at the market. Sam Smith's assessment of his own vegetable farming operation was both passionate and thoroughly uncompromising.

Caretaker Farm is located on a parcel of well-used land at the edge of the Berkshires in Williamstown, Massachusetts. It's beautiful country, a rough-and-tumble New England amalgam of steep sidehills and fields cut from hardwood and conifer forests, but it doesn't look like prime farmland. It isn't. Smith's thirty-five acres are bisected by a stream that floods every spring. The hills to either side are studded with pockets of clay so pure it could go directly into the kiln. The whole of his tillable acreage is contained in a ten-acre piece of loamy bottomland—Sudbury Fine Sandy Loam, to be precise (Class II Agronomic Capability), and Warwick Gravelly Loam (Class III). According to the Soil Conservation Service, soils in Class II are somewhat restricted, and in Class III severely restricted, in their suitability for agricultural production. "If I had to pick a perfect farm," Sam Smith admits, "this certainly wouldn't be it. But who can afford prime farmland anyway? This is my home."

Sam put in his first garden in 1970, a French Intensive style, double-dug, raised-bed affair worked entirely by hand. It occupied less than a half-acre. He was working then as a teacher and administrator at a nearby community college. Gardening was strictly a hobby. In the years that followed he began to garden more and administer less, until in 1975 he finally jumped ship, as he puts it, to concentrate exclusively on Caretaker Farm. Every growing season since he's increased the amount of land farmed, and by 1982 he had 10 acres in production. He still grows his vegetables organically on raised beds; these days, some of those beds are 250 yards long. And he still does much of the work by hand, if for no other reason than that machinery designed for his size and type of farm is practically unavailable in this country.

Caretaker Farm's resemblance to a well-kept garden is no coincidence. The difference between gardening and farming is more than just a difference in scale; it's a fundamental difference in concept. Gardening begins with an acceptance of limits: there's only so much space and so much time. Gardeners apply heavy blankets of mulch because they would rather spend their time reading than weeding. They plant intensively so as to obtain the greatest possible harvest from a small plot. They ritually till in compost and manure, the good ones do anyway, to preserve the fertility of their backyard's finite topsoil supplies. Gardening well demands a willingness to work within certain limits.

Farming, on the other hand, at least in its conventional incarnation, has tended to be expansionist and characterized by a refusal to accept limits. Many of its proudest triumphs have been acts of defiance, the opening of previously unfarmable terrain to farming. The arid Nebraska Sand Hills, for instance, long reserved for rangeland, are perforated now with deep wells and sport improbable crops, irrigated by gangly self-propelled center pivot sprinklers that sweep ponderously around huge circular fields like the hands of giant clocks. On those rare occasions when agriculture has bowed before natural limits, the tendency has been to leave them behind. The landscape of western New England, of which Caretaker Farm is a part, is at present thickly wooded. The state of Massachusetts is seventy percent forest. At the outset of the nineteenth century, however, Massachusetts looked more like Iowa. Scenic panoramas of that era depict bald hilltops, bare hillsides, blank valleys. Stone walls buried deep in groves of fully grown trees once bounded open fields. When the thin soil on those fields was exhausted their farmers moved on, to Pennsylvania, to Ohio, Illinois, Iowa.

The land they left is Sam Smith's farmland. If Caretaker Farm's lowly soils are to produce consistent and bountiful harvests they will have to be encouraged, nurtured, pampered. Like a garden. The cornerstone of his system is the permanent raised bed. He builds planting beds six or eight inches high and four feet across, divided from one another by eighteen-inch paths set exactly five feet on center, to match the wheelbase of his tractor. He enforces a strict injunction against any traffic on the beds themselves: tractors, carts, and boots are confined to the paths. Sam cultivates only rarely, and then just the top few inches of the bed, after mowing, to incorporate the residue from short-term green mulches (buckwheat, mustard, rye) or longer-term, deep-rooted leguminous cover crops (alfalfa, vetch, clover). Conventional mold-board plowing, which completely inverts a layer of soil and sod as much as a foot deep, compacts the soil below that depth and produces a phenomenon known as plow-pan, an asphalt-like impediment to the upward mobility of nutrients. By using shallow rotary tillage—initially with a rototiller, more recently with a tractor-driven implement called a rotovator—Sam blends the cover-crop trash into the surface of the soil but leaves undisturbed the network of root channels, cracks and fissures, and earthworm burrows below. The result is a soil that's firm but supple, absorbent, respiratory, almost sentient. The beds are Sam Smith's profoundest delight. Thanks to them, he says, "the farm is more than a lot of endless rows; it's a lot of endless beds. But beds, I've found, have more character than rows."

Sam contends that quality, not quantity, must be the small grower's trump; everything else favors large producers. Most of what Sam grows is sold to local restaurants, or to retail customers who drive a considerable distance to call at Caretaker Farm's stand. He does not feature cut-rate prices. Sam knows his vegetables have to look and taste better than anything available elsewhere, so his standards are exceedingly high. As a consequence, the per hour compensation is pretty minimal: Caretaker Farm grosses just less than $3,000 an acre; the net profit is about half that. But Sam has succeeded at something that others have tried and failed to do: he has converted a fallow patch of marginal land into a rich and productive small farm. And he's earning his living from it.

"I figure this is a ten-dollar breakfast," Sam announces. It's half-past eight on the second morning in May and he has returned to the kitchen, after chores, for breakfast with his wife, Elizabeth, and Cindy, their current hired hand. He is eating warm crêpes stuffed with home-made cottage cheese and marmalade. He's well along on his second or third plateful when he offers an impromptu economic analysis of his repast. Sam Smith is forty-eight years old, bespectacled, professorial. Before becoming a vegetable farmer he graduated from Yale, got a master's degree in education, spent a year at divinity school, taught high school and college, and early on suffered a brief stint as an international investment banker. "I didn't last long at that; it really wasn't for me." He savors another bite, then estimates that his sawbuck breakfast has cost him about fifty cents. He and Elizabeth have lately added a new sideline at Caretaker Farm, bed and breakfast to tourists. "I'll bet they won't get breakfasts like this anyplace else," Sam says, spooning a last dollop of marmalade onto what's left of his crêpe. "How do you compute the net worth of a year of these breakfasts as a fraction of the farm's total output?"

In the past year Sam and Elizabeth have made the decision to commit themselves to Caretaker Farm rather than look for another place that is agriculturally better endowed. The effects of their resolution show up everywhere. They've installed solar panels by the house (hot water, a concession to the bed-and-breakfasters). They are backfilling a gully to provide additional parking space and building a new farmstand beside the road, making the barn available for Sam's expanding stock of equipment. He has at last invested in a tractor, a fifty-two horsepower Massey-Ferguson diesel, small by conventional standards but a good forty-four horses more powerful than the rototiller that until now had constituted his one concession to mechanization. He bought an array of attachments as well: a front-end loader, a five-foot Howard rotovator, a bush-hog rotary field mower, and a cultipacker seeder that will simultaneously prepare the seedbed and broadcast seed for his cover crops. The whole of his cropland has been newly fenced with the last word in deer dissuasion, an electrified, seven-strand barrier that tilts outward on the bias, increasing its effectiveness by scrambling the animals' depth perception. (Elizabeth Smith, wearing yet another hat, has become a franchised dealer of such fences.) Most notably, since his appearance at the N.O.F.A. conference three years ago Sam has more than tripled the amount of land he has under cultivation. With the bottomland now being worked, his original beds behind the house seem almost irrelevant by comparison. They've been outgrown.

"Oh yeah, we're a real farm now," Sam remarks as we make our way down the fields after breakfast to begin the day's primary task: transplanting by hand a thousand strawberry crowns. "We've even got a farm dog." His whistle brings the instantaneous arrival of a small, eager mongrel named Strider, a piebald collie-shepherd mix rescued by Elizabeth from a doomed litter. I ask Sam if Wolfie, his big square-headed black Labrador retriever, isn't also a farm dog. "Oh no," he replies. "I don't think so. More of a gentry dog."

Planting the strawberries demonstrates Sam's meticulous approach. The field where they'll go takes up one corner of his new bottom ground. Seeded to a legume cover crop a couple of years ago and plowed down this spring, the field was then rotovated and beds were formed with the tractor—much easier, Sam grants, than forming the beds by hand. Today we will put strawberry plants into the formed beds. It's possible to purchase a mechanical transplanter for use with the tractor, but Sam does not as yet own one. Instead, he paces the rows with a fourteen-foot one-by-six plank marked off like an oversized ruler in six-inch increments. The crowns are to be planted two feet apart. Sam lays his measuring stick on the edge of a bed. Every twenty-four inches, with the heart-shaped blade of a long-handled hoe, he excavates a slight cavity from the soil beside it. He works with a practiced economy of effort, using only his forearms, folding his lanky frame like a heron fishing in the shallows as he stoops to insert a white tongue-depressor next to each hole.

I follow behind him down the row, bearing a bucket full of compost and fertilizer, depositing two scoops of the stuff at every tongue-depressor, taking care—as instructed—not to fill up the holes. Next comes Cindy, carrying the strawberries. She clips back their roots to promote vigorous growth, then sets them gently into place, tamping the compost blend in around them. There might ideally be another worker, taking up the rear with a watering can, but we lack a fourth so that duty falls to me. Cindy's assignment takes longest, and when I've gotten well ahead of her I circle back behind, soaking each transplant with a swimming-pool-blue solution of brook water and Peters soluble plant food. One watering can waters about ten plants. Replenishing my supply means traversing the field, slipping through the fence to the brook, dipping two five-gallon plastic pails (ostensible contents: Dunkin' Donuts Bavarian Cream and Apple Strudel fillings) into a pool, then clambering back up with full pails. "I was thinking about irrigating down here," Sam muses, "but I was hoping I could hold off until next year on that. Now I see this field already getting a little dry and I wonder if maybe I hadn't better do it now. I don't know."

The cause of organic agriculture has not been much advanced over the years by the tendency of its supporters to substitute philosophy for facts. For commercial organic farmers like the Engelkens and Sam Smith, the quest for reliable research information is frustrating and often fruitless. The existing agricultural research system, dominated by the U.S. Department of Agriculture's Agricultural Research Service, concerns itself almost exclusively with conventional chemical methods. Organic farmers must look elsewhere for help, and they have been turning increasingly to the Rodale Research Center, a 305-acre complex of offices and laboratories, barns, greenhouses, and test fields, located in the Berks County, Pennsylvania, hamlet of Maxatawny.

The Rodale Research Center is the brainchild of Robert Rodale, editor and publisher of *Organic Gardening* and *The New Farm* and president of Rodale Press. The Rodale name has become virtually synonymous with organic farming in the United States, and its mere mention is enough to raise the hackles of many conventional agricultural scientists. There is a three-by-five card tacked to the wall of the Greenmarket office in New York that reads, "Greenmarket Quote for the Day: 'People like Rodale get all hung up on things like broccoli.' Dr. R. Brian Haw, Professor of Agricultural Economics, Cornell University." Rodale himself concedes that some skepticism may be justified. "The old style of organic research was one where you'd run this plot one way and that plot another way, and after a while you'd compare them and announce that the organic was better. We did that for about thirty years," Rodale says, "and it was not a really rewarding type of research."

The Rodale Research Center is modeled on university experiment stations and represents a clear attempt to legitimize organic research. It employs a full-time staff of thirty, more than half of them credentialed professionals working in development of new crops, horticulture, nutrition, agronomy, entomology, and the like. One of the Center's principal aims is to investigate and document the biological mechanics of places like Barrington Hall and Caretaker farms.

The director of the Rodale Research Center is Dr. Richard R. Harwood, a ruddy, heavyset man in his mid-forties who came to Maxatawny after ten years in the tropics with the International Rice Research Institute. When he was recruited for the position, Harwood initially balked. "I told Bob I didn't really believe in organics," he recalls. "He kept asking how I'd run things. Finally, he was so determined and it seemed like such a challenge that I actually began to consider the idea. My main underlying concern, I guess, was that I was throwing my career away. This was back in 1976, when there was no respectability at all to this kind of research, at least from a scientific point of view."

Harwood eventually took the job on the condition that he would have carte blanche to redesign the Center's research agenda. "My feeling is pretty simple," he explains. "Either there are biological differences or there aren't. If there are, I want to know what they are. If there aren't any differences then there really isn't anything *to* organics. It's religion then, not science. There has to be a scientific base to it or there isn't anything there. Well, there's a lot of evidence out there now—fairly soft evidence, I'll admit, because we haven't documented it yet, but evidence nonetheless—that in fact there *is* something to it. Farmers are practicing organic techniques, and they're working, and we're getting bits and pieces of good hard scientific data to show why they're working. No, ninety percent of the scientists probably shouldn't be working on organics, but two or three percent should. We can't afford not to. If organics has the potential to reduce erosion by eighty percent, as the Lambert farm (an eight-hundred-acre organic wheat farm in the erosion-prone Palouse hills of eastern Washington) seems to show, then that's reason enough to look closely at it. And if it can reduce energy inputs by sixty percent, as Lockeretz says, or even by only thirty percent, then we ought to be finding out how and why."

Part of this inquiry is underway in a fifteen-acre field off Siegfriedale Road a half-mile west of Harwood's office. The Conversion Project, as it's called, is intended to explore the effects of organic management on chemically farmed land, but, ironically, there isn't any chemically farmed land left on the Rodale property. When Bob Rodale bought the old Siegfried place with an eye toward putting his research facilities there, he leased two-thirds of the farm's acreage to a neighboring Mennonite farmer, Ben Brubaker, who promised to farm it organically (though he used conventional practices on his own farm). By 1980, when the notion of the Conversion Project was taking shape in Dick Harwood's mind, the fields Ben Brubaker was farming had already been converted—so satisfactorily, in fact, that Brubaker had given up chemicals on the rest of his land as well. So an adjacent field, as yet unreconstructed, had to be leased for the Conversion Project.

For the purposes of dramatic metaphor the conversion field could hardly be better sited. It is literally sandwiched between opposing ideologies. To the west and north one neighbor cultivates two thousand acres of corn, soybeans, and small grains—mostly wheat. His fields roll westward in monotonous succession, unbroken by windbreaks or hedgerows, arranged for the convenience of large-scale planting and harvesting equipment. On the steep south-facing slope directly north of the conversion field this farmer two years ago planted winter wheat. He harvested his crop in July, turned the stubble under, then left the ground bare. It rained. Topsoil washed down in a muddy torrent laced with fertilizer and pesticide. The Research Center dug a diversion ditch to prevent the run-off from contaminating Conversion Project data.

To the southeast of the conversion field lies the land leased to Ben Brubaker. Brubaker has divided his 322 acres into some 94 distinct fields. His fields are compact, trig, variously shaped, no bigger than 3 or 4 acres apiece. They are tailored to the contour and character of the land, and to something less quantifiable but probably equally important: Ben Brubaker's intuitive sense of what will do best when and where. "He's strip-cropping," Dick Harwood says, "and he keeps his strips narrow to control erosion on the slopes. He has small enough equipment that he can do that. These guys with thousands of acres have to have huge equipment, so they can't strip-crop. They have to farm whole fields. Even if they wanted to break up the fields, they have nothing to break them up with. They plant corn, beans, and wheat, and that's that. With equipment that big you can't fiddle around with little fields. You have to put the whole thing into one crop—you don't really have an option." Ben Brubaker, by contrast, not only grows a variety of different crops, but grows different varieties of each crop. He has, for example, at least four sorts of hay: alfalfa, clover, a clover-timothy mix, and straight timothy. He keeps perhaps a hundred acres in hay, but his harvest is obligingly staggered. He'll cut his alfalfa first, then move on to his clover. The clover-timothy mixes come off next, and his pure timothy will wait patiently until last without lodging in the field. His haying is spread over six weeks, improving his climatic odds and absolving him of the need for large-scale equipment.

"The conversion field has been in chemical agriculture for at least thirty years," Harwood explains. "It's been pretty well taken care of. The K and P are good. The organic matter content is reasonably high and holding steady. Then you cross the fencerow to an organic field that's already been through the conversion process. It's got the same amount of organic matter as the conversion field. Last year we grew corn in both fields, without nitrogen fertilizer. In the organic field we had 137-bushel corn, which is good but typical, and there was 160 pounds of nitrogen in the above-ground plant parts. In the chemical field we got 37 bushels, with about 59 pounds of nitrogen taken up by the plants. Our soil tests showed the same thing. In the organic field we found twenty-eight parts per million of nitrate in the soil wash solution, indicating that there is a real source of nitrogen there, feeding soluble nitrogen into the system. The conventional field, unfertilized, tested out at three parts per million. With three parts per million nitrate there's no way your corn's going to get enough to survive. We have to conclude that the organic matter in the chemical field was inactive and wasn't supplying nitrogen."

Harwood thinks this may be one of the biological differences he's been hunting for. He surmises that the reason the conventional field's organic matter was inactive is that constant treatment with chemical fertilizers has undermined the soil's ability to extract usable nitrogen from natural sources. He's certain, he says, that there is a voluminous flow of nutrients through the insect and microbial phases of organic soil. A Ph.D. candidate in entomology at Michigan State is in residence at Maxatawny, investigating the habits of one microscopic species of bug, Collembola, which dines on microorganisms in the soil and in digesting them makes nutrients available to plants. This sort of activity, Harwood says, seems to be slowed or stopped by the presence of chemical fertilizers. What he has begun to suspect is that a conventional farming system encourages a net downward flow of nutrients through the soil structure: fertilizers applied as soluble salts rather quickly disappear, either washing off the surface or leaching down to the subsoil. In an organic system it seems that there may be a net upward movement of nutrients as deep-rooted leguminous plants—alfalfas, vetches, some peas and clovers—literally mine fertilizer from the lower reaches of the soil profile.

"That would be consistent with what we're finding on long-term organic farms," Harwood conjectures, "like the Lambert farm in Washington. Don Lambert's family has been farming that place for eighty years and they've never put on any fertilizer. They haven't even used any animal manures. His P and K levels are higher than his neighbors—his phosphorus is forty percent higher, and they've been fertilizing! He's self-sufficient in nitrogen. I would argue that if you go into one of his fields and take a deep core sample, go down forty or sixty inches, you'll find that he has fewer nutrients at that depth than his neighbors do, because that's where his fertilizer is coming from." And by logical extension, where theirs is going.

What captivates Harwood is nutrient flow. A 200-proof shot of soluble nitrogen might do more harm than good, he suggests, if it simply shuts down the biological activity of the soil, short-circuiting the nutrient flow. If you're going to use synthetic fertilizers, Harwood ventures, it seems sensible to mix them first with compost, thereby binding them into the topsoil and counteracting their deleterious effect on the soil biology. "When I explain it this way to soil scientists, they'll say, 'Well, that makes sense.' Then they think on it a bit, and a little later they'll say, 'You know, that would explain a lot of what we've been seeing.' "

It is difficult to find anyone involved in the Conversion Project who's willing to toe the rigid organic line. They'd rather you found your fertilizer somewhere on your own farm, of course, but they won't completely rule out synthetics. In the initial stages of a conversion they will go so far as to suggest that farmers keep up diminishing applications of chemical fertilizers. "Otherwise they'll probably close up shop," one staffer remarks, "and what good would that do?" They're opposed to insecticides on principle, but they'll countenance their use in a Integrated Pest Management system along with mixed croppings and releases of beneficial predators. They're even soft on herbicides. One of the more startling projects in progress here monitors conditions in a three-acre field that, having been successfully converted from conventional to organic management, is now being gradually returned to chemicals. "We want to drive the system in both directions at once," Harwood explains. "We want to see how rapidly we can destroy an organic system by pushing it backward."

Organic agriculture may actually demand a higher level of technical sophistication than conventional farming. The organic farmer has to stay on top of a host of biological interactions that are occurring simultaneously on his farm, from the microfauna and microflora in his topsoil to the livestock loafing in his barnyard. This management demand, and not culture or politics or even biology, may turn out to be the limiting factor on organic farm size. There's no biological reason why organic methods should not work on the grandest agribusiness scale, so long as the necessary management can be supplied. "What it takes is a direct link between management and biology," Harwood says, "whereas in a conventional system we've gotten completely away from that. You'll see a bank officer in Illinois writing out a formula for five thousand acres. The farmers just follow orders. There's no biological feedback whatsoever, because none is needed."

For his feature presentation Dick Harwood displays Ben Brubaker, whose own experiment with organics is both contained within and in a very real sense also contains the Rodale Conversion Project. "What you're looking at in a system like Ben Brubaker's is a much greater input of management time," Harwood comments. "He spends a fair amount of time just walking. You'll see him out there walking across his fields, tipping his hat back and scratching the top of his head. I love to go out there then, in the morning. He'll say, 'Dick, I just don't know what to do about this field. What do you think? Should I plant it now and go with corn, or wait another week to let it get rained on once more and put in soybeans instead?' Then he'll notice a few weeds, and he'll say, 'You remember last year there was this patch of weeds down here? I'll bet if I let it go for soybeans I'll have a terrible time with those weeds.' He knows exactly what's happening in each of his fields and he's predicting what the biological responses are going to be. He has a good sense for it, and he does well. He doesn't just drive by in his pickup and look over his shoulder. He gets out and walks the field, and he remembers what's happened there before. He'll say, 'Well, it's been a bit dry this year, and we're ahead of the dock down there, so it might not hurt us too much. I think maybe we can get away with beans.' He's always anticipating."

Ben Brubaker's cornfields yield approximately 120 bushels to the acre, 30 bushels better than the state average. His cost of production, meanwhile, runs to roughly half the state's mean. Pennsylvania's Corn Club farmers—the premier corn growers in the state—report production costs of $1.50 to $2.00 a bushel. A bushel of Ben Brubaker's organically grown corn costs him $.70 or $.80. "But the interesting thing—and I think it's more interesting than the low costs alone," Harwood says, "is that in Ben's case eighty percent of his costs are in labor and machinery time: his own machinery and his own labor. Only twenty percent was cash outlay. Those other guys are just the opposite, eighty percent cash and twenty percent labor. They aren't really getting much of a return on their investment in equipment. Their major return is coming on a cash investment in chemicals.

"That's one big difference between the two systems. A second difference is that Ben has a much lower horsepower requirement. The size of his basic units is smaller. On three hundred and some acres he'll plant maybe ninety acres to corn—his biggest single crop. That means he never has to handle more than ninety acres at any one time. Most farmers around here with three hundred acres have three hundred acres of corn. They need a big tractor because they have to cover a lot of ground in a hurry. So Ben can get by with smaller, older, and cheaper equipment. And he can adjust better to changes in the weather. He doesn't need all his machinery or manpower at once; he works over a longer period of time. His neighbor probably left two weeks ago for Arizona or someplace. I doubt he's even here now. Once he gets done planting, he's free until harvest time, and he doesn't have anything for his big tractor to do in between. It just sits up there in his barn. He works that machine about eight weeks out of the year and the rest of the time it's idle: a one-hundred-and-twenty-five-thousand-dollar investment sitting in a shed."

Harwood stops, suddenly conscious, perhaps, of having crossed the invisible line from science into something more closely resembling religion. "American agriculture has gotten used to that sort of thing," he says at last, "but in the future I don't see how we're going to be able to afford it. It's just too damn expensive."

An Easter blizzard in 1982 left Caretaker Farm under two feet of snow. The forsythias and daffodils have wisely waited until May to bloom. Sam says he'll have to forgo some of his spring crops altogether. His spinach and peas should have been planted weeks ago; if he puts them in now it will be high summer when they mature, and the odds are they'll bolt before they bear. He worries about his onions as well, and about the health of seedlings held indefinitely under glass while he waits for the weather to improve. Sam worries about everything. The phrase, "I don't know," serves him as spoken punctuation.

Sam's situation neatly illustrates why smaller diversified farmers like him and Ben Brubaker have slipped into the minority while large-scale single-crop specialists like Brubaker's neighbor have multiplied. Caretaker Farm is nothing if not diversified. Sam raises perhaps two dozen different vegetables and small fruits for market, plus several beds of flowers as cutting stock for his restaurant accounts, to say nothing of the various cover crops he includes in his rotations. He also keeps on hand an ark-like barnyard menagerie, mostly for home consumption: Clara, his Jersey milker, and Clara's heifer; a flock of laying hens, a small flock of broilers, four feeder pigs, three muscovy ducks, and two turkeys. And he's toying with the possibility of getting sheep.

It's true, as their proponents assert, that small diversified farms like Smith's and Brubaker's are generally resource-efficient, more conserving and more flexible than larger specialized operations. This endows them with certain advantages: low overhead chiefly, and the option of adjusting their production plans on fairly short notice to changing market conditions. In Sam's case these are not options so much as necessities. Caretaker Farm probably couldn't survive financially any other way. This is part of what makes places like his so important. If it were not producing his good vegetables, the land he farms would almost certainly be producing nothing at all.

But what small-farm advocates mention less often, and less loudly, is that farming Sam Smith's way is extraordinarily demanding. When Dick Harwood discusses management inputs, he is talking about some farmer's time and energy. One reason why big monocrop farms have proliferated, along with the agricultural chemicals and powerful tractors and sophisticated implements they require, is that this style of farming makes life a lot easier for the farmer. Ben Brubaker's neighbor goes to Arizona while herbicides keep his fields clean. Ben goes out and cultivates. His neighbor stays on in Sun City through Brubaker's six weeks of haying. The more diversified a farm is, the more management input it requires—which helps to explain why so many Corn Belt farmers jumped at the chance to get rid of their livestock and become cash-grain producers, banishing pigs and cattle forever from their farms and leaving the feeding to feedlots. The consequences of these decisions may well prove disastrous over the long haul, but the motivation behind them is entirely understandable. A 5,000-acre corn-and-beans kingdom in Indiana probably requires no more of its owner—and quite conceivably somewhat less—than Caretaker Farm extracts from

Sam Smith. "Being a good market gardener is like being a good woodworker, or a good writer, or a good anything," Sam said to me once. "You've got to have some skill, you've got to have patience, you've got to pay attention, and you've got to be suited to it. There just aren't that many people who are suited to it, especially in a culture where you can do just about anything else, where you can pump gasoline, and make more money."

As entertainment, transplanting strawberry crowns begins to pall after about two hours. It's stoop labor, for which Sam touts his elevated planting beds as partial relief, but the six extra inches don't seem to me to help much. Sam and I fall into synch and converse as we move along, talking across the bed about the expansion of Caretaker Farm. One difficulty he's encountered, he says, is that raised-bed planting on the scale he's attempting, while not uncommon in Europe, is without precedent in this country. This means that there is no technical support base here for his brand of agriculture, particularly when it comes to machinery and mechanization. American agricultural technology skips lightly from garden tillers to tractors too cumbersome to turn around on Caretaker Farm's tiny plots, much less perform any useful work. The middle is poorly served. Not only is there nothing new and shiny available on the showroom floor, there are no agricultural engineers attending to the special challenges of a system like Sam's, no graduate students building prototype machines, no breakthroughs in the offing.

Agricultural mechanization is the classic Catch-22. For innovative machinery to be introduced, manufacturers insist they must first be convinced that there will be a market for it. But markets have traditionally sprung up in response to—and not in advance of—the introduction of new equipment. Before World War Two, for example, hay on American farms was universally harvested loose, by hand, then loaded onto wagons and put up in the mow by strong men with hayforks—the farmer's sons usually, and his hired men. Frost's Silas was admired for his skill with a hayfork. In 1940, when the New Holland company brought out the first automatic baler, farmers reacted with skepticism. How well would the bales hold up in storage? How dependable would the baling machines be? Farmers' sons, predictably, reacted somewhat differently. They proceeded to acquire balers the moment control of the farm passed into their hands. Balers soon became ubiquitous.

Sam's problem is that the prospective market in this country for small-scale raised-bed truck farming technology has been considered and found wanting. It is a problem compounded by the fact that American farm equipment manufacturers, like American automakers, would rather sell limousines than compacts. (Agricultural economist Patrick Madden is fond of quoting a John Deere executive who told him, "Small tractors make small profits.") The likelihood of International Harvester's unveiling a new line of bed-tenders and small-meadow crop-harvesters any time soon is slim indeed, let alone the machine of Sam's dreams: a kind of hermaphrodite truck-tractor hybrid, able to do a tractor's job in the fields and a truck's on the road. Not that such vehicles don't exist. I have a glossy color brochure listing the many advantages of the Reform Muli 50/150, which looks something like a small but heavily built flatbed truck. The flier is in German, but as near as I can tell from the pictures it's just what Sam has in mind. Here's the Reform Muli at rest in an Alpine meadow, with a haybine attached to its rear and its body converted into a forage wagon, with a silage chopper mounted to its flank, as a manure spreader, and with a dump body on, dumping. Here's the Reform Muli on its way to market, with farmer Klaus, young wife Marlene, and little Werner riding merrily up front. "Perfekt im Detail—vollendeter Fahr und Bedienungskomfort." The trouble is the Reform Muli is manufactured and sold in Austria, and no United States sales network has yet materialized. Woe to the poor farmer whose Reform Muli hauls up lame and leaves him with no alternative save taking it round to his local John Deere dealer for repairs.

So Sam has had to assemble an inventory of equipment that is for the most part not quite appropriate for the work he wants it to do. Looking around at his new tractor, his new fence, his new planting beds, and his new strawberries, Sam sings a muted lament. He finds himself in a sort of no-man's-land, battling the agricultural establishment on the one hand but considered something of a turncoat by his own troops on the other. "I'm in hot water with the Wendell Berry wing," he sighs, "and I'm in trouble with Earl Butz too. I'm in trouble with everybody." (Later, standing by the brook mixing pails of plant food, Sam would be mildly chastised by a former apprentice who'd dropped over for the afternoon to help. "Sam," she asked, "are you sure it's safe to be using chemicals like that so close to the stream?" Sam glanced plaintively in my direction. "You see!" Farming is a business built on compromise, and nobody stays pure for long.

We are approached as we work by a large and apparently fearless turkey, the tom of the farm's pair, out for an unscheduled constitutional. This old bird has seen the far side of November often enough to harbor no nervousness about his mortality. He is a celebration of ego, ruffling his tail feathers, puffing out his chest, shaking his variegated wattles and comb. Sam sees him coming and groans.

"Eat him, Strider," he commands. "Go on. Eat that turkey."

The bird crowds in close, peering over Sam's shoulder, violating his personal space. He supervises. He considers the quality of Sam's work, gobbles disapprovingly. He steps on newly planted seedlings.

"Eat him, Strider."

"What's his name?"

"Turkey. He hasn't got one. Come on Strider, eat that bird."

Strider prudently concludes that he might be outmatched. The turkey, oblivious, stays on a full hour before Elizabeth comes to retrieve him and call us for lunch.

There is a ruminative air about Sam Smith, an echo of the lapsed seminarian surfacing now and then in the novice farmer. He is an admitted moralist. He habitually cross-examines himself. He is suspicious of his own motives. "Everyone's backed somehow," he said to me over lunch once. "The fact is you can't buy a farm anymore in the United States without being backed. There's nobody farming, no small farmers anyway, who aren't backed in some way. They've made money in previous occupations, or they've inherited the farm. Something.

"I think that people like myself, a lot of us very small farmers, know deep down that this isn't really a viable model. I don't know if any of us wants to admit it, and maybe I'm extrapolating too much from myself. Talk to me tomorrow and maybe I'll change my mind, but I just don't think that this is a model. Maybe for the very long term, yes, but not in the short run.

"So why do we do it? I suspect it's because we see in small farming the possibility of making a modest income in an honorable manner. Maybe it's a copout. I've been accused of that." He knows, he says, that he is not a "real farmer." If he were, if he had grown up on a farm and progressed through 4-H and Future Farmers of America and a land-grant college education, he would have been taught that what he is doing is impossible, and being a smart fellow he probably wouldn't have tried. Out of Sam Smith's ignorance came Caretaker Farm.

If Sam is in one sense liberated by his lack of an agricultural background, he is hampered by it as well. His handicap is most evident in his relationship with his equipment. He has had to teach himself in middle age what farm kids instinctively understand by the time they're twelve. This is not an intellectual process. Most of the equipment on most small farms is old, nursed along, and when it gives up the ghost it's replaced more often than not with something second-hand. Not least among the things we stand to lose if we let the small family farm become extinct is a tradition of innate handiness passed down through generations of farmers and farmers' sons. The drivers of quarter-million-dollar, fully computerized, air-conditioned grain combines cannot easily carry on that tradition. Neither can born-again farmers like Sam Smith, much as he wishes he could.

When Sam mechanized he bought new equipment, at great cost. When something goes sour, he's hard pressed to put it right by himself. Mechanical handiness is like a foreign language: proficiency is most simply attained if it's spoken at home when you're young. Now, when Sam fails to show up promptly for supper, I'm sent out to see if he needs help with the chores but he hasn't even begun the chores yet. He's hunkered down under his new tractor.

"What's up?"

"Well, a sort of a crisis."

The tractor's left front wheel has collapsed. The lug nuts

holding it unaccountably loosened; some of them must have fallen off in the field and when the last lugs gave way the tractor pitched forward onto its loader bucket. One nut was stripped out and another torn through the rim. Sam is distraught. "Of all the times for this to happen," he mutters despairingly, "why'd it have to be now?" We set about jacking up the front axle, so as to remove the ruined wheel, but a jack footed in compost has structural shortcomings. The job proceeds slowly. Sam rushes, gets angry, and counsels himself: "Slow down Sam, slow down."

We are about halfway through removing the wheel when a neighbor appears, by the name of Charlie, round of face and frame, a short man ornamented with a porkpie hat and an unlit pipe. Charlie's a retired dairyman who has come, at Sam's behest, to consult on the possible irrigation of Caretaker Farm.

"Hello Charlie," Sam offers mournfully, when he notices his neighbor's presence. "Look at this mess! This wouldn't happen to a real farmer, would it? It wouldn't happen to someone who'd owned a lot of tractors, only to new farmers, first time tractor owners like me."

"Happened to me in a truck once," Charlie says.

Sam summons the will to discuss irrigation—"I didn't feel much like it," he later acknowledged—and obtains the name of a reputable pipe and pump dealer in New York. They talk of fences and coons in the corn, and Sam casts an unhappy glance toward his new ground. "I'll bet there's a lot of coons down in that bottom part," he says.

"I'll bet so," says Charlie.

"The phrase 'organic farming' is itself redundant," Sam said to me late one afternoon. "I hope the day will come when no modifier is needed before the word 'farming,' when there'll just be good farmers and bad farmers. I'm inclined to agree with Eliot Coleman that it doesn't matter what you call your system of farming. What matters is whether, in the long run, your benefits outweigh your costs. In the very long run, which is the kicker. Organic farming can't be an end in itself. It's just one tiny window onto a much larger transition that has to take place in people's thinking."

What worries him most is the sense that the agricultural middle class is disappearing—that we are in danger of losing the size of farm that can adequately support a family without having to be subsidized. Sam said, "The disappearing middle suggests that eventually there will be only very large, mostly absentee-owned megacorporate farms, though corporate isn't really the right word, since a lot of family farms are incorporated for tax purposes, but big business outfits in which the farmers are just hired hands. Then we'll wind up with only two tiers: the huge operations run by businessmen, and the marginal operations, the very small, part-time farms that don't really count for much, and among which I count my own. And all the rhetoric, and all the N.O.F.A. conferences, and all the other meetings all around the country all amount to a kind of dream that we've got something to fall back on if that big system collapses.

"Well," he amends, "we do have a backup, but it's a mighty small backup, and it's not an alternative in any real sense. Driving into Williamstown, you can take the high road or the low. The high road is five miles and the low is five-point-two. The low road runs along the river, so it's a little prettier. That's an alternative. Small market gardens are by no means an alternative to conventional agriculture. They're the best we've got, but they sure won't get us to town."

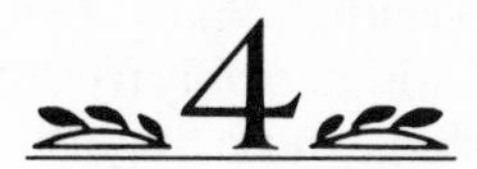

LOCALLY GROWN

Constance and Bertha are sisters. They keep house together in a small apartment in Queens, and they have acquired the telepathic consonance of old people long in one another's company. Addressed, they quite often answer in unison. They are fastidiously turned out today, in light coats, plain spring dresses, and wide-brimmed hats that shield their milky complexions from the sun.

They're not nearly so frail as they look. On Saturdays throughout the summer they double-line their ancient shopping bags and descend to the subway for the circuitous trip into Manhattan, changing trains twice before they surface finally here, at the Union Square Greenmarket, at Broadway and Fourteenth Street. Here, where the farmers come to sell their fresh produce, Constance and Bertha infallibly come too. They've stationed themselves just now before two bushel baskets brimming with green beans—nice-looking beans, first of the season, the only beans in the market. Constance and Bertha are in no hurry. They are selecting with care the beans they intend to purchase. They are picking them out one at a time.

I am fond of these two because they seem as irredeemably addicted to this experience as I am. On this warm June morning the northwestern border of Union Square is teeming with similarly afflicted New Yorkers. They're layered six deep at the farmers' trucks, stuffing their rucksacks and shopping carts with fine country provender, awaiting their opportunity to redistribute some of their city wealth. Some goes to Sandra Roman, the Long Island fish lady, for impeccably fresh Montauk fillets. Some goes to Bob Van Nostrand, whose fingertips are stained crimson with strawberry juice. Some goes to Frank Stiles, for vegetables grown in Gloucester County, New Jersey; to Don Keller, for Orange County, New York, vegetables; to Norbert and Barbara Kohlmaier for plump chickens recently deceased. Some goes for Rich Hodgson's eggs, the jumbos please, the ones in the pale heliotrope styrofoam cartons. Some little goes to me too, at the market manager's table, for sturdy white plastic shopping bags with the word *Greenmarket* emblazoned across them in italic lettering, above a bright green apple. I do a brisk trade in shopping bags. It's reassuring to note that most of these people are no more able to control themselves than I am, once they're here.

"Have you got shopping bags?"

"Could I have a shopping bag, please?"

"Two shopping bags, please. I guess I'll need two."

"They're reusable."

"How much are the bags this year?"

"Forty cents."

"Forty cents! How much were they last year?"

"Forty cents."

"They've gone up!"

"Are they strong, the bags?"

The woman who wants strong bags has her arms full of Greenmarket produce. She looks like the goddess Persephone as depicted on the frontispiece of a nineteenth-century agrarian tract. Bob Van Nostrand, beside us, has just added two pints of strawberries to her load.

"I never knew about this!" she exclaims.

She is a transient. Transients happen past the market on their way somewhere else and are drawn irresistibly in, like ducks decoyed to a pond. You can tell the transients by their surprised expressions, and by the fact that their arms are full. Regulars learn to bring their own shopping bags. They know, for example, that if they want one of the Kohlmaiers' chickens, they'll have to get to market before nine-thirty. They know that for a decent selection of cut flowers they will have to arrive even earlier. Regulars rarely look dazed; they look greedy.

"Are you here all the time?"

"Wednesdays and Saturdays at Union Square, but there are other markets around the city on other days. Would you like a schedule?"

At the manager's table we answer questions, disseminate information, sell shopping bags, take orders for Greenmarket T-shirts, accept suggestions and complaints, watch the variegated crowd ebb and flow. This being one of the season's first market days, there are a fair number of people stopping by, regulars and transients both, picking up schedules, asking the whereabouts of favorite farmers who seem to be missing from the ranks. ("He grows grapes. He hasn't got any grapes grown yet. He won't be in until September.")

Constance and Bertha wander over with their half-pound of perfect green beans and seat themselves on our bench, resting a moment in the shade of our purple-striped picnic umbrella. Jane Weissman, Greenmarket's assistant director and the manager of the Saturday market at Union Square, inquires after their health. "Oh," they reply simultaneously, "we've been well." Jane seems to know three-quarters of the people who come into the market, if not by name then at least by sight, and today she is spending a substantial amount of her time exchanging greetings and renewing lapsed acquaintances.

"This is the first day, isn't it?"

"No, last week was. Did you know we're having a Wednesday market in Union Square this year?"

"Are you in charge here?"

"No, not really." Jane has gone off to take a turn round the market. "Can I help you with something?"

"I want to make a complaint about the bacon." Stocky, stern, fiftyish, and well fed. "They say it's nitrite-free, but it isn't. We found a list of ingredients stamped on the covering." Her husband obediently nods. She repeats her accusation three or four times until I've written it all down and agreed to take up truth-in-advertising with Jimmy Van Houten.

"That's the infamous nitrite lady," Wm. Levine remarks. A part-time Greenmarket staffer and former market manager, Levine has this year crossed to the other side of the table, having put in a small truck garden in Westchester County. He sells on Wednesdays at Union Square, and he's attempting to get a Saturday market off the ground in suburban White Plains. He is here this morning strictly to socialize. He has met the nitrite lady before. "She comes around every year to complain," Wm. says. "I don't know why she bothers to eat bacon."

"Isn't this just wonderful?" Svelte, blonde, Adidas, and running gear.

"It's so reminiscent of Europe." Ditto.

"How much are the shopping bags?"

The past decade has seen a remarkable renaissance of agricultural direct marketing in this country. Ten years ago the debut of New York's first Greenmarket was still three years off. Today, with its eighteen branches generating a total sales volume approaching $4 million annually, Greenmarket has all the trappings of an institution.

The new direct marketing movement is broad-based and diverse, but farmers' markets are undoubtedly its most visible aspect. In 1982 *American Vegetable Grower* magazine estimated that there were fifteen thousand of them in the United States, half again as many as there had been just three years earlier. Over the same three-year period the gross receipts at these markets nearly tripled. *Fruit Grower*, another trade publication, editorialized in its June 1982 issue on the "coming of age" of direct marketing: "Indeed, the sheer number of pick-your-own operations and roadside markets virtually guarantees that they will be a considerable marketing force. There are 21,000 such operations now across the United States, a number that far exceeds the number of outlets of any major retail supermarket chain." The impetus for all this activity isn't difficult to discern. As the gap has widened between the wholesale prices paid to farmers for what they produce and the retail prices charged consumers at the supermarket, more and more people at either end of the food system have begun looking for ways to bypass the middle.

Nor is the new direct marketing limited to produce hawked from farmers' markets and roadside stands. In northern New England, for example, efforts to revive regional sheep farming have concentrated on boosting prearranged sales of freezer lamb direct from farm to consumer. In New York and California, and no doubt elsewhere as well, the proprietors of first-class restaurants and food shops have begun contracting directly with local farmers for supplies of high-quality, hard-to-find or exotic foods. In Nebraska, I met a farmer who raises small grains for direct sale. Forced back onto the last forty acres of what had been his father's much larger farm, Dick Dye has been weaning himself from borrowed capital. He is an organic farmer now, growing oats, rye, and wheat. He harvests his crop when it's ripe with an antique combine, salvaged and rebuilt for less than the cost of just once hiring a custom crew to come out and do his harvesting for him. He stores what he harvests in used grain bins on his own farm, rather than pay the cost of storage at the town elevator. Alongside the grain bins, under an improbable assemblage of scrap lumber, corrugated sheet metal, and black plastic tarpaulins, Dye has mustered a low-rent challenge to Kellogg's of Battle Creek. He cleans and hulls his own grain, and when an order comes in he mills it himself, into wheat berries, rye flakes, or rolled oats. Then he bags what he's milled, stacks the bags in his truck, and sets off across the prairie to deliver his cereal. On the day I visited he was getting ready for a nine hours' drive south into central Kansas with a load of rolled oats for a food co-op there. "Last year," Dick Dye said with unconcealed pride, "a hundred and eighty thousand pounds of bagged grain left this farm, and all of it left in that truck."

There is nothing novel about farmers' markets, of course. In parts of Europe, and more strikingly in Latin America, loosely organized farmers' markets still perform many of the same functions that wholesale terminal markets do here. In some ways, what may be most significant about the recent rebirth of direct marketing in the United States is the new sense of regionalism it represents. One of modern agriculture's principal wonders is the extent to which large-scale centralized food production and distribution has blurred regional dietary boundaries. For a long time this phenomenon was widely and uncritically welcomed. Paul Campbell, editor and associate publisher of *The Packer* ("The National Weekly Business Newspaper of the Fruit & Vegetable Industry"), recalls that when he joined the paper in 1967 the mood of the fresh fruit and vegetable industry was unrelievedly gloomy. "Frozen was in then," Campbell recalls, "and fresh was in trouble. It wasn't even a question anymore of *if* frozen would take over completely; it was a question of when."

I met Paul Campbell for lunch one day, at a restaurant tucked into a shopping mall near his suburban Kansas City office, and he talked about how the prognosis had improved since then. The social and dietary changes of the 1970s sparked a largely unanticipated reversal of the industry's sagging fortunes, Campbell told me. By the end of the decade the produce departments of supermarkets were the fastest-growing segment of the business.

When a waitress had taken our orders, Campbell and I joined the line at the salad bar. "Look at this!" Campbell commanded, as diners piled their plates with fresh spinach, lettuce, raw broccoli, cherry tomatoes, sliced mushrooms, and alfalfa sprouts. "How many salad bars do you think there were in 1967? Not many, I'll tell you that much. This is exactly the type of thing that's saved us."

The same wealth and prosperity that fueled the rise of the new agriculture—and concurrently hastened the demise of so many smaller regional farms—may turn out to be at least partly responsible for the tentative revival of regional agriculture. The American attitude toward eating underwent pronounced revision during the decade that saw the emergence not only of salad bars and new-style farmers' markets, but midweek food and cooking sections in metropolitan newspapers, and expanded opportunities for international travel. As the modern conventional food system matured and we began to take its abundance for granted, consumers were able to think of food not simply as a necessity but as entertainment. They began asking for variety as well as reliable availability, wanting fresh fillets in addition to frozen fish sticks, and locally grown leaf lettuces alongside the usual iceberg. Supermarkets and restaurants naturally sought to satisfy these demands, but the new agriculture's very facility for high-volume standardized production makes it unresponsive to a desire for more idiosyncratic local specialties. That desire, consequently, is increasingly being accommodated by newly revived small regional farms.

"There's definitely a trend on the wholesale level toward buying more local produce," Campbell says. "Not much has been made of this, but I personally think that the growth of roadside stands and farmers' markets, especially in the northeast, has had a lot to do with that development. Those kinds of operations began to provide real competition, so the supermarkets had to respond." I had imagined that Campbell, as a spokesman of sorts for a sector of the American food system that profited enormously from the switch to large-scale technologically advanced production and distribution, would probably have scant enthusiasm for the revival of small farms or enterprises like Greenmarket. I was wrong. "I should warn you," he'd written to me before we met, "that my views on the fruit and vegetable industry are fairly conventional." He was admittedly skeptical about the Rodale organization, but he was no flack for agribusiness. "Almost anything that gets too big runs into trouble sooner or later," he told me that day over lunch. Campbell discounts fears of total corporate control of agriculture, not because the corporations haven't tried but because they've tried and failed. "If you were to ask me whether conglomerates posed a threat to the produce business, I'd have to say no. They just haven't been successful enough. Agriculture is too complex. You can't run a field in California from an office in New York, and they've been finding that out the hard way."

It is Paul Campbell's belief that any increase in regional food production by comparatively small farms is all to the good. He envisions the relative revitalization of small-scale regional agriculture gaining momentum as more farmers' market customers bring their revised expectations with them to the supermarket. In the future, he says, produce managers confronted with such expectations will tend to seek out sources of locally grown vegetables, for purely pragmatic reasons. So much the better for everyone, Campbell contends.

It was August when Campbell and I talked, high season at Union Square. "This time of year," he said, "the California growers realize they're going up against a lot of competition back east, and there's not much they can do about it." They are having to get used to sharing the market, something new for most of them, but Campbell has no doubt they'll adapt. What he does concede is that high transportation costs, which have helped to make smaller local farms more competitive again, are not about to disappear, nor are the steep petrochemical prices that have cut into the profitability of conventional agriculture, making operations like Greenmarket and Caretaker Farm look less like anomalies than harbingers of what's to come. "Part of the attraction is simple economics," Campbell says. "That might not be the noblest of motives, but it works."

At Union Square this afternoon there are no vegetables. There are no farmers either; the Greenmarket season won't begin for another month. I am down on my hands and knees in the gutter, on Union Square West between Fifteenth and Sixteenth Streets, holding what a carpenter I once worked for described as the stupid end of a hundred-foot measuring tape. Jane Weissman, holding the smart end, is a half block to the north. She is reeling me in. Together we are taking the measure of territory into which an enlarged Saturday market will expand. The measurements are necessary so that the street can be divided, on paper at least, into the twelve-by-eighteen-foot spaces Greenmarket rents to farmers who sell at the market. Greenmarket, in turn, leases the use of the street from the city for a nominal fee, and the difference between what is paid out and what is taken in goes toward keeping the program solvent. Rentals collected from farmers comprise approximately eighty percent of the program's income. The spaces cost farmers $35 a week, but this may be the only address in New York where no one complains about the rent. On average, a space at the Saturday Greenmarket in Union Square yields a $20 return for every dollar invested in rent.

A pair of expensive heels clips past, topped by two well-preserved calves. I look up to find a stylishly dressed older woman strolling arm in arm with a young, slightly fey man, wearing a silk sportcoat over a pink polo shirt. They pause. The polo shirt speaks.

"You're doing this because you're going to make the Square beautiful, right?"

"Well," I say, "we'll be filling it with farmers and vegetables."

"That's beautiful."

New Yorkers tend to phrase questions as declarative sentences, appending an interrogative almost as an afterthought. I first noticed this one morning at the corner of 102nd Street and Amsterdam Avenue, another Greenmarket site, where I was slathering chrome yellow paint onto the curb in an effort to dissuade drivers from leaving their cars parked across the market's sole truck access route. "That's wet paint, right?" people would ask as they approached, and then two out of three would step in it anyway. They left a pattern of yellow footprints, like the choreography stenciled onto Arthur Murray's dance floor.

"Es pintura mojada, no?"

Once, at Union Square, I overheard a dialogue between the proprietor of Finch Factor Farm (Frenchtown, New Jersey) and a scholarly-looking gentleman in Bermuda shorts and horn-rimmed spectacles who had stopped to examine the lettuces. He was subjecting a head of romaine to intense scrutiny, holding it up to the light, revolving it in his hand. At long last he asked, "What kind of fertilizer do you use?"

"10–20–10," Dick Finch replied.

"That's a chemical, right?"

Judy Krones, managing Wednesdays at Union Square, once entertained a short, florid woman with jet black hair who wore purple sunglasses with bright fuchsia frames. "On weekends I like to go out to the Island," the woman volunteered. "I love it that you're open during the week now, but you know, there aren't any bananas here today."

"Bananas aren't locally grown."

"But nothing here is locally grown."

"Everything in this market is."

"That's impossible."

We believe what we choose to believe and we do what we damn well please. A woman complimenting Osczepinski on the tenderness of his carrots went on to complain about the tops. She said they were terribly tough. A man who had just acquired a dozen big heads of Kohlmaier's buttercrunch was asked by the person behind him in line what on earth he intended to do with all that lettuce. "Freeze it," he said. Freeze it? Barbara Kohlmaier listened in horror as one of her customers explained to another how well lettuce kept in the freezer.

The farmers, for their part, have not been slow to take advantage of the opportunities afforded by our behavioral quirks. Wildflowers are a perennial bestseller at market: roadside pioneers sold by the bunch. Bouquets of Queen Anne's lace. Bouquets of daisies, black-eyed Susans, and flinty blue cornflowers. Bouquets of goldenrod. Each fall a farmer from Long Island brings in his van filled with bittersweet. Bittersweet is a weed, albeit a lovely one—a rapacious climbing plant capable of annexing whole groves of healthy trees. At Union Square it fetches a dollar a branch and sells out fast. Brussels sprouts once came into Greenmarket loose, in boxes, snapped from their stems and sold by the pound. No more. Running late once, one farmer went out to his field with a corn knife and cut off the stalks at ground level. He brought them to market intact and sold them by the piece. Sales of brussels sprouts perceptibly picked up. Many of his customers, he later discovered, were not eating the sprouts. They were using them as decoration.

Not least in importance among Greenmarket's contributions is its service as a link between two estranged cultures. In May 1982 I attended an event billed as a "regional food symposium," sponsored by Rodale Press, titled "Building a Sustainable Food System." The conference brought together city folks and farmers, food activists and experts of every stripe, including, one afternoon, the secretaries of agriculture from four mid-Atlantic states. The men sat on a panel together, and if what they said was not startling, their mere presence was. Ten years ago no self-respecting state secretary of agriculture would have been caught dead at an event hosted by Bob Rodale.

The weekend's most telling exchange was not part of any prepared speech. It occurred on Sunday morning, when we gathered in groups segregated by state of origin, to lay plans for future activism at home. One of the few farmers present at the New York meeting complained that it had become all but impossible, in his neck of the woods, to keep livestock. It was getting harder and harder, he offered by way of illustration, just to get a pig bred. Beside me, a woman leaned toward her neighbor and asked, "What's a pig bread?"

Wendell Berry, in *The Gift of Good Land*, writes of the "absolute dependence of most of the population on industrial agriculture." Says Berry, "We have an unprecedentedly large urban population that has no land to grow food on, no knowledge of how to grow it, and less and less knowledge of what to do with it after it is grown. That this population can continue to eat through shortage, strike, embargo, riot, depression, war—or any of the other large-scale afflictions that societies have always been heir to and that industrial societies are uniquely vulnerable to—is not a certainty or even a faith; it is a superstition."

The rise of modern industrialized agriculture made it possible for the first time for large numbers of people to go through life being fed and clothed from a distance, to live comfortably with no understanding of farmers or farming. With modern agriculture's inevitable decline, and the emergence of a decentralized, more regionally self-reliant alternative, that gap between food producers and food consumers will have to be bridged. The new regionalism's most familiar features—its roadside stands, pick-your-own farms, and farmers' markets—cannot in themselves accomplish this transition, but to the degree that programs like Greenmarket foster fuller communication between a predominately urban populace and the rural minority, they provide something far more valuable than fresh produce.

For my love affair with Greenmarket, I have Barry Benepe to thank. Benepe is Greenmarket's founder, and after eight years remains its director. An architect and planner, Benepe had worked upstate as well as down. He knew where good carrots came from, and he knew, too, how hard it was to find such carrots in stores near his Greenwich Village apartment. He'd watched the rural economy collapse even as the quality of life in New York City palpably declined, and he began to wonder whether a marriage of convenience might be arranged between city people hungry for high-quality fruits and vegetables and the beleaguered farmers still struggling to scratch a living from the urban fringe.

In 1974 Benepe pried loose a small planning grant from the America the Beautiful Fund. He grafted his dream to the Council on the Environment of New York City, thereby acquiring non-profit status, and made the rounds of private philanthropies, looking for support. He recruited a staff and set about finding eligible farmers, and he embarked on a protracted municipal pilgrimage that eventually included stops at the departments of Real Estate and Transportation, of Traffic and Highways, and City Planning; at the Police Department, the Fire Department, and the offices of Consumer Affairs and Economic Development. He secured a posh East Side site, at Second Avenue and Fifty-ninth Street, and lobbied local residents and merchants. He plied the media with press releases, confirmed and reconfirmed his thickening sheath of official permissions, and, finally, at eight o'clock on the morning of July 17, 1976, he cut the ribbon for the first Greenmarket. There were seven farmers present. Six hours later they had all sold out.

Barry Benepe has graying blond hair and grown children. He looks perhaps fifteen years younger than his true age. He is athletic, paunchless, clean-shaven. On Saturday June 5, 1982, opening day for Greenmarket's seventh season, he greets the dawn in Union Square. Jimmy Van Houten is already there, unpacking and setting up. The rain is coming down in sheets and torrents, not falling so much as skidding along parallel to the ground, a standing wave of icy water propelled by a thirty-knot gale. Pete Hotaling's umbrella is airborne, headed north. Bob Van Nostrand has on Helly-Hansen foul weather gear, the preferred outerwear of Norwegian offshore fishermen, and he is smiling. "I'm surprised I have anything at all to sell today," he says cheerfully. "I've never seen half that much rain before. We had potato plants floating out over the road. It washed out most of our seedlings, all the cauliflower and nearly all the lettuce and beans. Now we've got another seventy flats waiting to be transplanted as soon as the weather breaks." He is putting out fresh herbs in bunches, pints of strawberries, glistening spinach.

Jane Weissman, soaking wet despite her yellow slicker, is negotiating with the driver of a late-model Chevrolet sedan. There are not supposed to be any cars in the market. He seems disinclined to move. Jane has apparently exhausted her reserves of patience. She notices Barry and yells.

"Barry! Help me out!"

Barry wears orange earphones. A wire descends from his chin into a pocket of his coat. He is listening to a Bach suite for unaccompanied cello performed by Mstislav Rostropovich. Especially lyrical passages cause him to sing along softly under his breath. He sizes up Jane's situation and beats a hasty retreat, which serves only to intensify her anger. The rain, upon hitting her forehead, seems to turn instantly to steam. Wisely, the offending driver rolls shut his window and backs out of the market.

By half-past eight the farmers are all in. Most of them drive trucks with their names written on the side, but one has come in a vehicle bearing the familiar logo of a truck leasing firm. Jartran Farms. The wet produce is moving fast. Rain or no rain, the market is crowded with shoppers. Bad weather might discourage transients, but not the regulars. Bob Van Nostrand sells out before one o'clock. His first customer of the day, he says, was a buyer for Dean & Deluca, a pricey SoHo gourmet shop. "How much are your herbs?" the fellow inquired. "Seventy-five cents a bunch," said Bob.

"How many have you got?"

"About a hundred."

The buyer peeled off three twenties, a ten and a five. He paid forty cents for a shopping bag and filled it with herbs. "He'll split the bunches into fourths and resell them for a dollar seventy-five apiece," Bob remarks. "I know. I went down once to look at his store."

The market looks fairly clean, which is to say that most of the produce changing hands is not obviously out of season. The agreement the farmers have signed with Greenmarket stipulates that everything sold at the markets must be locally in season, and that virtually everything displayed on a farmer's table must have been grown on that farmer's farm. Every farmer is permitted one item "bought in," so long as it originates within twenty miles of his home. The farmers adhere somewhat sporadically to these regulations. The temptation to bend the rules is strongest in the spring and toward the end of the season, when homegrown stocks run thin. The Greenmarket staff are deputized vegetable cops. They visit the farms to see what's growing, and then they police the markets. Sometimes they consult standard crop maturation tables and count backward. ("Let's see . . . green peppers . . . sixty-four days from last frost . . . well, maybe.") At today's market there are some questionable head lettuces, some asparagus that may have been reared on the opposite coast, but nothing really blatant. Philly Hoeffner, offering for sale mostly rhubarb and strawberries, vigorously protests the presence immediately to his left of a street peddler offering mostly Chilean grapes. Jane, calm now, reviews the problem with the peddler. The peddler leaves.

The woman who wants reassurance that Binaghi's impossibly early tomatoes did not come to Union Square by way of Hunts Point but were actually grown in Binaghi's New Jersey greenhouse is mollified by the news that two Greenmarket staffers were dispatched to Bergen County last week to watch those tomatoes grow. She has no inkling of what was required to get them here. She is not aware that in order to get to Union Square in time to provide her with three pounds of broccoli, Frank Stiles must leave his farm at three o'clock in the morning; nor that the peripatetic Van Houtens—participants in no less than four concurrent Saturday Greenmarkets—depend on a fleet of seven refrigerated trucks to keep themselves constantly in two or more places at once. She has not, if she's lucky, ever been caught in the middle when two police precincts claim jurisdiction over the same turf. She might have noticed in passing the parking meters behind the farmers' trucks, festooned as they are with No Parking notices, but she surely cannot imagine how difficult it is in the city of New York to evict the occupants of three dozen apparently legitimate parking spaces and install a farmers' market instead. She doesn't know any of this, but the Greenmarket staff does.

Greenmarket command central is the top floor of a Sixteenth Street brownstone. In late May, the office is pretty well filled. The staff has launched a full court press toward opening day, and the overall effect is of order only temporarily wrested from chaos. Jane Weissman pastes up the mechanicals for flyers announcing the opening dates of the various markets—a task complicated by the fact that some of those dates are still undecided. Barry Benepe reconciles the requests of farmers for placement in particular markets with the amount of space available at each market site. Ellen Chuse, Greenmarket's part-time bookkeeper, struggles valiantly to sort out the project's scrambled finances, while Marcy Roth, Barry's long-time aide-de-camp, places long distance calls to the farmers, scheduling farm visits, reviewing crop plans, and dunning them for payment of past due obligations.

"Who's feeling tough and nasty? Jane? Who wants to call these guys and ask what the hell they think they're doing not paying us the three thousand they owe from last year?"

"What have we gotten from anyone else?"

"Nobody who owes us anything has paid a cent since last month."

"What a bunch of deadbeats."

The Greenmarket office is not big. In warm weather the windows are opened wide and indoor activities sometimes spill out onto a fire escape that doubles as the back porch. An orphan sandal, pressed into service as a paperweight, anchors a stack of U.S.D.A. produce price bulletins to the top of a hopelessly cluttered table. A poster taped to a closet door depicts an unpaved lane running through a freshly planted field. The image is contained by a constricting frame of type. FARMLAND, it reads, NEW JERSEY'S SHRINKING RESOURCE. A large wall map nearby is perforated with colored pins denoting the locations of Greenmarket farms, and quite a few of the map's pins still puncture the decrescent Garden State. Mozart wafting from an unseen source competes unsuccessfully for aural attention with telephone conversations, huddled strategy sessions, and intermittent queries spoken aloud and left dangling unanswered in the air. A rectangle of heavy paper mounted above Barry's desk has the words, "Working Days Left Until Markets Open" written across it, and beneath them, on a detachable three-by-five card, today's number: 13.

"When you've finished fighting with the U.S.D.A. bureaucrats about Food Stamps, maybe you'd like to go over to Union Square and speak with the police?"

"Can Hawthorne Valley work out the back of their truck or only out the side?"

"But you won't have very much ready that early, will you?"

"When does a Hundred and Second Street open?"

"Peas?"

"If they're going to sell out the side they'll have to have a space and a half. I don't see any way around it."

"Strawberries too? Well, okay, I'll try to work you in earlier, but I can't promise anything, all right?"

"The eleventh?"

"What does the grape man bring down? A pick-up or something bigger?"

"The eighteenth, I think. It's either the eleventh or the eighteenth?"

"Everything? On the fifth of June? What's everything?"

Barry and Jane are making market assignments, attempting to ensure that every market will have enough farmers and every farmer enough markets. This is a not inconsiderable assignment. Greenmarket's markets come in all shapes and sizes. Some are small and perpetually in need of farmers, comparatively poor locations where there are always spaces to spare. Others, like Saturday's at Union Square, will forever be standing room only. The farms are a polyglot group as well, ranging from microchips like Wm. Levine's half-acre plot on up to outfits of five hundred acres or more. When plans for the farmers' markets were first proposed, finding enough farmers was expected to be a problem. No problem. News of the markets spread quickly through outlying agricultural regions, and these days the farmers find Greenmarket. "We get calls all year round," Marcy Roth says.

"We have farmers calling in late July with a big crop coming in. They've heard about Greenmarket from other farmers and they want to know how to sign up. People call in November, wanting to sell firewood. They can't understand why New Yorkers wouldn't want full cords." The problem now is not finding farmers so much as it is fitting farmers together with markets. This is a delicate and inherently subjective process, like making blind dates for friends, fraught with the possibility of disappointment.

Farmers who want to sell at Greenmarket must first submit applications on which they are asked to divulge a few particulars: the size of their farm, the variety of crops grown, probable dates of earliest and latest harvest, approximate quantities available for sale—factors affecting a market's composition and character. They may request space at specific markets, and most veterans do so, hoping to return to locations that have proved productive in the past, or to get shed of less profitable postings. "It's a chicken and egg situation," Jane Weissman explains. "At the Hundred and Thirtieth Street market people told us they'd been once but hadn't found much food, so they didn't return. The farmers complained that there weren't enough customers, and they didn't want to come in for that market. The customers said there weren't enough farmers, so they wouldn't go either." The mortality rate for newborn farmers' markets is very high.

"Has anyone signed up yet for Kings Plaza?" Jane asks.

"We'll have to look at the sheet," Barry answers, unfolding a poster-sized page fabricated from smaller leaves of Eye-Ease green accountant's ledger paper. This is the sheet: the master list of market assignments. On its vertical axis are recorded the names of all Greenmarket farmers. The markets, along the horizontal, are identified by address, day of the week, opening and closing dates. Notes made in cryptic shorthand at the sheet's interstices indicate who will be where when.

With the chart spread before them, Barry and Jane trace their fingers across the graph, counting the farmers who've volunteered to sell from a parking lot in a far-off province of Brooklyn. The total to date is disappointing. "We'll just have to assign some," Barry says. "What about D'Amico?"

"D'Amico," Jane mutters. "He's so big." Seven hundred acres

big, a hundred and forty of them devoted exclusively to the cultivation of *Coriandrum sativum,* making D'Amico Farms of Hightstown, New Jersey, the preeminent coriander grower east of the Susquehanna. Jane tends to favor the smaller farms.

"He was there last year," Barry counters.

"How about Keller?"

"Keller's in Harlem on Tuesdays."

The Harlem market is choice. A farmer would not willingly surrender space on 137th Street for a spot at Kings Plaza. In Harlem, the farmers say, they make good money. They make out adequately also at 67th Street, at the Flatbush Avenue market in Brooklyn, and most spectacularly at Union Square.

For a farmer, the sight of the Union Square Greenmarket on a midsummer Saturday is something not easily forgotten. I walked through Union Square once with a farmer who'd signed up to sell there on Wednesdays—at a market created partly to open the Square to more small growers. His crops weren't yet ready, so he'd come in to do some reconnaissance. His eyes spun, as if he was working the slots. He circled the market slowly, seeming intoxicated, mesmerized, maybe a little scared. Between the opening gun and the closing bell there might be twelve thousand visitors to the Union Square Greenmarket. The farmers who sell there tend to be the bigger ones not simply by virtue of squatters' rights but because the very small grower who sets up his scales in the Square risks being picked clean and put out to bleach.

Union Square is the major leagues, and on that diamond the big boys play hardball. The Van Houtens, for example, on a typical Saturday sortie, might bring with them twenty thousand pounds of pork and produce. They will not infrequently sell all of it before they go home. They employ a double-digit sales staff behind forty-odd feet of table frontage. They have sold, in the course of a single Saturday at Union Square, three and a half tons of tomatoes. ("It's a personal record," says Bob Van Houten with no hint of modesty, "and we think it's a market record too.") This is a high stakes game, and some of the largest farmers resist being assigned to sparser sites. Benepe is unsympathetic. Serving less lucrative locations seems to him a fair price to pay for the privilege of bellying up to the banquet at Union Square. This is a view that he will freely acknowledge is not universally shared by Greenmarket farmers.

"This is my complaint about Barry," Bob Van Houten declares. "I think he's an absolute genius at coming up with an idea and getting it started, but he's a complete disaster as a manager. The thing is, he's a planner, not a businessman. I think the markets could be run for half the money by a businessman instead of a planner."

"Bob," says Bob's wife Anne, "tends to make blanket statements."

"Say I had strawberries ready right now," her husband continues. "I might sell fifty pounds of strawberries at Fulton Street. I can't pay the cost of my trip from here to Fulton Street on fifty pounds of strawberries."

Today is the first day of June, and Bob Van Houten does not have strawberries ready. He does not have a whole lot else ready either. He is pleading his case with Jane Weissman, arguing that he should be allowed to go on selling imported produce, as he has been selling it throughout the winter, on the site of a new Greenmarket in lower Manhattan, at the foot of the Southbridge Towers apartment complex, near South Street Seaport. The building's residents have asked Greenmarket to assume responsibility for the market, which has heretofore operated independently.

"We built that market!" Bob protests.

This is at least partially true, but now that what had been an informal arrangement will be taken under Greenmarket's wing, Greenmarket rules apply. Which means, for Bob Van Houten, that whereas on Saturday, May 29, he could show up at Fulton Street with a full line of fruits and vegetables, on Saturday, June 5, he will be offering a few spring greens, radishes, and bedding plants. He does not find this prospect compelling.

"Don't you still sell a lot of meat?" Jane asks.

"I don't sell a hundred pounds of meat at Southbridge," Bob rather mournfully replies.

"Really!"

"In a predominantly Jewish neighborhood you just don't move a lot of pork."

Bob's conversation with Jane is conducted across the broad kitchen table of the Van Houten family farmhouse in Columbia County, Pennsylvania, three hours distant from New York. We are here on what is euphemistically termed a "farm visit."

"Southbridge just isn't going to work," Bob says, shaking his big head from side to side, stoking his pipe for emphasis and sending up billows of blue smoke. He is large, chunky, forty or thereabouts. "If we can't bring in a full line, we'll just have to quit. We'll go right across the street to where we've been for four years, building that market."

Like a number of Greenmarket farmers, Bob Van Houten and his brother Jimmy customarily extend the market season to twelve months, selling mostly home-grown goods between June and December, but peddling brokered produce from January through May at locations on or adjacent to Greenmarket sites. By selling through the winter, they say, they not only generate much needed income at a time when the farm's cash tends to flow out rather than in, but they maintain a high profile, which wins them more customers during the summer. The growers who do best at Greenmarket are salesmen as much as they are farmers. Once they've latched on to a steady market, they're loath to let it slip away. The Van Houtens' moonlighting is tolerated on the condition that when the Greenmarket season officially opens they will cease their trade in exotic imports.

The Van Houtens are highliners. In Columbia County they own three hundred acres, most of them tillable, and rent several hundred more. They own and operate their own roadside market in suburban Rockland County, New York. Their equipment sheds shelter a complete inventory of the latest in agricultural technology, and just this past winter they added a new six-row grain combine—in addition to their vegetable crops they devote a substantial acreage to feed corn and soybeans—because they couldn't resist the implement dealer's offer to let them have the $100,000 machine for $65,000. About fiscal specifics they are determinedly evasive—"I don't know any farmer that's ever going to tell you anything at all about how much he makes," says James

Van Houten, Sr., Jim to his elder son's Jimmy; "I won't, I know that much"—but they are plainly not hard-pressed, poverty-stricken, marginal holdouts. The debt the Van Houtens owe Greenmarket is a large one. "I don't even like growing vegetables," Bob complains. "I wish we grew nothing but field corn. I love field corn. But I know I can get to Florida on the vegetables, and on the field corn I could go broke."

Van Houtens have been farmers for as long as any of them can remember, but they bought this place only twelve years ago. They looked long and hard before they found it, and happily paid the then astronomical price of $500 an acre. As in-migrants, they are appropriately chauvinistic. "I grew up farming in Rockland County," Bob says, "which I'm sure they named for the rocks. If we want a rock here we've got to go out and buy one. I'd never move back to New York." It wasn't stony soil that drove the Van Houtens from Rockland County, however, but the relentless spread of suburbia. Their original farm was submerged by a reservoir that filled the swimming pools and irrigated the lawns of the houses that now separated their scattered rented holdings. They farmed for a time on bits and pieces, but combining the bits or buying a bigger piece proved impossible. So in 1970 they moved to Pennsylvania, keeping the family's ancestral home and their roadside stand as a staging area for their assaults on the city.

When Greenmarket came along they were moving as much as they could through the roadside stand and shunting the rest off to Hunts Point. They grew vegetable crops on contract for food processors, but they weren't making out very well. The increasing dominance of Southwestern agribusiness was cutting into their earnings, and into their market share as well. Greenmarket changed all that. "Greenmarket," Jim Van Houten confides, "is what's keeping us in business."

"These Greenmarkets are giving us an education in selling, too," Bob says, interrupting. It's lunchtime at the Van Houten household: self-service sandwiches constructed from plates full of ingredients on a heavily laden lazy Susan. Conversation around this table is a competitive affair, like the playing of rival jazz musicians gathered on a nightclub bandstand. Jim and his son trade solos, riffing, improvising, cutting one another. James Sr. is a conversational locomotive. There are long stretches when Bob can't insert a word edgewise. He stutters, stops and starts, and finally hollers, "Dad, I want to talk!"

He wants to talk about tomatoes.

"We have a lot of display space," he begins.

"Forty-four feet," Jane interjects.

"And what we'll do sometimes is we'll put a pile of tomatoes at each end. One pile we'll sell three pounds for a dollar. The other we'll price at, say, three pounds for a dollar twenty-five. They come out of the same box in the truck, but the dollar and a quarter tomatoes consistently sell better than the dollar pile. Some people just want a better grade of vegetable, and those must be a better grade—they cost more, right?"

Bob grins. Jane grimaces.

To say that the Van Houtens are industrious, even aggressive, would perhaps be to understate the facts. Obsessive is more like it. Fanatical, maybe. In an effort to beat the market this year they have raised 200,000 string bean plants under glass so as to be the first ones at Union Square with beans. "We plan to have everyone else at the market come screaming to Jane that we bought in those beans!" Bob yelps. "I swear I'm going to drive Barry out here myself to see them growing," says his father, dropping one palm explosively to the table.

Earlier, driving through his fields, Bob had pointed out the passenger's side window of his truck. "We had all this in tomatoes last year," he said, "but we never picked a single tomato from that field."

"Why?"

"Another field came in that was better, and we didn't have time to pick them both."

I asked if the farm follows any particular crop rotation.

"Sure," said Bob. "Our rotation is that we plant whatever field is ready for planting with whatever crop we need."

After lunch we peruse greenhouses full of flowers and houseplants, full of peppers sweet and hot ("Your Thursday market," Bob says, meaning the market at 175th Street and Broadway, "they'll take as many of these jalapeños as we can bring in. The

Spanish love 'em. They're hot enough to make the devil blush."), full of assorted cole crops and leggy, root-bound tomato seedlings ("Here's more tomatoes that got ahead of us," says Bob). We walk through empty greenhouses whose contents have already moved outdoors. We drive, in a convoy of trucks, through acres of fields, from a silty bottomland plain where rows of root crops are laid out laser straight, up a steep slope to a shaly, south-facing sidehill: the better part of ten acres planted entirely to early tomatoes. Like Jane, I'm partial to the smaller farms, but it's hard not to admire the unbridled ambition of the Van Houtens' operation.

A day spent in the company of vociferous Van Houtens is exhausting, and we don't talk much during the long drive back to New York. It had been overcast all afternoon, then the skies split open just before we left the farm. It rains off and on the whole way. We hiss down black, soaked pavement, past solid oak barns and sagging sheds and sprawling Easter-colored clumps of purple and white phlox, massed hazily in the low spots beside swollen streams. At dusk I watch the lights wink on in a milking parlor just up a hill from Interstate 80. As we close in on the city the farms give way to factories and the fields are first flecked and then clotted with monotonously similar houses. The bridge that is Greenmarket spans a considerable distance.

We arc over the Hudson, onto the West Side Highway, and down toward Greenwich Village. I am driving and thinking of something Jim Van Houten said to us as we were leaving. He was standing in the kitchen with Bob and Anne's children dancing around his feet. It was the kids, he said, who got the best deal of all. Growing up on the farm, going to rural schools, they were being raised with the good country values he wanted for them. But as members of the family sales force they were coming into the city as well, to the markets, meeting all kinds of people, learning more about life in the city than many city kids would ever know. That was the thing he liked best, said the patriarch of Van Houten Farms—what Greenmarket meant for his grandchildren.

5

THE GOVERNMENT FARM

Bud Kerr is yelling into the telephone. He holds the receiver clamped between his right shoulder and his cheek while he stirs instant coffee into a mug of hot water. It is twenty minutes before nine on a midsummer Wednesday morning, and Kerr's desk is already awash in yellow call-back slips. He shuffles them as he talks, weighing their relative importance, alternately arching his eyebrows and grimacing. "Well goddammit!" he hollers. It's not clear whether this expletive implies enthusiasm or anger.

Howard W. ("Bud") Kerr serves as northeastern regional coordinator of small farms research for the United States Department of Agriculture. He has been known to describe his position somewhat more succinctly by saying, "I *am* the U.S.D.A.'s small farm program." On the phone this morning he conducts the usual business of government: lobbying, extracting small promises, calling in past-due obligations. This is a practical skill, like fishing, and he is its master. Just now he's brought the conversation round to one of his favorite topics, the peaches he grows in his own orchard near Baltimore. When Bud Kerr goes fishing, he uses peaches for bait. "You haven't had any yet this year?" he exclaims. "Well, hell, I'll bring some in for you tomorrow." He has provoked a rise. "Of course I can," he says, setting the hook. "Sure I will." He leans back in his chair to listen, glancing first at his watch, then at the stack of call-back slips and the steaming mug on his desk, wondering if he can successfully conclude this call before his coffee cools.

Among the ranks of middle-level managers at the sprawling suburban Maryland campus of the U.S.D.A.'s Beltsville Agricultural Research Center, Bud Kerr is regarded as something of a curiosity. There is, for starters, the matter of his peaches. "You want to try one of these?" he offers, gesturing toward three fat tomatoes and a half dozen blushing peaches queued up on the window ledge behind him. He doesn't wait for a reply. "Here," he insists. "Let's eat this peach right now." He unfolds a penknife and bisects the ripe fruit, then hands a perfect hemisphere across his desk. It's a delicious peach, tree ripened, still firm but explosively juicy. Kerr beams. He extends a helping handful of Kleenex.

Much of the irrepressible energy of the small farmer's man at Agriculture seems to stem from the fact that he is himself a small farmer, with a small farmer's gritty pride. Kerr has half seriously referred to himself as the only career bureaucrat with calluses on his hands as well as his backside. He grew up working summers on his aunt's Maryland dairy farm, got actively involved in 4-H, and managed two years of college before being sent to Korea. Upon his return he enrolled at the University of Maryland, staying long enough this time to earn a master's degree in agricultural economics, then signed on with the U.S.D.A. For the next dozen years he was strictly a desk-top farmer. His conversion, as Kerr tells it, came in 1970 when he represented the Department at the National Peach Growers' Convention in Atlantic City. He listened to industry officials ranting about "carport operators who got twenty-five cents a pound for their peaches and lived in nice houses, while commercial growers were getting seven cents a pound and going out of business." Carport operations sounded pretty good to Bud Kerr. He went back to Maryland and began planting trees. Today, after he leaves Beltsville but before he goes home to Annapolis, he will put in what amounts to a second work day at his farm in Randallstown, where he grows twenty acres of fruit and berries for sale to pick-your-own customers and at farmers' markets. "It's a good thing I'm a workaholic," he concedes. "It would never work otherwise."

Bud Kerr could not be called bashful. "People remember me," he says. They could hardly help it. He has the size and build of a National Football League lineman, and he nurtures his iconoclastic reputation. He habitually eschews protocol, but he has perfected use of the interoffice memo as a protective device. He lards his monthly activities reports with everything from guest lists ("I was pleased to host for several hours, two visitors from Egypt, Dr. Abdel-Hamid Talaat Higazzi, Head, Egyptian National Research Centre, Botany Department, Cairo, and Dr. S. M. El Naggar . . .") to gleanings from his mail ("I was pleased to receive the enclosed article, 'Small Farms, Big Comeback,' from the editor of the *National Future Farmer*. . . ."). His memos might intimidate by their sheer bulk. They bristle with attachments: newspaper and magazine clippings, copies of correspondence, reproductions of Kerr's crowded appointments calendar, and in one instance a cartoon from *The New Yorker*, showing a diminutive witch about to touch her wand to the forehead of a farmer on his tractor. "Every twenty minutes another small farmer disappears," the caption reads. "You're next."

The mortar in each memorandum is a paragraph or two of unsolicited editorial comment. "Small farms and the people who constitute this segment of the agricultural industry are daily becoming a more potent, productive, and political force," he writes in one entry. "It now appears certain that it will be necessary in the very near future for agricultural leaders—many long devoid of a sense of having to responsively deal with small farms—to initiate action to further assist them. Such action will ultimately result not only in an overall strengthening of domestic agriculture, but, perhaps, will have an impact on agricultural systems worldwide." The monthly Kerr report goes out to several such agricultural leaders, his superiors at Beltsville, who may be surprised to learn of Kerr's plans for their future. Bud Kerr has transformed a tedious procedural necessity into a platform for his campaign. He knew he'd struck paydirt when a U.S.D.A. librarian called to ask if his memoranda might be entered into the archives at the National Agricultural Library.

As the small farmer's roving advocate at the U.S.D.A., Kerr is an unofficial troubleshooter. He is responsible for seeing to it that at least some portion of the Department of Agriculture's massive research expenditure is devoted explicitly to the needs of American small farms. For this endeavor he has been allotted slightly less than $2 million a year. He has also been charged with uncovering and making accessible any information that, while not aimed directly at small farmers, might nonetheless prove useful to them. He has his fingers in innumerable pies. At an institution accustomed neither to ambiguous job descriptions nor to worrying much about small farms, Kerr's assignment alone sets him apart.

The plight of the small farmer has never loomed large on the list of priorities held by this country's agricultural research establishment. In 1911, just twenty-two years after the U.S.D.A. attained cabinet status and only a half-century since the founding of the first land grant colleges, the Dean of the College of Agriculture at Cornell University already saw cause for concern. "We are now in the midst of a process of the survival of the fit," Liberty Hyde Bailey wrote. "Two great movements are very apparent in the agriculture of the time: certain farmers are increasing in prosperity, and certain other farmers are decreasing in prosperity. The former class is gradually occupying the land and extending its power and influence . . . notwithstanding that this is the very time when agricultural colleges and experiment stations and governmental departments have been expanding knowledge and extending their influence. The fact is that all these agencies relieve first the good farmers. They aid first those who reach out for new knowledge and for better things. The man who is strongly disadvantaged by natural location or by other circumstances is the last to avail himself of all these privileges. . . . The failure of a great many farmers may be less a fault of their own than a disadvantage of the conditions in which they find themselves. It is fairly incumbent on the state organization to provide effective means of increasing the satisfaction and profit of farming in less fortunate areas as well as in the favorable ones."

What worried Dean Bailey was an emerging pattern of disproportionate influence in the new discipline. He feared that as agricultural research matured into a fully fledged science it would lose sight of small farmers and concentrate its attentions on larger and more powerful operators. His fears were well founded. In 1968 Dr. Don Paarlberg, who had left Purdue University to become Director of Agricultural Economics for the U.S.D.A., suffered a rare seizure of public misgiving. "Many years ago in England the industrial revolution resulted in dislocations and social problems that were largely ignored," Paarlberg wrote. "It has become common to criticize the leaders of that day for their callousness. It may be appropriate to ask whether we who promote today's agricultural revolution may in time come under a similar indictment." Organized agricultural research almost from the beginning applied itself less to trimming the burden borne by small farmers than to trimming the number of small farmers. As agricultural progress became synonymous with expansion, small farms were left behind. Bud Kerr's budget for direct research represents less than one-half of one percent of the total spent each year on research by the U.S.D.A., yet small farms—those with annual sales below $40,000—comprise more than three-quarters of all the farms in the United States. As Kerr matter-of-factly puts it, "It's a hell of a lot more prestigious to develop a corn harvester that'll pick forty rows at once than it is to invent a better knife for cutting corn one stalk at a time." If it's true that science necessarily chases money, then there is considerably more money to be made chasing big agribusiness than small farms. The biggest ten percent of all United States farms ring up more than half of the nation's total agricultural sales. Inevitably perhaps, agricultural research has tended to skim that cream first, serving the rest of the farm community only incidentally.

No one has more persuasively argued this case than a garrulous Texan named Jim Hightower, an avowed populist who in 1982 confounded political odds by getting elected Texas Commissioner of Agriculture. In the early 1970s Hightower worked for the Agribusiness Accountability Project, a Washington-based public interest research group that scrutinized the food and agriculture industries, especially the effect that agribusiness dominance of farming had on consumers in general and on rural communities in particular. In *Hard Tomatoes, Hard Times*, the project's 1973 report, Hightower minced no words:

> If economies of scale, integrated food systems, and assembly-line efficiency are the products of research at land grant colleges, so are hard tomatoes and hard times. There have been many untabulated costs of land grant research, and those costs make clear that taxpayer-financed mechanization has not been the bargain many have claimed. Indeed, in terms of wasted lives, depleted rural areas, choked cities, poisoned land, and maybe poisoned people, mechanization has been a bad investment. It can be a good investment. It is not that mechanization is wrong, but that it has been wrongly applied. The land grant community, working too intimately with its agribusiness colleagues, is accountable for that failure. . . .
>
> The basis of land grant teaching, research, and extension work has been that "efficiency" is the greatest need in agriculture. Consequently, this agricultural complex has devoted the overwhelming share of its resources to mechanize all aspects of agricultural production and make it a capital-intensive industry; to increase crop yields per acre through genetic manipulation and chemical application; and to encourage "economies of scale" and vertical integration of the food process. It has generally aimed at transforming agriculture from a way of life to a business and a science, transferring effective control from the farmer to the business executive and systems analyst.

Agricultural research conducted since World War Two has consistently served agribusiness to the detriment of small family farms. The bulk of that service has come in the form of increased mechanization, either through the invention of new planting, harvesting, and processing equipment, or by the development of new crop varieties better adapted to rough mechanical handling. Considerable effort goes into the search for chemical amendments intended to make normally recalcitrant crops more compliant. There is Ethrel, for instance, a synthetic growth stimulant, which when broadcast over a field of immature green peppers will fool them into ripening, thus making possible a mechanized harvest of the whole crop with a single pass. Almost without exception this mechanization research has been undertaken in the name of improved efficiency, but efficiency, like productivity, is an elusive and highly subjective concept.

In a family garden where ragweed and lamb's quarters have

got a head start on the lettuce, a sharp hoe in the hands of an older child is an efficient weed killer. On a thousand irrigated acres of Imperial Valley iceberg and romaine, a schedule of specially formulated herbicides sprayed from a crop-duster may be just the ticket. Both are efficient, but the two efficiencies have very little in common. The former equates efficiency with an economy of means; the latter with an economy of ends. The lettuces get weeded in either case. What separates the two divergent methods might serve as an introduction to the purposes and consequences of modern agricultural research. Again, from the Hightower report:

> The land grant community would insist that all of its research is targeted toward the consumer, that he is the ultimate beneficiary. Considering the cost of mechanization research, that assertion is at least questionable. It is true that the consumer enjoys an abundance and wide variety of food products, and that he enjoys these products at a relatively cheap market price. But the connection between the price of tomatoes and the tomato harvester is a bit strained. Assuming that there are cost savings on mechanized production, and assuming that the producer's savings are passed on to the processor or marketer, it is unlikely that the savings comes intact from there to the consumer. The consumer is not the primary beneficiary, he is not consulted by the land grant community when the research is designed, and at best he enjoys the benefits of that research only after it has passed through a fine sieve of "trickle down. . . ."
>
> The land grant community has done approximately nothing to extend the benefits of technology and management techniques to the vast majority of farmers and other rural Americans. The fact is that the land grant colleges are expending their resources on mechanization that primarily is useful to the highest income growers, focusing attention on those producers with the necessary acreage, capital, and management to achieve economies of scale. . . . The mechanization research is either irrelevant or only incidentally adaptable to the needs of some 87 to 99 percent of America's farmers. The public subsidy for mechanization has actually weakened the competitive position of the family farmer.

Efficiency as defined by the agricultural research establishment has by and large meant the substitution of capital, in the form of technology, for labor. The ideal of mechanized efficiency depends on a number of assumptions: that labor is more expensive than capital, that reduction or elimination of labor is efficient, that producer expansion lowers consumer costs, that there are no limits to growth, and most crucially, that all these conditions will hold true indefinitely. Modern agricultural research developed around these assumptions, and if they have seldom been challenged during the comparatively brief history of modern agriculture it's not so much because agribusiness and the research establishment have maliciously conspired to keep the truth under wraps as because most Americans were content until quite recently to take their validity for granted.

In 1973, few Americans not directly involved in agriculture saw any reason to worry about its condition. As far as that goes, there weren't many farmers worrying either. Mechanized efficiency as an agricultural ideal may have reached the apex of its ascendancy during the tenure of Earl Butz, who served as Secretary of Agriculture from 1971 until 1975, when an ill-timed off-color joke led to his abrupt resignation. U.S.D.A. policy during the Butz years was based on the belief that the best of all possible farms was that which employed the least labor to produce the most goods. (It was also a tacit, if not explicit policy of the time that an appropriate equity position for ambitious farmers was to be eighty percent leveraged and twenty percent liquid—a position that subsequently sent many such farmers into bankruptcy.) In 1973, when *Hard Tomatoes, Hard Times* was first released, it seemed Jim Hightower was lecturing to an empty room.

Fortunately, Hightower's homily did not pass entirely unheard. One man who listened was Bob Bergland, the northern Minnesota grass-seed grower, three-term Democratic Congressman, and one-time Midwestern regional director of the U.S.D.A.'s Agricultural Stabilization and Conservation Service, who was nominated by Jimmy Carter to be his Secretary of Agriculture. It would be difficult to overstate the differences between Bob Bergland and Earl Butz. Both men can fairly be called exemplary products of the American farm system. Butz grew up on a farm in Indiana. He climbed the professional ladder to become Dean of Agriculture at Purdue, and had served a stint as an assistant secretary of agriculture under Eisenhower before Nixon awarded him the top job. Bergland was raised in Minnesota, near the Roseau River, on land passed down to his father from his father before him. He bought his own place in 1950—260 acres, which by the time he took over the secretary's office he had parlayed into 600. American agriculture had made both men wealthy, and neither had been given much cause to second-guess the system that had treated him conspicuously well. But where Butz was an indefatigable booster, Bergland was inquisitive. Where Butz saw infinite opportunities, Bergland saw limits. Where Butz was eager to get government out of agriculture, Bergland worried that government was not exercising enough authority. Butz was a true believer. Bergland, to say the least, had doubts.

At home in Roseau County he'd watched the number of farms dwindle as their average size increased and the cost of getting started soared. When he left for Washington he leased his place to his daughter and her husband, aware that even had he wanted to sell it, the farm's earned income could not cover the debt service on its sales price at fair market value. For six years in Congress he'd helped to write legislation intended to aid the small family farm, but now he wondered what he'd accomplished. "I was always troubled," Bergland has written, "during those hours and hours of testimony and negotiation that we never seemed to get off the same familiar, circular tracks: the levels of price and income supports, the levels of exports, the constraints of the budget. We didn't know exactly who was being helped or who was being hurt by the measures before us." He later wrote, "The problems were seldom clearly defined. If they were, they were cast as narrow but immediate crises that needed patches quickly. Other than a dime a bushel here or a few pennies a pound there, the remedies were either politically unacceptable or simply made no sense.

"We thought—we hoped—that if we helped the major commercial farmers, who provided most of our food and fiber (and exerted most of the political pressure), the benefits would filter down to the intermediate-sized and then the smallest producers. . . . I was never convinced we were on the right track. We had symbols, slogans and superficialities. We seldom had substance."

That remarkable incidence of candor is drawn from Bob Bergland's introduction to *A Time to Choose, The Summary Report on the Structure of American Agriculture*, rushed into print and hurriedly distributed in the waning days of the Carter presidency. The report culminated an exercise in official introspection that extended the full four years of Bergland's term. As secretary he channeled his disquiet into a departmental task force endowed with unprecedented independence and simple instructions: to turn American agricultural policy upside down and see what shook out. "No subject was to be considered off limits," Bergland wrote. "If the Federal tax code affected the structure of agriculture, for example, I wanted it explored. . . . The research was undertaken to establish *what* was happening and *why*, what the true problems were as a result, and what the likely needs of agriculture would be in the future. . . . The underlying issue explored in this report is the question of control. Who controls the land, and in turn our food supply, by default or design? Who controls the prices and access at each step of the food system?"

Departmental reports do not normally set the blood racing, but *A Time to Choose* is a pretty extraordinary document. Its authors concluded that virtually every facet of United States farm policy overtly or tacitly aided large-scale agriculture at a measurable cost to small family farms, politically expeditious rhetoric to the contrary notwithstanding. Tax policies, they found, "on balance . . . are biased toward the larger farmers and wealthy investors." The conventional marketing system is "oriented to better serve the larger producers." Commodity and credit policies "have been of greater benefit to the larger producers, and this too has affected structure. . . . At the same time, it has become increasingly evident that the gains to the nation that remain to be captured from the continued shift to larger and larger farming operations have become smaller over time. When the net losses to farming communities associated with the continual decline in the number of farm families are taken into account, we have passed the point where any net gain for society can be claimed from policies that encourage large farms to get larger."

It is far from certain that any clear choice was prompted by *A Time to Choose*. It sank without a ripple within weeks after Jimmy Carter went home to Plains, leaving the White House to Ronald Reagan and the Department of Agriculture to an Illinois grain farmer, John Block. But there can be no negating Bob Bergland's legacy. He left, in addition to the structure report, the unexpectedly favorable *Report and Recommendations on Organic Farming*. He fostered full participation by the U.S.D.A. in the landmark National Agricultural Lands Study, a comprehensive multi-agency review of the outlook for American cropland resources. And he left Bud Kerr.

"I'm a thorn in John Block's side," Kerr readily admits. "Not something he can just pick out, but one that's broken off, in deep and festering."

Bud Kerr's thorniness is somewhat enhanced by his position as a twenty-five-year man at the Department. Civil service diplomacy being what it is, that makes him prodigiously difficult to get rid of. "The Carter administration was very concerned with the well-being of small family farms," Kerr recalls, "and they persuaded Congress to allocate $3.5 million in the 1979 fiscal year, targeted specifically for Agricultural Research Service work for small farms." Of that total, Kerr administers about half, with most of the rest handled by the A.R.S.'s southern regional research center in Booneville, Arkansas. So far Kerr's funding has held steady. "I got the same dollars this year that I did in '79, and I'm supposed to have the same in '83 as I had in '82," he says—then adds, "but you never know."

Zealous as he is, Bud Kerr recognizes that in allocating funds to assist small farms, Congress did not intend to change the course of American agriculture, or even to rearrange the research priorities at the Agricultural Research Service. The idea, rather, was to put out a fire by throwing a little money at it. Much as he hopes to keep that fire burning, Kerr has few illusions. "Look," he said to me one day as we drove past long rows of drab laboratories on our way to one of Beltsville's experimental orchards, "you've got seven thousand acres here, a thousand scientists, four thousand four-legged critters, and fifty million dollars a year being spent on research. It would lower the image of a place like this to say it was a small-farm research center—it's supposed to be the foremost agricultural research center in the world—so they hired a coordinator instead."

The coordinator first had to figure out just what needed to be done. There was consensus on the need to help small farms, but little if any agreement on what form that aid ought to take. "My job was to make small-farms projects accountable, tractable, visible, and yield tangible results," Kerr explains. It seems that $1.8 million won't buy a whole lot of research, so some sort of institutional triage would be needed to ascertain which farms could make best use of the help. In 1979 and again in 1981 Kerr polled county extension agents in his twelve-state northeastern region to solicit their views on the present character and future complexion of local small farms. Both surveys showed large-scale commercial agriculture in the region retreating under pressure from several sides, while small farms—often very small, part-time farms—were proliferating. Further, the studies confirmed Kerr's suspicion that large numbers of these new farmers were turning their backs on traditional livestock and forage crops in favor of fruits and vegetables and alternative marketing strategies. He found that among such farmers off-farm incomes were not the exception but the rule, and that to some extent this fact dictated the type of farm they would have. If a farmer relied on regular paychecks to help cover bills at his farm, then like it or not he couldn't afford to be married to milk cows.

Where these new-style farmers could compete was with variety, and especially with quality, offering not more and cheaper goods but different and better ones—selling them either directly to consumers through farmers' markets or pick-your-own operations, or obliquely, through local specialty shops and restaurants. Kerr's surveys hinted that these people were a force to be reckoned with—a new variety of farmer, one who could not be dismissed as a hobby farmer (that most derisive of appellations), but who wasn't employed full-time in agriculture either. What's more, extension service personnel were unanimous in their conviction that this was not merely an aberration but an identifiable trend, which could be expected to continue into the future. These new-fashioned small farms were by all accounts a vanguard of impending agricultural change.

That was all Bud Kerr needed to hear. As far as he was concerned he'd found his ministry. "Let's call it limited-resource agriculture," he says, "or part-time farming. That's what we're really talking about here, some guy who starts out with strawberries, gets some raspberries, adds a few hives of bees, and all of a sudden he's farming." Some guy, in other words, not at all unlike Bud Kerr. Kerr contends that the limited-resource farmer, in the Northeast anyway, is the farmer of the future. "The real thrust of what's coming has only begun to show up in the past two years," he says. "What you're seeing in the small-farm movement today is like the rumbling of the ground before Mount Saint Helens erupted." He predicts that the increasing expense of conventional centralized agriculture will lead to higher prices, opening a hole in the marketplace into which diversified, flexible local growers will pour their products. He grants that in the coming decade some of the more remote pick-your-own farms might also be hurt by higher gasoline prices, but over the same period he envisions centrally located farmers' markets growing like Topsy. As a weekly participant in the big Baltimore market, Kerr is not exactly a disinterested observer of this phenomenon. Hearing him rhapsodize, it is impossible to separate Bud Kerr the small-farms research coordinator from Bud Kerr the limited-resource farmer. His two selves are inextricably entwined. The tomatoes arrayed on his office windowsill were picked from a research plot at Beltsville. The peaches are windfalls collected last evening at his farm, during a final sweep of the orchard's lanes. "I cry," he confides, "every time I see a peach hit the ground."

The Beltsville Agricultural Research Center, more familiarly known simply as B.A.R.C., covers twelve square miles of rolling Maryland countryside straddling the Capital Beltway fifteen miles northeast of the Washington Monument. In a state where development pressure has steadily eroded the farmland base, Uncle Sam owns far and away the biggest farm. It is an androgynous sort of place, half farm and half laboratory, where the manipulation of genetic minutiae goes hand in hand with the mucking out of stalls. B.A.R.C. researchers claim credit for the miracle of everbearing strawberries, the domestic high-bush blueberry, and the bird of choice among commercial turkey farmers nowadays: the Beltsville White, a plump, high-breasted, early-maturing gobbler notable for being small enough when fully grown to fit into an average-sized oven. There is a pear tree there, alone on a hillside overlooking a neighboring industrial park, that as Bud Kerr puts it is "the grandaddy of all pear fire-blight resistance." There are side-by-side nursery plots, each a year old, one of them festooned with dangling lightbulbs like an Italian street festival, the other left dark. The plants on the lit side are taller. Researchers are trying to figure out why. Visiting Beltsville can provoke a nagging sense of dislocation, as if, on your way from Baltimore to Washington, you'd somehow strayed and ended up instead in Iowa, surrounded by the low growl of tractors, the sight of combines combing fields of soybeans or corn, and the velvet dark smell of manure hanging thick in the morning mist around a barn.

"Let's take a ride," Kerr says, leading me from his office down the back stairs to his truck. It's late afternoon. We stop first on Entomology Road, to have a look at Bill Cantelo's tomatoes. They don't look at all well. They look, in fact, as if they have been run through a shredder. Cantelo, a research entomologist, has been searching for some way to slow down the advance of the Colorado potato beetle. Greedy little gourmands no longer confined to Colorado nor content to dine only on potatoes, the bugs have lately shown an appetite for tomatoes, the highest value vegetable crop grown in the northeast. "They may be the region's major vegetable pest," Cantelo says. Colorado potato beetles have shown appalling evolutionary prowess, outdistancing one pesticide after another. According to Cantelo, "If this thing develops a resistance to pyrethroids we could be in real trouble." Pyrethrum insecticides are forbiddingly expensive in any case, and the more they're used, the more opportunity the beetles will have to adapt to them. Cantelo has shredded his tomatoes in an effort to determine the threshold of damage before which it doesn't make sense to spray. He's also breeding beetle-proof plants, and trying out nonchemical controls, like the bacteria *Bacillus thuringiensis*, which some tests have shown to be as much as eighty-five percent effective.

If bacteria won't do the trick, another insect might. Cantelo revels in the discovery of a tiny parasitic wasp that likes nothing better than feasting on potato beetle eggs. Bob Schroder, an entomologist at B.A.R.C.'s Beneficial Insect Introduction Laboratory, has been studying the wasps. He has also transplanted a parasitic mite from El Salvador that does battle with another stubborn pest, the Mexican bean beetle. "My mission, somewhere in the back of my mind," Schroder says, "is to reduce the need for pesticides." Schroder's mites live in lidded Tupperware trays just down the hall from the cluttered lab of Dr. Suzanne Batra, keeper of imported Japanese bees, who when she is not out with them pollinating the fruit on small farms, spends much of her time rearing wonderfully selective insects that eat only weeds: a moth with a taste for spurges, among others, and a family of weevils inordinately fond of thistles. The Beneficial Insect Introduction Laboratory is not an especially prepossessing place. It's housed in a ramshackle one-story building that seems to have sprung up around a trailer. The laboratory is bordered by a lush unmown swath, where Suzanne Batra's moths and weevils have taken up residence. A notice tacked to one of the lab's exterior walls reads, KEEP OFF THE WEEDS.

For three hours Kerr restlessly crisscrosses B.A.R.C.'s extensive grounds, pausing here to examine an experimental crop of purple okra, there to sample a cherry tomato sweeter than a seedless grape. He talks incessantly, part tour guide and part philosopher, bouncing back and forth between buoyant optimism and a sort of weary resignation. "I'm bucking constantly," he complains. "I don't have a hell of a lot of support. If it doesn't get done by me it doesn't get done." Moments later he is launching into a confident forecast of sweeping political change, a new administration borne into office on the backs of disgruntled small farmers.

Kerr's schizophrenia is understandable. The fact that his office exists holds out the possibility of real change in government agricultural policy. The fact that his mandate is mostly symbolic makes that hope untenable. What his job comes down to is playing the middle against both sides, making loaves and fishes from smoke and mirrors. He is uncommonly good at this trick, but it cannot be easy or very often inspiriting. He spent the better part of a year, for instance, convincing the Department that it ought to sponsor a special symposium on small farm research, which it finally did in November 1981. He then had to devote another six months to ushering the proceedings of that conference into print. He knows he can't make great gains while he's busy protecting his flanks, and he must understand, though he seldom betrays it, how slim are his chances of reversing the inertia compounded by decades of deliberate policy. He will have a hard enough time helping even his chosen few, the limited resource farmers, never mind the rest of the small-farm sector. All he can do is hold his ground, consolidate his gains, and holler. Bud Kerr has no more power over his circumstances, and yet he is no more dispensable than the Dutch boy with his finger in a bulging dike.

Our tour culminates in the orchards. Kerr seems to relax there, among dwarf fruit trees no taller than shrubs, engineered for easy picking without ladders, and apples trained to trellises like grapevines. He indicates a column of apricots pruned into two dimensions, fan-shaped and flattened, as though they'd been espaliered against a courtyard wall that's since been removed. "They bear almost as well as standard trees," he says, "and you can plant about twice as many to the acre." One of Kerr's pet projects is the development of a vehicle for the mechanization of an orchard of such trees, a sort of multipurpose rolling scaffold from which all picking and pruning can be done.

He forages through cumbrous blackberry bushes laden with thumb-sized berries. "I'm getting a buck seventy-five a pint for these at market. I can't stand to see them going to waste." Returning to his office, he cannot resist one final detour, swinging impulsively off the paved road along a lane leading into a peach orchard. He hauls the truck to a stop halfway up the steep, south-facing hillside, and we climb out to fill our hats. I wonder if absconding with government fruit is a criminal offense, like pocketing Post Office pens. We are picking Richhaven peaches, globular, softly cleft, unblemished, all but glowing. They average three inches in diameter. We stand beside the truck and Kerr goes to work with his knife. The government grows a creditable peach. It is as good as any I've ever eaten. It is as good, even, as one of Kerr's own.

"It ought to be," Bud Kerr allows between bites. "It was grown by a bunch of Ph.D.'s."

HOLDING GROUND

Every year, according to the National Agricultural Lands Study, approximately 3 million acres of farmland are converted to non-agricultural uses—a total 23.4 million acres in the eight years from 1967 through 1975. The greater and more noticeable portion of that conversion occurs in what are known as S.M.S.A.'s, or Standard Metropolitan Statistical Areas. The S.M.S.A. is a creation of modern economic geography, the product of pulsing population dynamics, embracing the city itself as well as the suburbs and exurbs that serve as its buffer zone, its catch basin, and, until fairly recently, its breadbasket. Perhaps a fifth of all American farms are contained within S.M.S.A.'s. Arrowhead Farm, where Bud Kerr raises his superior peaches, is in the City of Baltimore's Standard Metropolitan Statistical Area. The Beltsville Agricultural Research Center rides the cusp between Baltimore's S.M.S.A. and Washington's. Most of the customers for the farmers' markets and pick-your-own orchards of Kerr's new-wave, limited-resource farms live in S.M.S.A.'s, so it follows that most of these farms will need to be located in or near S.M.S.A.'s as well. This may be more easily said than done. "Since 1970 the price of farmland has increased at two-and-one-half times the rate of inflation," writes Chuck Little of the American Land Forum, a Washington policy study organization concerned with land use and land tenure. "In 1970 the average price per acre was $196—an average made up of areas ranging from the 'garden state' prices of New Jersey at over $1,000 to some arid areas of the West where farmland could still be bought for less than $50 an acre. But by 1980, farmland was fetching a U.S. average of $640 per acre—including $2,400 in New Jersey." There is almost no place left in New Jersey that isn't part of an S.M.S.A.

These are paradoxical times for metropolitan farmers. On the one hand, as Bud Kerr persists in telling anyone who'll listen, and as the success of Greenmarket would seem to confirm, Standard Metropolitan Statistical Areas are just the place to be. "We may have this whole thing backward," Chuck Little remarked during a seminar he'd convened on the future of metropolitan farming and farmland. "Maybe metropolitan agriculture should not be defined as a set of problems but as a set of opportunities. Here is this big marketing opportunity and an agriculture around it that is starving to death. That is ridiculous. Maybe . . . things . . . could be handled better by the Department of Commerce rather than the Department of Agriculture. Why don't we have programs to realize this terrific opportunity?" If a small farmer's capital consists mostly of flexibility and responsiveness to changing conditions, then the best return on that investment would undoubtedly derive from a captive market of consumers. Presumably the farmer who tethers his farm to an urban market stands to profit from the city closing in around him.

He also stands to be run over. As the advantages of near-urban agriculture become more conspicuous, so do its frustrations. It has gotten harder and harder to get started. Larry Orman, executive director of People for Open Space and a participant in the American Land Forum's colloquy, made a spot check of real estate prices in the San Francisco Bay Area and found agricultural land values as high as $6,000 an acre. It is harder still to stay in business. "Our experience is that ever since the minibike was invented, housing and agriculture—at least in Montgomery County—have not been compatible," Maryland planner Perry Berman told the same meeting. Abutting the District of Columbia to the northwest, Montgomery County, Maryland, is part of Washington's S.M.S.A.

Before 1960 Montgomery County held more than three hundred working dairies. Fewer than fifty remain. One of the last to go was owned by a lifelong dairyman named Charles

Savage, who hung on to his hundred-acre farm until it was completely surrounded by suburbs, then put the place on the block at $15,000 an acre. He wasn't doing it for the money, Savage told a reporter—he'd already sold off enough bits and pieces to make himself wealthier than milking cows ever could. And he wasn't doing it because he had no choice. Montgomery County has one of the best small-farm and farmland preservation programs in the country. He was doing it, Charles Savage said, on account of his cows. "There were some kids beating on my cows with sticks," he explained. "Another time, some kids sicced their dogs on my cows. . . . I've had two cows shot. . . . I got sued once when a car hit one of my cows that had gotten out, another time when the cows got out and played hell with this lady's yard. . . . The cows would get out in the middle of the night and run through the developments. It got so I couldn't sleep at night. I was so close to those cows. That was the worst thing I ever had to do in my life, giving up those cows."

"In 1968," Chuck Little recalls, "I ran an organization called the Open Land Institute. We published an article then called 'The Vanishing Farm,' and it reads now as if it was written yesterday." In the intervening years the dilemma of disappearing near-urban farms has at least insinuated itself into popular awareness. Forty-eight of the fifty states have enacted differential assessment legislation, lowering property taxes on agricultural land. Sixteen states have some sort of right-to-farm law on their books, to protect farmers from nuisance lawsuits and unreasonable local legislation, or exempt them from suburban environmental niceties (so that a dairy, for example, won't have to dig a herd-sized septic tank). Hundreds of counties and municipalities have pushed through zoning requirements that provide either incentives to agriculture or disincentives to development, or both. A half-dozen foresighted states have full-scale agricultural districting plans that combine most of the preceding elements, and a handful have even started down the costly road of funding the purchase of development rights to endangered farmland, or the purchase of the farmland itself, so as to keep it in agriculture.

All this has had depressingly little impact. The attrition continues, scarcely abated.

Once, in Iowa, I drove west from the campus of Iowa State University in downtown Ames out through concentric rings of subdivisions to the University's research farm in an adjacent county. My host, a professor of agricultural engineering, called attention to our surroundings.

"Do you know what this is?" he asked.

"A housing development," I answered.

"No," he corrected. "What this is is the climax crop for an Iowa cornfield."

In areas where development pressure puts land values at a premium, a climax crop of townhouses will indisputably yield more dollars per acre than anything else a farmer can legally plant. As Montgomery County's Perry Berman reluctantly concedes, "There's no way we can justify ag preservation strictly on the products, although we made a good sales pitch that one-third of our milk comes from our dairies. You can sell a lot more expensive houses on that land than a farmer can make selling milk." Townhouses, of course, can be harvested only once, whereas well-tended fields or an adeptly managed herd will provide an income indefinitely. But the bait dangled by developers can be mightily seductive. The selling price for Charles Savage's farmland was one hundred and fifty times its purchase price. Indifference to such temptations cannot be based solely on anticipation of future agricultural earnings. It must also be rooted in an abiding love of the land and a deeply felt commitment to the craft of farming. No conceivable incentive can substitute for those very subjective qualities. Small-farm support activity, public or private, can only augment the determination to continue farming where such a resolve already exists. And in some cases even that may not be enough.

What happens when the rural-to-urban ratio slips out of balance is that farming, never an easy occupation under the best of circumstances, becomes markedly more difficult. For all their commendable intentions, right-to-farm laws are probably powerless to prevent this. It's not always the obvious annoyances—

the marauding bands of pubescent neanderthals attacking cows with sticks and dogs, the beer cans expelled from passing cars that stick inextricably in a baler's intricate craw—that make the greatest difference. It may not even be legal hindrances or hobbling taxes. Sometimes what matters most is that the local café is replaced by a quiche palace, leaving no place in town to go for a proper cup of coffee. What planners insist on calling "the agricultural infrastructure" begins to atrophy. A dairy farmer, for instance, cannot continue to milk cows unless a truck comes to pick up his milk. There must be a veterinarian available whose practice is not limited to household pets. It helps considerably if the farm-and-feed store hasn't metamorphosed into a home-improvement center; if the roving independent farm hardware salesman still makes house calls; if the local implement dealer still stocks a full line of parts—assuming there still is a local implement dealer. Having to travel fifty miles each way in the middle of haying to replace a two-dollar bushing can nudge even the most dedicated farmer toward retirement. As one farmer after another gives in and moves out, the demand slackens for agricultural goods and services. After a while the farmers who hang on may be left with nothing to hang on to. "When enough problems . . . accumulate, what has been called 'the impermanence syndrome' sets in," writes Chuck Little. "Farmers give up on making substantial improvements on their farms, hoping to sell out when the price gets right."

The high dropout rate is especially demoralizing because its effects tend to be irreversible. In rural, predominantly agricultural regions, when a small family farm goes belly up it is more often than not absorbed into a larger neighboring place, which when it too folds will be swallowed in turn by an even larger neighbor, and so on. "I suppose there must be a practical limit to that," Chuck Little comments, "but we haven't found it yet." There are, of course, a host of pernicious problems associated with such agricultural cannibalism, but at least the land stays in agriculture, keeping alive the faint possibility that it might one day be divided again among family farms. When a lingering near-urban farm goes under it tends to give way to a distinctly non-agricultural replacement. Converting a pasture into a parking lot is no big deal. Turning concrete back into cropland is like trying to get toothpaste back into the tube.

The route to Ralph Grossi's ranch, near the town of Novato in Marin County, California, amounts to a short course in the mechanics of suburbanization. Just across the Golden Gate Bridge from San Francisco, Marin County divides uneasily into three distinct geopolitical entities. Its coastline, now almost totally secured within the boundaries of the Point Reyes National Seashore and the Golden Gate National Recreation Area is a certifiable environmental treasure. To the east, the county boasts an affluent and educated commuter class and some of the most sought-after developable real estate in the United States. To the west, the cobbled hills of the Coast Range foster an active and productive agriculture that supplies much of the Bay Area's fresh milk. The three regions coexist in precarious harmony. They interact mostly at the margins, on contested terrain. Ralph Grossi ranches such terrain.

To get there you drive north on U.S. 101, along Marin's eastern flank and through its commercial heart. Gas stations, fast-food restaurants, low-rise office complexes, undifferentiated light industrial expanses, mini-malls, malls, and mammoth malls: the dreary sequence unspools on either side of the highway, crests around the city of San Rafael, and then tapers off. In Novato, at the junction of U.S. 101 and San Marin Drive, an insurance company's vast warren of offices rises from a bulldozed field. San Marin Drive proceeds through unbroken miles of suburban housing, distinguishable only by slight variations on ersatz vernacular themes. The dominant motif is soft-spread Spanish: white stucco and red tiled roofs, interspersed with thickets of hundred-thousand-dollar, pseudo-rustic, shingled sheds. You can reliably gauge a suburb's age by the size of its trees. The trees lining San Marin Drive are for the most part dwarfed by the wires and stakes that support them.

The country opens up some around Novato Boulevard. You still see street signs and sidewalks, but you see neatly fenced hillside pastures too, with stout cows lazing about in them, munching. The first farm past the last clutch of split-levels belongs to Ralph Grossi's Uncle George. It presides from its high berm over a county recreation area, complete with artificial lake, tame mallards, and picnic tables. Ralph's place is around the next bend, on the left, in a little hollow shaded by big live oaks. MARINDALE DAIRY, the sign out front announces, RALPH AND JAMES GROSSI. 4025 Novato Boulevard, insists the City of Novato, California—population 43,916 at last count and still growing.

As small family farms go the Grossis' is pretty substantial. The many barns and outbuildings are in good repair, ample and uncrowded. The enclave of tidy farmhouses has seen yellow paint in the not too distant past. This being mud season, the cows milling around behind Ralph's free-stall barn are rather heavily made-up, but they're fit and healthy and a long way from gaunt. With 900 acres owned outright and another 2,500 leased, and five full-time employees milking nearly three hundred cows, Marindale Dairy stretches the limits of what could be called, by New England standards anyway, a small family farm. To look at it, you'd never know that new bedrooms for Novato's fashionable San Marin neighborhood displaced the cows that had been the Grossis' neighbors, and have for some time seemed poised to displace the Grossis as well.

"It was just an accepted fact," Ralph says, kicking off his gumboots to go indoors, "something we knew as we were growing up. Someday this all would be houses out here, and we were going to have to leave. That's a common feeling in agricultural areas threatened by development, and a lot of farms go out of business prematurely because they're afraid to make the kinds of long-term investments necessary to keep going." We have just completed a tour of Marindale Dairy, where there is no evidence at all of impending failure, and plenty to indicate long-term investment. Ralph's latest investment, longer-term than most, strains noisily at its mountings in one spotless corner of an equipment shed attached to the barn. It is a converted Walker-Shaw gasoline engine, burning methane gas pumped from a swimming pool–sized black plastic bladder fifty yards away outside. The methane is produced from milk-making's most abundant byproduct, removed in copious quantities from the floor of Ralph's barn, digested and converted into gas. The gas runs the engine. The engine runs a generator. The generator runs a meter fixed to the wall of the barn by the Pacific Gas and Electric Company, runs it backward, at the rate of approximately forty-five kilowatts per hour, pumping electricity back into the grid.

Nobody who expects to go out of business soon installs a methane digester in his yard. "I've never seriously considered doing anything else," Ralph confides. "I enjoy this. I enjoy the challenge." As a junior partner on his father's farm, he is following the classic itinerary of the farm sons toward agricultural self-employment. It is one that has attracted fewer adherents in recent years, and that today promises far less security than it once did. So it is worth noting that Ralph Grossi is not anomalous in Marin County. "Most of the dairies I know around here have junior partners now," Ralph says, "and that's a real change from ten years ago."

Indeed, the outlook for Marin County farms has brightened over the past decade. In 1973, a Countywide Plan adopted by Marin's elected Board of Supervisors unambiguously rejected rampant development, and advocated the continued presence of agriculture. The county backed up its rhetoric with sixty-acre zoning for West Marin grazing lands, and quickly provided financial and technical assistance when farmers were forced by tough state environmental regulations to install water quality controls on their farms. A California state law known as the Williamson Act discourages the development of agricultural lands by blessing parcels under contract to locally administered "agricultural preserves" with tax abatements, and Marin County enrolled in the Williamson Act program. The county's dairy industry was helped along by self-imposed production quotas, investment in modernization, and the rapid growth of the population of greater San Francisco. As Grossi puts it, "We're right next door to our market. There are five million people in the Bay Area, and they drink milk. That's got to mean something in the long run."

What has meant the most, however, has been the appearance in Marin County of a vigorous coalition of ranchers and farmers, environmentalists, and local government. "Forget agriculture for a moment," says Larry Orman, the author of *A Search for Permanence: Farmland Conservation in Marin County, California.* "What happened first in Marin was that people got tired of having freeways punched through their backyards and threw out a traditionally pro-development Board of Supervisors." As Orman explained it to the American Land Forum meeting, "This was not done primarily for agricultural reasons but for growth management reasons. The agricultural element emerged later on, and it turned out to be the best thing in the world for the dairy industry. The public appreciated the open character of West Marin. There were a few key leaders who appreciated the agricultural values." Now, he says, "There's no question that local conservation groups have adopted agriculture as an issue."

As the coalition took shape odd things began to happen. Environmental activists trooped to Sacramento to testify on the ranchers' behalf at milk price support hearings. Ranchers—very few at first, but more as the fight wore on—found themselves in the unfamiliar position of stumping for strict zoning. The elected officials of a county whose future prosperity would seem to most observers to depend on continued development have for ten years had the political stamina to stare down some of the region's most powerful developers. The most recent offspring of this unlikely alliance is called the Marin Agricultural Land Trust (M.A.L.T.). Ralph Grossi is chairman of its board of directors.

In the arsenal of farmland protection, land trusts are at once the most effective and most problematic of weapons. An agricultural land trust seeks to secure land for agriculture in perpetuity. It has as its principal means the conservation easement, a legal device that when written into a deed forever restricts the uses to which a piece of property may be put. Easements are generally used to exclude development, and they thereby lower the market value of the land. Ownership of the actual property is unaffected. Only the rights to development of that land, individually tailored and exhaustively spelled out in each easement, change hands. Such rights, intangible though they may seem, are by no means inconsiderable. In Marin County they may amount to better than a thousand dollars an acre—the difference in market value between land used to raise beef, sheep, or milk, and land used to raise houses. When transferred from the landowner to a legally incorporated nonprofit community land trust, a conservation easement can provide its donor with certain tax advantages while guaranteeing that no crop of townhouses will ever grow on that land.

The Marin Agricultural Land Trust had its genesis in the spring of 1978, when two determined middle-aged women converged on the office of Jennie Gerard at the San Francisco-based Trust for Public Land, an organization that assists in the creation of community land trusts. One of Gerard's callers was Ellen Straus, who with her husband Bill and her son Albert runs a dairy in West Marin. Ellen had already led Marin's ranchers in support of sixty-acre agricultural zoning. (*Led* is perhaps the wrong word. Mrs. Straus often commanded an army of one. "During the hearings," her husband remembers, "I got up to speak in favor of the proposal and ninety percent of the ranchers in the room got up too—and walked out.") Though the measure eventually passed, Ellen had since become convinced that zoning alone was insufficient. Gains made there could too quickly be reversed by a minor shift of political power. What she was looking for was something permanent, something that once done would be as difficult to undo as a housing development. "It was obvious to me that zoning wasn't going to do that over the long term," Ellen says. "To me it was all very logical."

It is apparently slightly less logical to the Internal Revenue Service. The preservation of open land does not in and of itself constitute a "charitable purpose" and will not confer tax-exempt status on an organization established to do so. To be judged tax exempt a trust must accept an added responsibility, such as educating the citizenry about land conservation—education apparently being unarguably charitable. Without a tax exemption, a land trust cannot accept tax-deductible donations of easements.

What's more, agricultural lands may not be granted easements on their agricultural merits alone, but only if their preservation serves other closely defined "conservation purposes" as well. Land trusts established to preserve agricultural lands accordingly tend to steer clear of the word "agriculture" in their corporate identities, emphasizing the word "conservation" instead. M.A.L.T.'s founders, however, were resolved that their trust would be explicitly agricultural, and they located a small window in the rules through which it seemed they might be able to pass. An allowable conservation purpose, as defined in the Internal Revenue Code's section 170 (f)(3)(b) and (h), subsection (iii), includes "the preservation of open space (including farmland and forestland) where such preservation is (I) for the scenic enjoyment of the general public, or (II) pursuant to a clearly delineated Federal, State or local government policy."

West Marin's undulating hills seemed sure to qualify as scenic under subsection (I)—though depending upon your point of view a square mile of cut-over Iowa corn stubble might not—and, given the existence of the Countywide Plan, M.A.L.T.'s easements ought to be eligible too under subsubsection (II). One of the chief frustrations of boosters of agricultural land trusts is the need for all this hedging of bets. The American Farmland Trust, backed by the Rockefeller Brothers Fund, works in Washington to have the tax laws clarified, but thus far no change has been forthcoming. The Marin Agricultural Land Trust snuck into existence through a regulatory transom left slightly ajar by the Internal Revenue Service.

"It's easy to talk about starting an organization like this, but doing it is something else again," says Paul Maxwell, who has been doing it for several years now as M.A.L.T.'s executive director and only full-time employee. "We've got some of the most productive forage land in the country here," Maxwell says, "and we're trying to keep it from looking like the East Coast. If they'd started planning there for the preservation of agricultural land a hundred years ago they'd have a better land use mix now. We can't afford to wait much longer."

The Marin Agricultural Land Trust shares a sparsely furnished office with the Marin County Farm Bureau, in Point Reyes Station, near the entrance to the National Seashore. Point Reyes Station is the sort of town where battered pickups compete with late-model Mercedes Benzes for parking spots on streets lined with boutiques, galleries, and gift shops geared to the tourist trade. M.A.L.T.'s office is spliced in between a florist's shop and a custom-made clothing store. A few blocks away, at the intersection of Fourth and B Streets, a working dairy farm goes about business as usual.

Paul Maxwell is sandy-haired, soft-featured, and soft-spoken. He wears pale blue chinos and cowboy boots. He has impeccable conservationist credentials, having served before coming to Marin as a planner for Boulder County, Colorado, where he helped to shape one of the nation's most ambitious greenbelt preservation plans. But he grew up on a California farm and, like many of Marin's new generation of ranchers, trained in agriculture at Cal Poly in San Luis Obispo. He does not believe, as some conservationists do, that farmers and environmentalists must necessarily be at odds. "If you talk to young ranchers you'll find they learned a conservation ethic in ag school," Maxwell contends. "They just don't think of themselves as conservationists. A conservationist is a liberal."

Not surprisingly, conservation easements for wildlands protection have been employed mainly by those who stood to gain the most from available tax benefits: corporations and wealthy individuals. But farmers seldom inhabit the I.R.S. stratosphere. "Most ranchers around here have cash flow problems," Maxwell grants, "and I don't expect we'll see a lot of donated easements." Tax incentives aside, the real drawing card of an agricultural land trust may be its value for estate planning. "You've got second- and third-generation ranch families with very different ideas about how the land should be used," Maxwell says. "For them, estate planning becomes a central issue." Marindale Dairy, for example, will one day have to be equitably divided among four Grossi children. Only Ralph is as yet committed to a future in agriculture. His elder brother, James, Jr., is a civil engineer and developer who lives in a handsome modern house up the hill from the dairy. To realize their rightful inheritances Ralph's siblings might reasonably request that part of the ranch be sold. To keep on ranching, Ralph will need every acre he's got, and buying more is out of the question. The Grossis' rented grazing land, with an agricultural value of perhaps three hundred dollars an acre, has been put on the market. "He's asking a thousand an acre," Ralph says. "He won't get that, but he'll get seven or eight hundred, and that's just too much for us to pay for grazing land. It won't add up."

Even in an ideally uncluttered case, where a farmer's sole heir wishes to continue farming, inheritance can pose tremendous barriers to that ambition. An acre of West Marin grazing land bought in 1955 for $125 might fetch ten times that much today, with three-quarters of its new sticker price allotted to pure potential: the value it might have with a house planted on it. It is not uncommon for the development rights on a typical Marin dairy ranch to exceed the combined worth of everything else on the place. Assuming that the inheritor of such an operation was sufficiently savvy to avail himself of every I.R.S. loophole, he could still be liable for annual estate tax payments well in excess of the income he could hope to net from a year's ranching. He will not need a trip to H & R Block's to figure out that he'll have to put his ranch up for sale simply to pay the death duties due on it.

Paul Maxwell wishes he would first drop by the office in Point Reyes Station to discuss the possibility of a conservation easement. M.A.L.T.'s purchase of an easement at a bargain rate—say, half the market value of development rights to the ranch—would simultaneously limit the rancher's taxable estate while providing a cash reserve with which to defray the taxes that remain. More importantly, it would ensure a future in agriculture for ranch and rancher alike.

When he's not out trying to persuade ranchers to sell him easements, Maxwell pursues the operating capital to buy them with. "We won't get by on bake sales," he admits. "All my life I've hated asking for money," Ellen Straus says. "This is the first time I don't mind." She not only doesn't mind, she is the Trust's treasurer, and she's honed her skills at a seminar on nonprofit fund-raising. M.A.L.T.'s costs to date have been covered by grants from a local foundation, which has also provided seed money for a $200,000 revolving loan fund with which to purchase easements. But much more than $200,000 will be required to secure very many of Marin County's 130,000 agricultural acres. "What we're looking for," Maxwell explains, "is projects that pay for themselves."

One option is a concept known as T.D.R.—Transfer of Development Rights—in which a developer covetous of higher density on a site than local zoning allows could earn a variance for his parcel by buying the development rights for another piece of land and turning them over to M.A.L.T. A more aggressive and more controversial scheme envisions the land trust acting as a de facto developer, peddling limited development rights to the highest bidder—on land poorly suited to agricultural uses but contained within a larger, agriculturally useful whole on which the trust holds an easement—then applying the profits from such sales toward the purchase of more easements. "I think that's a long way down the road," Larry Orman predicts, but Paul Maxwell is enthusiastic nonetheless. "The beauty of it," he says, "is that it would let us act as a catalyst. We'd be using free enterprise to fill a niche."

Maxwell may find some encouragement in the experience of the Massachusetts Farm and Conservation Lands Trust, begun in 1980, which has enjoyed success with just such techniques. The threat posed by a dwindling farmland base has probably been most keenly felt in New England, where the regional agriculture has been allowed—some would say compelled—to atrophy in the face of lower-priced competition from the South, Midwest, and West. Small family farms are more than a romantic ideal in New England. They are for all practical purposes the only kind of farm possible where climate and topography rule out the highly mechanized agriculture practiced elsewhere. Over the years New England's farmers, with the partial exception of its dairymen, have bowed to economic reality. Massachusetts alone lost eighty percent of its working farms between 1948 and 1978. That state's commissioner of food and agriculture, Frederic Winthrop, Jr., contemplated this bleak statistic in a recent magazine article. "It is scant cheer for the dairyman who has just lost a rented hundred-acre cornfield because the owner sold it for an industrial park to know that several million acres of corn land exist somewhere else in the United States," Winthrop wrote.

"It is likewise not altogether reassuring for the consumers of New England, whose food bills are already higher than those in other regions, to know that when our nearby land is gone, land remains in production two or three thousand miles away. Most consumers know what's been happening to energy and transportation costs and how they affect the price of food shipped across the continent."

Massachusetts instituted differential assessments for active farmland in 1973. A 1977 bill authorized state funding for the purchase of development rights to endangered croplands. The legislation enabled the state to issue bonds to raise the money it needed to pay the larger share, in partnerships with individual towns, of the purchase price of Agricultural Preservation Restrictions—essentially, conservation easements—on qualifying properties. The bill's effectiveness, however, has been hampered by the amount of time consumed in inevitable bureaucratic review. Hot properties will generally have been and gone before an A.P.R. application can be completed and approved. The Massachusetts Farm and Conservation Lands Trust (M.F.C.L.T.) emerged to fill that vacuum. Backed by a revolving loan fund and commercial lines of credit, it buys lands that seem certain to qualify eventually for an A.P.R., holds them until the paperwork is done, then sells the deed restriction to the state and the restricted farmland to local farmers.

The fact of that state funding, of course, sets M.F.C.L.T. apart from M.A.L.T. There is no California appropriation for the purchase of development rights; M.A.L.T. must foot the bill for easements on its own. But M.F.C.L.T. has completed several projects that seem to bear out Paul Maxwell's hunch about the usefulness of limited development and transfer of development rights for farmland conservation. The particulars of one case, gleaned from the Massachusetts trust's 1981 annual report, should serve to illustrate both the method's potential and the immensely complex logistics involved.

In the fall of 1980 the scattered legatees claiming rights to an estate mired in probate petitioned for settlement, which necessitated the sale at public auction of eighty-seven-year-old Ralph Barton's seventy-seven-acre dirt and dairy farm. It happened that Barton's farm was one of the very few remaining honest-to-goodness farms in the town of Sudbury, Massachusetts, twenty miles north of Boston—a wealthy mink-and-manure-belt suburb where sentiment in favor of conservation and environmentalism runs nearly as high as the price of real estate. In April of 1981 the Sudbury Town Meeting approved an expenditure of $110,000 to go toward the preservation intact of Ralph Barton's farm.

The M.F.C.L.T. was called in to figure out what to do next. In consultation with a private planning firm, the Trust determined that just more than half of the land had real agricultural value and ought to be protected with an A.P.R. Another fifteen acres or so, encompassing a pond and brook and some low marsh, could revert to the town's conservation commission for preservation as a recreational area. The remainder, including the farm's original house and barns, was deemed developable, with its development not infringing on the continued presence of agriculture nearby. Thirteen potential house lots were identified—exactly half as many as local zoning would have allowed.

In October of 1981 the Massachusetts Farm and Conservation Lands Trust bought Ralph Barton's farm from the Barton Estate, and immediately began preparing to resell it in somewhat different form. An A.P.R. application was filed with the state. A developer was recruited who would buy the thirteen homesites and build on them. Area farmers were interviewed at length, and two agreed to purchase portions of the restricted farmland. The Trust's annual report, published before the final closing, shows this summary:

BARTON LIMITED DEVELOPMENT PROJECT

Interim Accounting — Closing: February 25, 1982

ANTICIPATED EXPENSES

$537,500	Purchase from Barton Estate (80.52 acres; $6,125 per acre)
31,160	Planning, survey, appraisal, legal, interest, administrative costs, and contingency reserve
26,875	M.F.C.L.T. overhead fee (5 percent of purchase price)
$595,535	

ANTICIPATED PROCEEDS

$272,300	Sale of 21.91 acres to builder-developer ($12,422 per acre)
99,650	Sale of 15.13 acres conservation land to Town of Sudbury ($6,582 per acre)
200,350	Sale of A.P.R. on 43.47 acres to Commonwealth of Massachusetts and Town of Sudbury ($4,609 per acre)
23,235	Sale of 43.47 acres restricted land to farmers ($534 per acre)
$595,535	

For land trusts already testing the limits of bureaucratic tolerance, this can be a dangerous business. "What it comes down to," Ralph Grossi explains, "is that in the eyes of the I.R.S. we can't be developers and conservationists at the same time." Tax law is ambiguous at best, and subject to maddeningly whimsical revision. Potential donors or sellers of easements may hold back for fear of I.R.S. reprisals. "No easement has been disallowed yet," the Trust for Public Land's Jennie Gerard cautiously says, reviewing the record of land trusts around the country, "but when you claim a conservation easement you're subject to an audit, and it's just possible that the I.R.S. agent will come in and say, 'That's shuck and jive. This isn't scenic or natural, it's plain farmland.' At which point the donor could be hit with fines, back taxes due, and—if you can believe this—a gift tax on the value of the easement."

In the face of this unhappy prospect the Marin Agricultural Land Trust has proceeded at dead slow, awaiting promised I.R.S. clarifications, detouring its every action across the desk of an esteemed San Francisco tax attorney beforehand. More than three years passed after Ellen Straus and Phyllis Faber first declared their intentions to Jennie Gerard, before M.A.L.T. took title to a single conservation easement. (M.A.L.T., unlike M.F.C.L.T., does not have the benefit of an established state repository for deed restrictions, and so must go through many more maneuvers in advance of accepting them.) "If we don't do it right it's not fair to anyone," Ellen Straus says, "but I don't think we realized how long it would take to do it right."

The agonizingly slow pace reflects both the difficulty of the undertaking and the thoroughness of M.A.L.T.'s approach to it. Lawyers scrutinized the trust's proposed structure to verify its legal inviolability. An accountant at Touche Ross and Company was persuaded to prepare elaborate hypothetical financial projections of the estate tax implications of conservation easements, a precaution that later proved valuable in winning the support of an uncertain Marin County Farm Bureau. M.A.L.T. had a dozen transactions under way by fall of 1982, but with every easement having to be custom made a lot of time is inevitably taken up, and there's no good way to hurry the process along.

"It usually takes a year or two to do any deal, even when a trust is well established," Jennie Gerard says. "I'm impressed with their progress."

Gerard suggests that the real measure of M.A.L.T.'s success should not be confined to a count of the number of acres it's rounded up. What may be more important is the ripple effect it's had on the agricultural land trust movement, and on the agricultural community as a whole. She cites as evidence a quantum leap in the volume of requests her office has been receiving for information and technical assistance. She notes with pleasure that these requests no longer emanate exclusively from liberal environmentalists, but come more and more often from traditionally conservative farmers themselves. Last summer, at the Marin Farm Day festivities, Gerard was collared by Hank Korda, a dairyman who succeeded Ralph Grossi as president of the Marin County Farm Bureau. She had by then finished her attendance at M.A.L.T.'s birth and had turned her attention elsewhere. Korda couldn't wait to tell her all about Marin's new agricultural land trust. "It was clear to me that as far as he was concerned it was *his* land trust," Gerard recalls. "I was delighted. It was as if the graft had taken."

"I'd feel more comfortable talking to you if we had a couple of easements under our belt," Paul Maxwell admits, "but on the whole I'm pretty confident." Even Ralph Grossi, whose own wish to put Marindale Dairy into trust may be clouded by the complexities of joint ownership with his siblings, remains resolute. "I'm optimistic," he says. "You've got to be optimistic. If you're going to get involved with something like this you have to believe it's going to work out in the end."

If you ask Ralph Grossi whatever possessed him to get involved with something like M.A.L.T., he will shake his head, grin, and pronounce a single two-syllable word.

"Ellen."

"Ralph Grossi was really instrumental out there," Larry Orman says. "Ralph and Ellen."

"If Ellen Straus offers you dessert," Jennie Gerard advises, "do not pass it up."

I am engaged in hand-to-hand combat with a slice of mocha buttercream cake only slightly smaller than the plate it balances on. Sunlight washes through clean windows, warming the kitchen where we sit. Outside, bright early primroses bloom in the dooryard. "I only just bought them," says Ellen Straus, half bashful. "I couldn't resist." The surface of Tomales Bay, partly hidden behind a tall eucalyptus grove, glitters and refracts. A big peacock crosses the driveway trailed by a bevy of drab hens. I am encouraged to tackle another slice.

"I have to believe it's only a matter of time until we recognize the importance of preserving agricultural land," Ellen says. She has been discussing the Marin Agricultural Land Trust, the only enterprise she's ever come across whose appetite for time and energy surpasses a dairy farm's. "We have to remember how to use land well," she says. "We have to preserve the skills as well. I learn all the time, from every farm I visit and whenever I look around our own place. I walk over our land and I see where we've done things wrong, where we kept too many cows by the barn and ruined the soil. All over Marin County we can see the mistakes of the past."

She refills my coffee cup and advances the cake toward me.

"I think we're finally learning to talk to each other," she says. "I think the environmentalists may have finally learned how to speak to farmers, but for a long time they didn't know how, and they really fell flat. So we knew we didn't want the Trust to be sponsored by environmentalists, or by the county. We wanted it to come from the ranchers themselves, and I remember, at one of the very first meetings we had, we were asked some pretty tough questions about what good a land trust would actually do for ranchers. That's changed now. There's still one neighbor who says to me, 'Where's the money in it for me?' but most are more willing now to wait and see, to listen, because, really, they don't have many options left."

When I've cleaned my plate, Ellen takes me for a walk around the farm. Bill and Ellen Straus live at the base of Bolinas Ridge, a few miles north of the town of Marshall, in a neatly kept Colonial house—white clapboards, spruce-green shutters and trim—that looks incongruous here on the northern coast of California. Eucalyptus and live oak grow where the sugarbush should be. Pillowed coastal hills swell up behind the Strauses' milking parlor, carpeted in new green, punctuated by wild blue irises. The slopes are steep, and wet weather this past winter has left the hillsides so soggy that spring grazing had to be held off for more than a month. Today, though, the pasture is freckled with Holsteins gathered in amiable pairs and quartets, save for one seeming recluse who claims her solitary summit, prone, almost ornamental. The ladies eat at their leisure, lifting their huge heads from time to time to gaze across Tomales Bay: cobalt, fjordlike, a slender incision left in the landscape by some ancient earthquake, marking the precise location of the San Andreas Fault.

"Overall I'm encouraged," Ellen says as she surveys the surrounding territory. She indicates neighboring ranches bought up by speculators but rescued for ranching after the passage of sixty-acre zoning. "I know of five on the east side of the bay alone," she says, "all family farms. Now we're seeing a lot of young people coming back."

Far below us, in the shadow of our ridge, Ellen's son Albert crosses the barnyard carrying a sickly calf. Albert is a shareholder in the farm now. A graduate of Cal Poly, he's begun taking the reins of the operation into his own hands. He has installed a home-built computer in his living room to help him keep track of the farm's affairs. He's planted new acreage to barley and oat hay, reducing his dependence on expensive imported alfalfa, and in what might once have been considered an act of dairy heresy he has trimmed the size of his milking herd, bringing it more into line with the carrying capacity of the range.

Telling me all this, Ellen seems almost to glow. Her husky European accent acquires a different, deeper timbre. She traverses the hill's narrow spine, leading me into a field where luxuriant clover has at last won out against a colony of thistles. Ellen kneels there and runs her hand through the thick fodder, fondly, as if it were the tousled head of her child.

"Oh," she exclaims, "this is exciting! This makes me feel very good."

7

THE SURVIVAL OF SMALL FARMS

"Farmland preservation," Marty Strange rules, "is very, very much an urban liberal phenomenon." He speaks with the authority of a man who lives and works in Walthill, Nebraska, population 860, an hour and a half north of Omaha and eight miles west of the Missouri River. In Thurston County, between Winnebago and Rosalie. Nearer to Rosalie. Liberals in Thurston County, never mind the urban variety, are in conspicuously short supply. Marty Strange is himself one member of that minority, though he would doubtless dispute the appellation. He shares an office with most of the others. The building where they work was once the town's hotel, and their office was its lobby. Then the hotel became an apartment house and the lobby became a tavern, and in successive incarnations, a package store, a grocery, a social club, and a head shop. Two years ago it was transmuted once more, into an office for the Center for Rural Affairs, of which Marty Strange is co-director. Through all of its multiple identities the building's capacious first floor has clung fast to one saving architectural grace, an elegant and ornate stamped-tin ceiling, at which Marty Strange, tilted back in a battered office chair with his feet up on the desk, is apt to stare as he talks.

"We lose about twice as much farmland, in terms of productive capacity, to topsoil erosion every year as we do to urbanization." It isn't that Marty Strange favors the wholesale development of metropolitan farmland. What rankles him is that its preservation has gained the gloss of a politically correct crusade, like saving whales or baby seals, while equally deserving but less glamorous goals get short shrift. There's not much glamour in Thurston County, and it will be some time before urban sprawl poses any real threat to the farmland there. In the meanwhile, the resource that most needs preserving is not farmland but farmers. There's as much land as ever being farmed, but by fewer and fewer farmers, and if the effects of this trend are not as dramatic or obvious as what happens when the last suburban farm is paved over for parking, they are no less pernicious.

During the 1970s the small family farm in the Midwest was increasingly endangered by the tendency of larger and more affluent operations to expand, capitalizing on the equity value in their landholdings and adding to that equity with each expansion. As the price of farmland continued to rise without reference to the level of earnings the farmland would yield, nonfarm investors flocked to farm states in search of a piece of the action. More recently, the price of prime Farm Belt cropland has declined. Since loans for the purchase of land are generally secured by other land previously purchased, this decline worries bankers and borrowers alike. "The ones who are really hurting now are the people who took advantage of high land prices to leverage themselves way out on a limb," Marty Strange says. One young Illinois farmer racked up 15,000 acres before he turned forty, took a long look over the precipice of bankruptcy, then went out behind the barn and shot himself. An Indiana man named Eugene Smith left Purdue University in 1968 equipped with a master's degree in agricultural engineering and a powerful ambition. Over the next dozen years he assembled an empire that included 16,600 acres of Midwestern farmland and $1.25 million worth of new farm machinery. By the time his credit ran out he was $35 million in debt. Stories like these receive prominent play in Farm Belt newspapers, to sobering effect, but the land rush is far from ended. If farmland no longer qualifies as a growth stock, it has acquired new luster as a blue chip for investors to whom the possibilities of "tax-loss farming" seem compelling. These new-style investor-farmers farm mostly from a distance, over the telephone. They often replace small family farmers who'd been leasing the land with contract farm management services. The investors aren't villains. They are businessmen. They employ farm management services for the same reasons that they employ stockbrokers—to make a profit from their investments. The expansionist farmers can't really be considered villains either. They're playing to win, but they're playing by the rules. The real villains, Marty Strange would contend, are the rules themselves—those rules that ever since the New Deal have frankly advocated the consolidation of small farms into large ones, and the transfer of agricultural authority from labor to capital.

"If the family farm represents anything," Strange says, "it's a very intimate and fundamental relationship between people and resources." It's all very well for Bud Kerr to tie the survival of small farms to off-farm income and well-heeled urban consumers, but in places like Thurston County there aren't any well-heeled urban consumers, and the only off-farm income available is farm-related. Fewer farms mean fewer farm service jobs and more people wanting them. Fewer jobs mean less money spent, so nonfarm business suffers as well. And as families leave to look for work elsewhere, they leave behind schools without students, churches without congregations, and towns without citizens. It's a matter of critical mass. Ten 3,000-acre farms may produce the same amount of food as one hundred 300-acre farms, but one hundred 300-acre farms will keep a community the size of Walthill happy and healthy. Ten 3,000-acre farms won't.

The Center for Rural Affairs exists to preserve that critical mass. Unlike the Marin Agricultural Land Trust, however, it disavows any narrowly defined mandate. "We don't have a special relationship with the farmers of this county," Strange says. "We're not really a local organization. Our business is political economy. Our job is challenging institutions to examine themselves and their behavior."

Policy study projects typically have urban or academic underpinnings and tend to spring up where there's a proven market for their wares. Walthill, though, falls somewhat short of being metropolitan, and there is no university sponsoring the Center's efforts. Several other agricultural reform efforts, like Rodale's Cornucopia Project, or Acres U.S.A. ("A Voice for Eco-

Agriculture") are rooted in a quasi-religious allegiance to organic farming, but the Center for Rural Affairs professes no such devotion. "What we are concerned with is changing the way food is produced in this country," Strange says. "We see farmers—conventional farmers—as our natural constituency." The Center's board of directors includes at least ten representatives of that constituency, along with a small-town banker, a businessman, an attorney, a country priest, and the editors of a couple of rural weeklies. (One of these is Norris Alfred, editor and publisher of the Polk, Nebraska, *Polk Progress*, whose motto when he assumed control was "A Progressive Paper for a Progressive Town." "Neither one is," Alfred concluded, so he adopted a new motto: "Slower Is Better.") "Walthill is a perfect place for us to be, precisely because there's no good reason for us to be here," Strange remarks. "If we were in a center of power we'd probably be doing something wrong. Here we can't get away with saying the kinds of outlandish things about farming that people in DuPont Circle can say."

That would depend, of course, on your definition of what is or is not outlandish. In fact a great deal of what Marty Strange and his colleagues have to say would strike the nation's agricultural policymakers as outlandish indeed. "The Secretary of Agriculture essentially presides over that segment of the populace which is most victimized by current agricultural policy," he comments. "It's an untenable job." In the middle of the day, in the middle of summer in northeast Nebraska, the air temperature in Strange's office has passed the melting point. He is performing emergency surgery on an antique "Eskimo" table fan, poking at its innards with a Swiss army knife, dribbling 3-in-1 oil into any likely looking orifice. He glances up. "When we've got the top six percent of our farms producing forty percent of our food, we begin getting into what I call the Chrysler syndrome. We start believing that we can't afford to let them go under."

Strange questions the wisdom of an agriculture that weds its financial stability to the market for exported grain. "Twenty-eight percent of all the farmland in America changed hands between 1972 and 1979," he says, "at an enormously high cost predicated on continuing high corn yields and continuing high corn prices. The fundamental problem with corn in America is that we're committed to it."

Neither Marty Strange nor his co-director, Don Ralston, have agricultural backgrounds. "Of thirteen staff at the Center," Strange says, "only Don and I aren't from Nebraska, and most of the others grew up on farms." Ralston grew up in Cincinnati. Strange was raised in Dalton, Massachusetts, in the Berkshire foothills. He came to Nebraska as a V.I.S.T.A. volunteer in the late 1960s to work in the racially divided city of Scotts Bluff, on the state's western border. On his way back east he paused inWalthill and took what he thought would be a temporary job. He hasn't left yet.

"We don't have any blueprint for the future," Strange admits. "The Center spends much more time trying to ask the right questions than it does trying to come up with answers."

The right questions are most often questions of policy. What makes asking them so difficult is that our agricultural policy inevitably reflects our schizophrenic view of agriculture. One of the crises of modern agriculture is an identity crisis. "The discipline of farming has a low public standing," observes Wendell Berry. "The term 'agribusinessman' is used partly as a euphemism for 'farmer,' and, not surprisingly, many farmers aspire to be 'agribusinessmen.' " The difference between a farmer and an agribusinessman may entail a substantive difference of purpose and style, but it is also the difference between an image of farming lodged in the collective unconscious of that ninety-seven percent of the population which no longer lives or works on a farm, and the reality of American agriculture as it is practiced by the three percent that still does. The farmer's calling, according to the myth, is the application of a kind of practical compassion: nurture, stewardship, husbandry. Expertise without need of formal education. Skillfulness rather than high technology. Abundance as the just reward of thrift. This is the image of agriculture preserved on the covers of drugstore calendars and in the contents of illustrated children's books. It is the same image, for that matter, that is implicitly purveyed along with the fresh produce at urban and suburban farmers' markets. It's not a bad image—it is an image, in fact, that fairly (if incompletely) depicts a numerical majority of small family farmers—but it is an image at odds with the new agribusiness ideal.

With the postwar emergence of large-scale industrialized agriculture came the need for a refurbished agricultural ideal. The new image would emphasize technical training (recasting farmers as agricultural engineers), efficiency and productivity, profit rather than thrift. If it is the pragmatic magic of farmers to plant seeds and harvest plants, it has sometimes seemed that the agribusiness ideal, fully realized, would dispense altogether with the planting of seeds and the harvesting of plants, planting pennies instead, and harvesting dimes. The agribusiness ideal appears in supermarket advertising and high school filmstrips, and in pre-dawn television programs with names like "Agriculture on Parade." It is an up-to-date, Rosie-the-Riveter, patriotic sort of image that hastens to prove that the making of meat and potatoes is a technological masterwork, like air travel or telecommunications. This isn't a bad image either. It has a certain streamlined, businesslike appeal, and it is surely better suited to the tenor of the times than the myth of the family farm, but it is also demonstrably less romantic, and it enjoys no comparable warm spot in the heart of popular culture.

This is significant for several reasons, not least being the policy implications. It is a political truism that no agricultural legislation will ever make a successful passage through Congress without first trumpeting its support for the family farm. It's equally apparent, however, that the bulk of agricultural policy has not lived up to its advance billing, and that much of it has had quite the opposite effect. Farm policy—or more to the point, the absence of any coherent small farm policy—has been generally injurious to small family farms.

"As farmers became more and more dependent on fossil fuel energy, a radical change occurred," Wendell Berry has written. "It may turn out that the most powerful and most destructive change of modern times has been a change of language: the rise of the image, or metaphor, of the machine. . . . And so the farm became a 'factory,' where speed, 'efficiency,' and profitability were the main standards of performance. These standards, of course, are industrial, not agricultural."

For all its deleterious influence on the formulation of agricultural policy, there is a less conspicuous effect of the incremental transformation of farming from a craft into an industry that may turn out in the long run to be more serious. We have saddled the farmer with a split personality. In the eyes of the public—and often in his own eyes as well—the farmer must combine the compassionate virtues of the family farm myth with the more mercantile attributes of the agribusiness ideal. Some have fared better at this than others, just as some have resisted and others have wholeheartedly embraced the change in image, but what is amazing is that the fabric of American agriculture has been entirely rewoven within their lifetimes. Farmers in their fifties today were born and raised under circumstances much more closely resembling the old image than the new. They were reared as family farmers, cast from the same mold as their farmer fathers before them, and they have had to adjust as best they could to the advent of agribusiness ideals. As recently as 1950 there were four times as many Americans living on farms as there are today, comprising one out of every six citizens at the time. Now the ratio has fallen to one out of every thirty. The average farm size then was about two hundred acres; it has more than doubled since. Before the Korean war the overwhelming majority of American farms were small- to moderate-sized family-run operations. They still are. But in 1950 that majority contributed most of the nation's food, whereas now, though they still constitute fully seventy-eight percent of all the farms, farms whose gross receipts amount to less than $40,000 annually—too little, many agricultural economists think, to adequately support a family without some off-farm supplement—take home not quite nineteen percent of the total agricultural income. Today's family farmer may still perceive himself in terms of the tradition he comes out of, but he is likely to have adopted the means and ends of agribusiness, if only because he can see no other way of keeping up with his neighbors, and no way of keeping his farm if he doesn't.

The progressive industrialization of American agriculture has happened too gradually to provide any easily identifiable turning point, before which things seem to have been going all right and after which the trouble began. Some insight into the character of this transformation may be gleaned from a slim booklet entitled *Take Hogs, for Example*, written by Marty Strange and Chuck Hassebrook for the Center for Rural Affairs. "Family farming dies in small pieces, one enterprise at a time," the authors comment in their foreword. "Much of the change is promoted by a complex of public policies, many with unintended effects. . . . For that reason it is sometimes easiest to piece together the story behind the industrialization of agriculture by looking at the changes taking place in one commodity."

A wondrous animal is the pig. "I eat pork," Goethe declared, "and I turn it into Goethe." Which is a neat trick, but is as nothing by comparison with the pig's own talents. The pig eats almost anything and turns it into pork, and he does so with unparalleled efficiency. Under favorable conditions a hog will gain 1 pound for every 3 pounds it's fed. A pampered steer, by comparison, might manage a pound of beef from 8 pounds of feed. Pigs, moreover, do a dandy job of making more pigs. A cow can be bred only once a year and the issue of that union will likely be a single calf, but a good sow farrowing twice yearly will yield two drifts of eight piglets each. Within six months her offspring can be expected to reach their market weight of about 250 pounds. Thus has the hog won its place in the agricultural pantheon.

Pigs, we learn from Wheeler McMillen's marvelously idiosyncratic *Feeding Multitudes: A History of How Farmers Made America Rich*, accompanied Columbus to the New World in 1493. They traveled with Cortes in Mexico, and with De Soto through Florida. There were pigs at Plymouth and Jamestown, and there have been pigs on American farms ever since. They've evolved from eating mainly nuts and grasses to eating mainly Midwestern corn, from rooting about in open pastures to living their whole lives indoors. They've survived epidemic outbreaks of disease and have outlasted changing tastes. Nowadays a lilting chorus serenades radio listeners with the message that "America is leaning on pork." So impressed was he with the pig's ability to adapt that Wheeler McMillen was moved to prophecy. "With one possible exception—the rat—the hog in some form will probably be the last surviving quadruped on earth. He is omnivorous, suspicious, adaptable, intelligent, and, aside from the machinations, temptations, and overwhelming forces presented by man, ever able to defend himself. . . . The hog will never become an endangered species."

The hog farmer, it seems, may not be so lucky. Hogs have historically done best what they naturally do well on small family farms. Few other animals integrate as comfortably into the polymorphic pattern of small-farm production. Hogs are comparatively independent—as opposed to dairy cows, for instance, which demand several hours of the farmer's time twice daily. The hog wants attention mostly during farrowing, when sows give birth to their large litters. Happily, farrowing can be scheduled for the month or so before field work begins in the spring, or in the six weeks after fall harvest, when a farmer has few competing preoccupations. A small herd of brood sows fed the year round will supply a regular crop of market pigs for not much more than the cost of their feed. And hogs, as Wheeler McMillen notes, are indiscriminate eaters. They'd prefer corn, of course, but they'll eat almost everything. I know a vegetable farmer who keeps a few pigs for his table. Being stingy with bought feed, he supplements the animals' grain with cabbages, carrots, broccoli, or squash—whatever he's culled from the day's picking and packing. Bob Van Houten, who sells both pork and vegetables at Greenmarket, first harvests his sweet corn, then fences the field and lets his hogs loose inside. "It's our version of pick-your-own," he says. A pig asks for little by way of housing—a few rough hutches scattered about the pasture—and requires no specialized equipment. In the reductive idiom of economics, the hog represents a low-capital, labor-intensive enterprise. This is just what the small farmer is looking for. He has a fonder description of his pigs. He calls them "mortgage burners."

Alas, the very qualities that have made the pig so appealing to small farmers may lead to its removal from small farms. Small- and medium-sized Corn Belt farms have tended to be so fond of hogs because hogs are so fond of corn. Keeping pigs increases the farmer's flexibility. When corn prices are high, he can sell his corn. If prices fall, he may choose to feed the corn to hogs and sell it instead as pork. Increasingly, however, that option is being foreclosed. *Take Hogs, for Example* chronicles the ominous rise of a new style of hog production that eliminates farm and farmer both, substituting total-confinement buildings—great hangarlike hog barracks where tens of thousands of animals can be reared by a handful of hired technicians. Confinement production relegates the noble pig to service as the end product of a manufacturing process, much like the mass-produced Central Valley carrots that Carmine sells, stripping him of his laurels as a provident component in a diverse and interrelated farm scheme. Control of the hog market is rapidly passing into the hands of a few extremely large operations. University of Missouri research cited by Hassebrook and Strange suggests that by 1989 farmers marketing fewer than a thousand pigs a year—who in 1974 comprised ninety-seven percent of the nation's hog farmers and produced three-quarters of all the hogs—will be left with only twenty-five percent of the market.

What's happening to hogs isn't new. It has already happened to chickens. Like hogs, chickens are admirably efficient converters of feed to meat. They tolerate less than luxurious lodgings, cost little to raise, and can be sold for cash. Like hogs, too, chickens were once integral to most small farms. Before World War Two the nation's broiler chickens were almost without exception locally fed and marketed. Chicken production then was a study in resource efficiency. The cycle that ended in an in-town oven began on an outlying farm and paused only briefly at the butcher's counter in between. The system was decentralized because it worked best that way. In the next twenty-five years, though, as the demand for chicken rose, chicken farming changed. When it was all over the chickens were gone from the barnyard, and farm families with a yearning for fricassee lined up like everyone else at the supermarket checkout counter.

The first milestone was passed in the late 1940s when it was discovered that dosing the birds' feed with antibiotics would curb the virulent outbreaks of disease that had previously stymied any attempt to raise large flocks in confinement. This development greatly interested feed companies, who realized that there was more money to be made from specially formulated medicinal feed than from cracked corn. In an attempt to establish markets for specialized medicated feeds, they funded prototype large-scale poultry operations, which they found to be so successful that some of them branched out into the chicken business. Not unexpectedly, chickens grown on the company farm, fed company feed, and slaughtered and distributed to retailers by company personnel arrived at the marketplace priced lower than birds bred on small farms and sold to the corner butcher. As chicken factories proliferated, small producers were forced to sell their birds below cost if they wanted to stay in the business. Many chose not to stay in the business. As of 1970, the aggregate contribution from small flocks to total commercial chicken production had slipped below the threshold of statistical visibility.

The extinction of the small-farm broiler flock came to pass courtesy of a standard business procedure known as vertical integration, in which a single corporate entity gains control of most or all of the independent steps in a product's manufacture and distribution. If you were a hot dog vendor, for instance, and you were dissatisfied with your profit margin, you might consider vertical integration. Your profit is constrained by the butcher's desire to make a profit too when he sells you a hot dog, so you'd want to buy out the butcher. You'd buy the meat packer who made the hot dogs and the beef processor who supplied his trimmings to the packer. You'd buy the feedlot that fattened steers for the processor, and the cattle ranch that shipped cattle to the feedlot. Just for good measure you'd want to acquire the bakery that supplies your buns, and you'd take a controlling interest in a condiment company as a hedge against the rising price of relish and mustard. You wouldn't be a hot dog vendor anymore, of course. You'd be a food service industry executive.

So it went with chicken farming. A feed company whose function had formerly been limited to the sale of feed to farmers now forwards contracts for the direct delivery of grain, grinds and mixes the grain into feed, feeds it to chickens, then slaughters and processes the chickens and delivers them on contract to supermarket chains. Whereas decentralized chicken production had involved a multitude of independent entrepreneurs, vertically integrated chicken production involves very few. For those few there are distinct advantages, and now the vertical integration of hog farming is well under way.

The most tiresome and time-consuming aspect of pig farming is undoubtedly farrowing, but it is also the most important, for without a reliable supply of feeder pigs there would be no way for a farmer to market his corn as pork. After it had been demonstrated that hogs could be raised successfully in confinement, it occurred to some ambitious farmers that they might escape the odious task of farrowing by collectively investing in a confinement facility whose sole function would be to provide them with young stock. That would free them to farm more land (to raise more corn, to feed more pigs), which, they reasoned, would soon offset their investment in the farrowing facility. But removing the farrowing of pigs from their feeding (or "finishing") was only the beginning. It wasn't long before the finishing moved indoors as well, and it soon became obvious that farmers in search of feeder pigs were by no means the only investors interested in confinement hog production. The construction and operation of pig factories turns out to be a superlative tax dodge.

When a small farmer raises pigs he does so as cheaply as possible. His principal investment is his labor, which is of course what makes the opportunity so appealing. Confinement production, although it requires very little labor—perhaps one-fourth as much per pig as a conventional operation—ties up a lot more capital. Gone are the crude hutches in the farmer's back pasture. A modern facility must be designed and equipped with mechanized feeding systems to move food in to the pigs, and with manure-handling systems to move it out again. There are employees to be paid and medicated feed to be bought. All this is not inexpensive—a decent-sized, up-to-date confinement farrowing facility may cost more than a million dollars to build—but the high price only enhances its allure for investors.

An investment in a pig factory provides an impressive array of tax benefits, including accelerated depreciation (allowing investors to trim their taxable incomes by writing off proportionately more of their investment early on in the life of the facility); cash accounting (making possible a year-end juggling of the books so as to technically erase any profits subject to taxation); an investment tax credit (amounting to ten percent of the investor's initial ante, deductible from his first year's income taxes); and the customary deduction of interest paid on loans or mortgages. Such enticements, needless to say, mean a lot to investors with inflated incomes, for whom a harvest of tax deductions is likely to be more valuable than a supply of feeder pigs. They mean nothing at all to the small farmer who raises his hogs without any substantial capital investment. "They are subsidies to capital," write Hassebrook and Strange, "and they encourage both expansion and the substitution of capital for labor. If your primary asset is your labor, this works against you by subsidizing your capital-intensive competition."

How this affects the high cost of bringing home the bacon is worth a brief look. The authors of *A Time to Choose*, in their investigation of the structure of American agriculture, took care to distinguish economies of scale, as they relate to actual efficiency of production, from market economies, the economic advantages that accrue to those in a position to buy and sell in huge quantities. Enhanced production efficiency, it seems, does not inevitably go hand in hand with expansion. Most types of farms come very close to theoretical technical perfection while they are still fairly small. A typical Midwestern corn and soybeans operation, for example, achieves 90 percent of its potential efficiency with $60,000 in sales and 300 acres under cultivation. To hit 100 percent it would have to add another $85,000 in revenue and 340 more acres of land. That last 10 percent tells the story. It's there that the market economies are hiding. "The increasing average size of farms does not necessarily imply the existence of attainable economies of size," the report notes. "It only implies the absence of significant *diseconomies*. . . . Based on the observed diversity of farm size, it may be that no significant economies of size exist in agricultural production; any enterprise that exhibits significant economies of size breaks away from agricultural production to become a separate industry."

Which is exactly what happened with chickens, and what seems to be happening with hogs. In fact, Hassebrook and Strange contend, production efficiencies actually decline as market economies are sought—a decline that would be more obvious were it not for the purely financial advantages of large-scale production. "Hogs," they observe, "don't love confinement. At least they are not physiologically well suited to the conditions in hog factories." Lacing a pig's rations with antibiotics may keep him from getting sick, but it won't make him healthy. Hogs in confinement exhibit measurable stress. They nip at each other's necks and bite off their companions' tails. They ignore their feed and don't gain weight as efficiently as their pastured cousins, despite the fact that the liberated hogs presumably shed potentially salable calories running about out of doors. Confinement hogs haul up lame from standing all day on concrete and steel. Their libido wanes. They are, anthropomorphically speaking, dreadfully unhappy, and any good farmer knows that an unhappy animal won't perform. The hog's displeasure dissipates any efficiency that might be gained by his confinement. When the University of Missouri tallied up the tab on both sides it found that the real cost of factory pig production was $1.50 higher per hundredweight than its old-fashioned counterpart.

But if factory pork costs a bit more to produce, that cost is distributed among many, many more pigs. A farmer will farrow his animals twice yearly, in spring and fall, on a schedule that suits his own convenience as well as the hogs'. His costs are for the most part simple production costs, and they are the same per pig whether he markets fifty pigs or five hundred. He adjusts his rate of production to market conditions, increasing it in times of high prices and cutting back when they drop off.

The factory can't afford to be so flexible. Most of the costs of confinement production are fixed costs: payments due on loans and mortgages, weekly payroll obligations. The pig factory will always have sows farrowing, and it will always be sending pigs to market, come high prices or low. It has to. The small farmer's pig production costs more or less disappear if he stops producing pigs, but not the factory's. Even in a soft market the factory will be obliged to meet production quotas, because the more pigs it generates the lower will be its costs per pig. The factory is insulated from low prices by its very high volume, and not incidentally by the tax advantages it passes along to its investors. *Take Hogs, for Example* reports that a small farmer, simply in order to hold his own with the high-tax-bracket investors in a confinement operation, would have to sell the equivalent of thirty percent more hogs. "Other developments seem likely. Public markets used primarily by small and average-sized producers will suffer a loss of business as more hogs are marketed directly by large producers to packers, or as other forms of vertical coordination—contracts, integrated operations, bargaining associations—replace open markets as a means of moving hogs from one stage of production to another. As the markets suffer, the fortunes of the smaller producer will, too."

So the industrialization of hog farming may lower the price paid for pork by consumers, if only temporarily; but the savings are largely illusory. They fail to take into account the revenue lost when the investors in a confinement hog operation realize their profits as tax deductions instead of as cash. More seriously, they ignore the price we pay for the loss of small family farms, the damage to rural communities, and the social and environmental costs of industrialized agriculture. If such costs could be factored in, cheap bacon would begin to seem like less of a bargain.

"The very special relationship to other kinds of production on diversified farms that earned the hog its affectionate nickname has been altered," Chuck Hassebrook and Marty Strange conclude. "Restoring that relationship will require fundamental reconsideration of all agricultural policies and all policies that affect agriculture. Economically, the hog might be the family farmer's mortgage burner. Politically, it may be family farming's last line of defense."

THE MACHINE IN THE GARDEN

In November 1981, when Bud Kerr convened the U.S.D.A.'s special symposium on small farms, he put together a topical palette sufficiently diverse to encompass "Sire Evaluation in Dairy Goats" and "Use of Composted Sewage Sludge for Turfgrass Production," "Herbs as a Small Farm Enterprise and the Value of Aromatic Plants as Economic Interplants," as well as "Concepts in Technology Transfer for Small Farms Research Internationally." Sam Smith was there to talk about the evolution of Caretaker Farm. Dick Harwood appeared on behalf of the Rodale Research Center. Bill Cantelo came over from his office on Entomology Road, and Suzanne Batra discussed the prodigious pollinatory talents of her imported Japanese bees. In all, some six hundred registrants showed up at the Beltsville Agricultural Research Center to sample from sixty-odd papers and panel discussions presented over the course of three days, and the symposium's centerpiece was a sumptuous evening banquet, following which participants pushed back in their chairs to listen to a keynote address entitled, "Responding to the Technological Challenges of Small-Scale Agriculture."

The speaker was a slight, soft-spoken, silver-haired septuagenarian whose principal agricultural credentials consisted of his having grown up on a south-central Nebraska farm. He was William C. Norris, chairman, chief executive officer, and founder of Control Data Corporation, a computer company that reported revenues for 1981 in excess of $4 billion. His audience might have been forgiven for wondering what the chairman of Control Data could find to say about small farms, but Bill Norris found plenty. "The perception that small-scale farming has great potential is not the prevailing view," he conceded. "Most experts agree that social benefits would be derived by improving the lot of the small farmer, but few believe that smaller farm units would produce attractive economic benefits or become significant contributors to the food chain." Mr. Norris, it was soon apparent, believed differently. While acknowledging the expertise of those who think it unlikely that the small farm as a species will survive this century, much less multiply and thrive, he nonetheless contended that "there is a growing body of evidence that the so-called experts are wrong; and better solutions to many of the problems plaguing the nation's food chain *can* be realized by means of the small family farm rather than through large, capital-intensive, fossil-fuel-based operations."

Quite a few of the so-called experts had just finished supper and were having some difficulty digesting this speech. The agricultural research establishment, Norris scolded, had shown the small farmer a disinterest that bordered on contempt. Purported advances in agricultural efficiency were too often promulgated without regard to their consequences. "Practically, then," he said, "these 'efficiencies' have been achieved at an added cost to society and are really subsidies to big agribusiness. Often, the government and universities have been the vehicles providing such subsidies. . . . One good example is the channeling of most government agriculture R&D funds into programs which benefit large- but not small-scale production."

This was not Jim Hightower speaking, nor Marty Strange, but the chief executive of a Fortune 500 corporation. Norris cited the U.S.D.A.'s own findings that small- and medium-sized farms were in most cases at least as efficient as the much larger and ostensibly more streamlined models touted as farms of the future by government agricultural planners. He predicted that as soon as we began having to pay the true cost of our already inefficiently oversized and centralized agriculture we would realize the folly of our ways. But Norris was not about to wait around for that realization to sink in. The failure of this country's agricultural research and extension system to apply itself to the maintenance of a healthy decentralized network of small family farms stood as an indictment of that system's worth, he contended, and if the research establishment wasn't prepared to make this commitment, somebody else would. Control Data, for instance. By now his listeners were sitting up straight. Norris's message was met at first with consternation, and then, as its full import dawned, with some indignation. "It sounded," one member of the audience later recalled, "like the room was full of buck deer in rut, all of them huffing and snorting."

"Whenever I see everybody going south," Bill Norris once told a reporter, "I have a great compulsion to go north." He grew up in Willa Cather country, along the Republican River in Webster County, Nebraska. He still keeps his grandfather's homestead claim framed on his office wall. As a young engineering student at the University of Nebraska, Norris was called home during the Dust Bowl years to take over the family farm after his father's sudden death. Most of the crops had failed. Faced with the imminent loss of the farm, Norris resolved to feed his cattle the only thing that was growing in any abundance: Russian thistles, the scourge of the pasture. The livestock, he'd observed, were not averse to nibbling on thistles so long as the plants were tender and young. He hired incredulous neighbors to harvest the immature weeds. The cattle survived. He still owns the farm.

Later, having served out World War Two as a Navy cryptographer and gone on to head up the Univac computer division of the Sperry Rand Corporation, Norris founded Control Data and parlayed a hunch into his company's dominance of the growing market for "number crunchers," massive supercomputers sought by science and the military to tackle impossibly complicated mathematical chores. This proved enormously profitable. In the early 1960s he began diverting some of those profits into the development of an ambitious computer-based education plan, nicknamed PLATO. Norris had long had ambivalent feelings about his own rural schooling; he was proud of that heritage but at the same time dissatisfied with the quality of instruction he'd received. Computers, he reasoned, could be used to expand

and improve educational opportunities at a reasonable cost. Observers scoffed, and their skepticism seemed justified when declining enrollments eliminated the public schools as the system's primary consumers before PLATO was off the drawing boards. Norris shifted course, pushing PLATO as a cost-effective employee training tool. The tactic worked. "PLATO has been one of the pet projects of Bill Norris," a Paine-Webber vice-president told *The New York Times* in April 1981, "and, after a lot of people thought that was just folly, he is about to be vindicated."

Now Norris has directed a sizable chunk of Control Data's resources into another pet project: the provision by the company of support services for small-scale agriculture. The agricultural research establishment is dominated by a monopoly, the U.S.D.A.'s cooperative extension service, and monopolies, he notes, are vulnerable. "The extension service isn't using technology to any great extent," he says. "They haven't developed the data bases. All we're doing is filling a need. If it happens to compete with them, so be it."

Mr. Norris does not consider himself an altruist. He expects to make money at this. He is not, however, in any hurry. He waited twenty years for PLATO to turn a profit, and he is prepared to wait again. "I never predicted instant success," he says. "I've always made it clear that it might take fifteen or twenty years of continuing research—and a lot of other things too—to get small-scale agriculture into a completely viable position. But start! Get on with it!" He is aware that neither his passions nor his patience are unequivocally endorsed by executives within his own organization. "But at Control Data," he explains, grinning, "being the founder of the company, I'm a little harder to throw out than your average chief executive."

Control Data's shimmering high-rise headquarters on the outskirts of Minneapolis is sheathed in golden green reflective glass. Looking at the building from the outside on a bright day can cause temporary blindness. Looking out from inside is slightly disorienting too, like watching the world through sunglasses. From his high corner office, Bill Norris commands a spectacular tinted view. Open countryside extends deep into the distance. Farmland begins where the parking lots end: flat, loamy, alluvial upper Mississippi floodplain, threaded through with meandering tributaries, gridded into a familiar Midwestern geometry of rectangular fields and unswerving rural roads. Here and there neat clusters of buildings appear, farmhouses and barns. In dry weather, rooster-tail plumes of dust eddy up behind working tractors. A hawk cruises past at eye level, riding a thermal. From this lofty perspective the scene spread out below seems exceptionally tranquil and beautiful.

When Bill Norris looks out his window he sees small farms struggling to stay competitive, hampered by outmoded equipment, ineffective management, and inadequate technical support. The Norris view holds that small farms suffer not so much from any systemic inability to compete as from having been systematically denied the information and technologies that might enable them to compete more effectively. This is a belief shared by rural activists like Marty Strange, but they do not occupy the executive suites of corporate headquarters, and they are less sure than Norris that this imbalance can be redressed with a simple technical fix. They point out that modern American agriculture is a game played with a stacked deck—that policies of every description have long favored large-scale production—and they suggest that a few shiny new technological toys will not appreciably affect the odds against small farms. Norris disagrees. "The thing that a computer offers above all else is the ability to put technology into the hands of the individual," he says. "Just because you're a farmer, shouldn't you get that technology, the same way a scientist gets it, from a computer? Of course. The problem for the small farmer, and for a lot of other individuals, is that nobody ever packaged the technology so that he could get his hands on it."

The contents of Control Data's package have been rolled out for review in a little room a few floors down from Norris's office. The room is done up with rough wood paneling and Astroturf-green wall-to-wall. A coffee table in one corner is strewn with farm magazines. Bucolic color photographs hang on the walls. Though a sign in the hallway window identifies this as a Control Data Agriculture and Business Services Center, it's actually only a mockup for demonstration and training. There are, to date, no Control Data Agriculture and Business Service Centers in operation, but Norris happily imagines a time in the not too distant future when centers like this one will open in rural communities across America, incorporated into hardware and farm supply stores, feed and grain dealers, small country banks. He told the Beltsville banquet that a dozen trial centers would be operating by 1983, and promised that before 1990 there would be ten thousand of them nationwide.

The Agriculture and Business Services Center suggests a rurally inflected cross between a video arcade and H & R Block's, equipped with a computer terminal with its own display screen, a couple of disk drives, a high-speed printer, a videodisc player, a videocassette deck, and a color television set. Today's lesson is "Baby Pig Management," one module of a complete course on feeder pig production. "It tells you just about everything you need to know to raise pigs," ventures Peter Grant, the clean-cut young man assigned to show it off, "except the smell. Maybe we ought to include a scratch 'n' sniff with the manual." He feeds a cassette into the Betamax and an amiable-looking fellow materializes on the television. He is wearing a royal blue Control Data seed cap and wheeling a supermarket shopping cart full of squealing piglets through an immaculate confinement barn. An invisible, sober-voiced narrator reviews the fundamentals of tail-docking, needle-tooth extraction, and proper nutrition while weaning—all to the alegretto accompaniment of a Muzak bluegrass soundtrack.

After the film is over, Grant plugs a floppy disk into the disk drive and punches up the appropriate exercise. A series of multiple choice questions rolls onto the computer's display screen, and I'm suddenly taking a quiz on hog-ration balancing. This latest generation of hardware boasts touch-sensitive screens: to indicate my answers or proceed to the next section of the test I can bypass the keyboard by applying an index finger directly to a tiny glowing pig on the screen. This is strangely mesmerizing, a sort of agrarian Pac-Man, and I'm soon caught up in the game. Bill Norris hopes that farmers will be similarly snared, and that those too busy or too stubborn to attend scheduled classes will gravitate toward PLATO's flexibility, upgrading their present operations or exploring new options.

Money management is the second of Control Data's concerns. Small family farms, whatever their other attributes, are not as a rule much esteemed for their bookkeeping. As a means toward more effective money handling, Control Data has concocted AGCHECK, a computerized accounting and cash management service. Farmers who sign up for the program get specially designed checks and deposit slips on which expenses and sources of income can be designated with individual account codes. At the close of each month the farmer delivers his canceled checks and deposit slips to the nearest Agriculture and Business Services Center. Control Data's computers then generate a running record of the farm's finances, broken down into income and expense accounts for each enterprise. For example, a dairyman who also fed hogs for market and raised an acre of pick-your-own strawberries would receive a separate accounting for each of the three endeavors, and within each accounting the attribution of income and costs can be quite specific: so much paid out for fertilizer, so much taken in at the livestock auction, so much allotted proportionately for each endeavor's share of total debt service, and so on. The farmer can compare actual monthly or cumulative totals to his own budget projections, recorded in an adjacent column on the printout. Using the center's terminals or his own home computer, he can refer back to a prior year's figures or work up adjusted estimates of profit or loss.

Information, third of Norris's chosen tasks, is by any estimate the most formidable. Control Data has set about amassing a comprehensive agricultural data base centered on small farm needs. AGTECH, as the system is known, attempts to provide plain English answers to a farmer's routine or emergency questions. It is an appealing concept: a complete, instant-access agricultural reference library. Say you're in the middle of farrowing when you notice that one drift of piglets are suckling but not gaining weight or strength as they should. With AGTECH, you would switch on your home computer, dial up the data base, and start asking questions. Type in "Baby Swine" and "Nutrition" and the intersection of those two categories produces a nifty menu of tech-unit titles. Requests from the menu bring brief abstracts of those reports deemed most relevant. ("Importance of quantity and quality of colostrum first milk for new-born swine," or "Symptoms of internal parasites in baby swine and effects on efficiency.") The likeliest might be selected for presentation in full. Complete reports run about three hundred words. They're cross-indexed to related reports in the data base, and they come with a selective directory of people and places where you might turn for further assistance.

In theory at least, AGTECH could nip a lot of problems in the bud, but the system has a long way to go yet before it will be of any real use to real farmers with real problems. For the moment, for instance, AGTECH is an on-line service, tethered to a central computer, which permits regular revision and addition of reports and makes possible electronic bulletin board and note file functions that let users exchange information directly among themselves via the computer. But on-line capability is also very expensive. In order to plug into the system a farmer must place a long-distance call to the central computer, connecting his home computer to the data base. This could tend to be prohibitively costly in remoter rural regions. He also has to have on hand a modem, a high-priced electronic gizmo that allows two computers to carry on a telephone conversation. Alternatively, of course, he might travel to his local Agriculture and Business Services Center to use the equipment there, but that would undermine AGTECH's greatest advantage: its immediacy. Control Data insists that the data base will eventually be made available on floppy disks compatible with most home computers, but it's hard to see in that case how the entries could be kept up to date or expanded.

It's hard to see too, for that matter, how enough information will ever be accumulated and organized to make the data base really useful. Practical agriculture is the bailiwick of skilled generalists. Its finest exponents are people like the Rodale Research Center's Mennonite neighbor, Ben Brubaker, whose expertise is founded on constant and intimate contact with his surroundings. It's doubtful that a computer data base, no matter how vast, could ever supplant that intimacy. The variety of possible responses to an agricultural dilemma is nearly infinite, and the best farmers make a lot of intuitive choices. Some of Control Data's critics—including some who welcome AGTECH's challenge to the U.S.D.A. monopoly—suspect that the whole effort will be abandoned before it has a chance to prove itself one way or another. Bill Norris dismisses such predictions, pointing to his company's history of developmental patience. For the foreseeable future, he says, AGTECH has enough promise to warrant its continued development.

Don Polly is one of the handful of farmers who have actually sampled what Control Data has to offer. "It might be useful someday," he says, "but it isn't yet, not for us anyway." Since 1980 Polly and a few of his east-central Minnesota neighbors have operated small farms along lines advanced by Bill Norris. Polly leases his farm and fields from the Control Data Corporation. His house and barn were built by Control Data, and his initial business plan and several subsequent revisions were hammered out in conjunction with Control Data advisers. Company administrators closely monitor his progress, and he receives aid and counsel from consultants on the staff of Rural Ventures, Inc., a Control Data spin-off. "I guess you could say we're Control Data's guinea pigs," Don laughs, not entirely without rancor. I've been staying with Don Polly and his family for the past week, helping out on their farm. We are having breakfast this morning in a back booth of the K-Bob Café in Princeton, Minnesota, discussing what has come to be known as the Princeton project: a life-sized experiment designed to test Bill Norris's hypothesis that in technology lies the salvation of small farms.

In early 1980, agents of the Control Data Corporation began casting about for agricultural property. They were looking for a total of approximately fifteen hundred acres, either all of a piece or in several large parcels, the whole of it to be contained in a circle whose radius could not exceed five miles. This circle had to be situated adjacent to a four-lane highway and within an hour's drive of Minneapolis, to facilitate regular round trips by Control Data personnel and visitors. The site should be bare, unimproved and unequipped, and the land, most peculiarly, could not be prime farmland. To be eligible for consideration a parcel had to have a lower than average agronomic capability rating. "We felt it was important to use poor land," Norris has explained, "because if we did it on good land, then everybody would say, 'Hell, any damn fool could succeed there. That's prime land!' "

Control Data finally found what it was looking for near the town of Princeton, on the Rum River, northwest of the Twin Cities. There they planned to establish a prototype Agriculture and Business Services Center and fifteen model farms. Before it could take title to a single acre of Sherburne County farmland the company had to agree to divest itself of its holdings within ten years and at no profit, so as to comply with strict state statutes prohibiting nonfarm corporations from owning agricultural land. That done, the project went ahead. An Agriculture and Business Services Center was installed in downtown Princeton, first in a vacant pizza parlor and later in a new shopping mall. The company's land was divided into farmsites of 75 to 150 acres each, and work got under way on houses and barns. Applicants were screened and selected from a pool of potential candidates. When I visited Princeton during the summer of 1982 there were eight farms in operation, and three more scheduled to start up soon.

Don Polly lights a cigarette and confesses that he was most attracted to the project not by the Norris philosophy but because it offered him the chance to get started in farming for no money down. Don rents his farm from Control Data for an annual fee of five percent of its total assessed value—in his case, roughly ten thousand dollars a year. Should his venture prove successful, he will have the option of buying the farm. Eighty percent of his past rental payments could then be applied to a purchase price figured by adding the cost of improvements made by Control Data (Polly's home and outbuildings, his irrigation system, and sundry other items) to the price the company originally paid for his land. In effect, he is capitalizing his farm by paying rent.

Don is tall, lanky, and raw-boned. His conversation is punctuated with the rattling throaty cough of a heavy smoker. A prominent jaw and deep-set eyes give him a haggard look, especially when he's tired. He is often tired. Don Polly is a limited-resource farmer of precisely the sort so extolled by Bud Kerr: a part-timer who juggles his farm work around a full-time job. Don is employed as a production engineer supervising the manufacture of pacemakers for a company called Medtronics, located in Fridley, forty-five minutes south of Princeton. In his spare time he tends forty acres of pick-your-own fruits and vegetables and thirty-five acres of hay and grains. (Last year the grain went to feed five thousand geese, which the Pollys raised on contract for a processor. That enterprise was abandoned after a neighbor's dogs repeatedly demonstrated their fondness for foie gras. This year the grain will be sold.) Don's farm is named Polly's Pickin's, and while he is away making pacemakers the operation falls under the direction of his wife, Nita, and to no small extent, of his twelve-year-old son, Dennis.

Breakfast at the K-Bob is a special treat, this being the Fourth of July weekend, and we linger longer than we should. When we get back to the farm a line of cars is already parked along the newly blacktopped county road that bounds the Pollys' fields. Don and Nita have 5 acres planted in strawberries, and this is the height of the season. The pickers awaiting the opening of the fields are for the most part heavy (often very heavy) older women in polyester pantsuits who bring nested stacks of 5-quart ice cream pails. They move through the rows in phalanxes, gleaning, vacuuming up berries. Nita charges $.60 a pound for strawberries, and two ladies yesterday lugged home 214½ pounds of succulent Bounties, Redcoats, and Sparkles. That's what went onto the scale, at least. What went directly into the pickers is harder to calculate, but Nita's Law stipulates that for every berry eaten while picking, a weed must be pulled in atonement, and the rows those women picked were absolutely pristine when they left.

Don has the holiday off, and he spends it moving irrigation pipe and catching up on cultivating the vegetables. If it was poor soil Control Data was after, they came to the right place. After four days of dry, hot weather Don's tilling turns up a dusty tumult, dust that is for better or worse his soil. It's thin, sandy—"blow away sandy," Nita says—and only in the most charitable sense of the term does it deserve to be called "topsoil." When a wind comes up, Don says, his soil sometimes blows so hard that it cuts seedlings off at ground level. It scrubs the paint from buildings and equipment and stings exposed skin like airborne sandpaper. Water passes through such soil without stopping to say hello, and irrigation here is practically a necessity, especially on vulnerable high-value vegetable crops. At Polly's Pickin's, a well 175 feet deep supplies 600 gallons a minute to Don's traveling gun, a sort of oversized lawn sprinkler with a rotating whirlybird head attached to a hose and a length of braided steel aircraft cable. The gun, on a wheeled carriage, is set at one end of an irrigation lane. A tractor parked at the other end serves as an anchor, and as the cable retracts onto its reel the sprinkler is winched slowly up the lane. The gun distributes moisture over a circle 400 feet in diameter. It will lay down an inch of artificial rain on 10 acres in the course of one 8-hour run. Then it must be moved and run again.

The system is maddeningly fallible, prone to leaks and blowouts and inexplicable mechanical fits and starts. Some of its maladies are more easily diagnosed than others. Water flows to the gun's feed hose through jointed sections of eight-inch aluminum pipe. Last winter, Don tells me, a woodchuck happened upon his neatly stacked irrigation pipe and thought it a fine place to hibernate. When Don moved the pipe in the spring the rodent neglected to leave. In June, when he first switched on the pump, a furry brown missile shot through several hundred feet of pipe and two hundred yards of hose until it came to the hose's coupling with the gun, where it stopped and quite firmly lodged. "I was back watching the pressure gauge on the pump," Don recalls. "The pressure is supposed to stay at around eighty pounds while the pipe is filling, then go up to a hundred and fifty when the gun starts. Instead it went straight up to one-fifty and right on past. I couldn't see the gun from where I was standing, and I didn't know what was happening, but I sure knew something was wrong."

I am assigned hoe duty among the melons. I follow along after Don has been through on the tractor, cutting out the weeds that grow close around the plants, where the rotovator can't reach. Most of the weeding here is done by machine or with herbicides. The Pollys are by no means organic farmers. In the living room of their home, tucked between the microwave oven and the electric dehydrator, they hoard an illicit jug of Poast ($108.00 a gallon, retail), a new herbicide shown to be effective against some of their stubbornest herbaceous adversaries, but not yet approved in Minnesota for use on vegetable crops. (The new Federalism is alive and well where pesticide regulations are concerned. Most states set their own standards, and the Pollys' gallon of Poast was smuggled in from out of state.) Meanwhile, they spray regularly with other herbicides, and rely on the rotovator to clean up between the rows. What remains, alas, must be hoed by hand.

Hoeing is the sort of hand work that makes small-scale vegetable farming so labor-intensive. It isn't a difficult job, but it's dreary and unrewarding. The slight flush of pride you feel on looking back at a long, weed-free row does not fully counteract the boredom that accumulates after a few hours behind a hoe. This, of course, is why increased mechanization and pesticides have tended to be so popular with vegetable farmers. I step and hoe, step and hoe, step, hoe, and stop again to sharpen the hoe's blade. In a more perfect universe it seems to me there would be a lucrative market for ragweed and wild proso millet, for quack grass and mare's tail, for pigweed, field bindweed, thistles, and lamb's quarters. Step and hoe. It's late in the day before I finish the melons and move on, as instructed, to the tomatoes. Step and hoe. The air is still and steamy. My shirt is veneered to my back. Step and hoe. The only real indication of oncoming dusk is the bugs: deerflies, gnats, no-see-ums, and mosquitoes massed for an evening offensive. Step, swat, and hoe. The mosquito, Dennis Polly informs me, is the Minnesota state bird.

After a week or so in Princeton it becomes apparent that Bill Norris's farm of the future is not a whole lot different from farms of the present or past. The kind of operation that the head of Control Data has outlined would be tightly managed, orderly, and attentive to detail, showing a high regard for the bottom line biologically as well as financially, and it would make use of the latest in computer technology to ease the management burden, freeing the farmer to spend more time farming. It would, in short, be a superlative small farm. But superlative small farms—or superlative large ones for that matter—have always been few and very far between, and nothing I've seen in Princeton has led me to believe that the introduction of computers will change that. Computers, in fact, seem to have had strangely little impact here. All of the project's farmers use the AGCHECK accounting system, some more reluctantly than others, but I can find no one who admits to much enthusiasm about the rest of Control Data's offerings.The Princeton Agriculture and Business Services Center—reserved for the exclusive use of Project farmers—is quiet as a church whenever I stop by. When I asked one project participant who is about to begin feeding slaughter pigs if he had studied the swine management materials I saw in Minneapolis, he replied that the thought had never even crossed his mind. Though the project's farms vary greatly in plan and purpose, only a couple have wholeheartedly embraced the mix of conventional and specialty crops that is a key component of the experiment. "I've always felt that was a thorn in my side," one farmer told me. "I've tried my best to get around it for two years." This same man also expressed the gripe I've heard oftenest from the project's farmers. "I just wish they'd let us farm like normal farmers," he groused. "We're always having to try out some kind of oddball thing."

Part of the problem has to be that the management structure of a large corporation and that of a small farm have little in common. The farmers complain of the company's unreasonable demands, of interminable delays and insensitivity to their needs. The company cites unrealistic expectations, intransigence, and a general refusal to cooperate. The man in the middle is Barry Werner, who directs the Princeton project for Rural Ventures, Inc., and acts as the liaison between Control Data and the project's farmers. I met Werner at his office in Princeton, upstairs from a chiropractor's in the Rum River Professional Building, and he directly suggested that we go out for coffee. "Let's get out of here before the phone rings again." For Barry Werner, drinking coffee is an occupational hazard. He spends his days stopping to chat with farmers, and he inevitably winds up having coffee. Riding with him from farm to farm, I have watched him consume almost a full gallon in under three hours' time. As often as not he conducts business from a table at the K-Bob, where we are now headed, and where he will order coffee. For a man with so much caffeine in his veins, Barry Werner is remarkably relaxed. He is an affable fellow, big and blond, a former dairy-man with a bad back who is given to using the phrase "you bet" as an affirmative.

"Have there been problems with the project?"

"You bet."

"You'll get some of the guys telling you flat out that this is their chance to get into farming," Barry acknowledges, "and for that they're willing to put up with Control Data for three years." The company, he grants, must shoulder a portion of the blame for this combative attitude. It has changed its plans often and without warning, switching support staff in and out of Princeton with a frequency that has left the participants gun shy. It has also invested less effort than it probably should have in conveying to the farmers the reasons why they should bother to use new technologies. "Most farmers still think that technology is some-thing you can hook up to a tractor and drag out into the field," Barry Werner says. The representatives of Control Data, like a lot of technocrats, cannot fathom why an innovation whose use-fulness is obvious to them would not be embraced with equal enthusiasm by everyone else. "Farmers are crisis thinkers," says Werner. "When the weeds get too tall, they decide it's time to do something about them. We're trying to change that, but it isn't easy." Another more serious source of friction derives from the fact that the technologies Control Data has available are far from their finished form. It is common for much more to be promised than can be delivered. The Pollys, for instance, spent several months working with a succession of Rural Ventures and Control Data staffers, attempting to mold the AGCHECK system to their particular needs—with only marginal success. This tends to breed frustration and distrust, and there's plenty of both in Princeton.

"I don't honestly know why they're here," Nita Polly says. "I suppose they're using us to test their program, but then I can't really tell what their program is either. A lot of us don't even call them anymore with our questions. We call someplace where we can get answers. When we've got trouble in the field we need help now, not in a few days."

It seems clear that although computer technologies could make an enormous contribution to the development of a decentralized small-scale food system, Control Data's efforts so far have not done so. A computer-based marketing network, for example, might enable a number of smaller farms operating in concert to match the crop consistency and quantity guarantees that up until now have been offered only by the largest growers, but without the negative social and biological side effects associated with present day large-scale monocultures. Computers could aid in the widespread adoption of integrated pest management techniques, or organic or biological farming methods: practices that demand a farmer keep track of large amounts of specific information. The Princeton project's participants protest that they're forced to do things differently from so-called "normal farmers," but that may not be what's really wrong. Maybe the real problem is that they're not doing things differently enough.

Like so many conventional large-scale farms, the farms in the Princeton project tend to be overcapitalized. They have an average assessed worth of some $300,000—far more than most of the farmers could afford were it not for their deal with the company. What's worse, according to some, is that this capital has not all been well spent. Too much of the investment seems to have gone into new-age window dressing: the odd-looking, ostensibly energy-efficient earth-bermed farmhouses, for example, the solar-powered grain dryer built on one farm and the windmill on another—accessories whose expense could hardly be recouped even if they worked. I was driving with Barry Werner one afternoon when we passed the field where the solar grain dryer stands, and I asked him how well it worked.

"Not at all," he said.

"What's the matter with it?"

"We don't exactly know, but it doesn't dry well enough or fast enough, and there's too much moldy corn."

Control Data's solar grain dryer, designed and constructed at a cost of many thousands of dollars, serves now as an embarrassingly expensive storage shed. In stark contrast, I met a farmer in Nebraska who built himself a solar-powered grain dryer for practically nothing. He had help from the Center for Rural Affairs' Small Farm Energy Project, and he scavenged most of the materials from around his farm. He made a big, flat-plate panel, a forced-air system equipped with various ducts and fans. For grain drying he couples the unit to a standard grain bin. It works like a charm. "Last year I harvested my corn at twenty-eight percent moisture," Gary Young told me, "and the dryer took it down to fifteen and a half." He has mounted the panel on a trailer, and when he's done drying corn in the fall he wheels the collector across the yard to his house and plugs it into his basement. "It makes the downstairs livable," he reports. "Delores, my wife, didn't want a collector built permanently onto the house, so I figured, why not build it portable?"

It would seem that instead of following the small farmer's first commandment, to make the most with the least, Control Data has been trying to impose the capital-intensive form of conventional large-scale agriculture on smaller-sized farms. My clearest sense of this conceptual failure came, oddly, on a visit to what appeared in most respects to be the Princeton project's finest farm.

George and Tammy Walker's place is set on a wooded hilltop a few miles northeast of the Pollys'. The Walkers do not need a scratch 'n' sniff to complete their education in hog farming. George raises feeder pigs in a small confinement building, and Tammy refuses to let him into the house with his barn clothes on. The couple are in their early twenties, the parents of a two-year-old boy and a newborn daughter. Tammy is slim, pale, and pretty. She works part-time as a bank teller to earn extra cash, and she unselfconsciously breast-feeds her baby as we talk. George is beefy and roughly cubical, the son of a Lutheran minister, and he spent four years working at the research farm of a big feed and grain company before coming to Princeton. The Walkers would make good neighbors. They are open and easy to be with, blending tolerance and conservatism in a way that often seems unique to farm country people.

Almost alone among the project's participants, Tammy and George offer unqualified praise for the mixed crop production plan. "It's been fun and rewarding," Tammy says, "and there's a great potential for income. We would probably never have tried the specialty crops otherwise, and I'm really glad we did." In addition to their regular crops of new piglets, the Walkers keep seventeen hives of bees and an eight-to-ten-acre market garden. Their vegetable patch is a testament to the virtues of diligence and the extraordinary potency of pig manure: innocent of weeds but unsullied by herbicides, it sports resplendent broccolis with main heads ten inches across, expansionist squash and melon vines, and basketball-sized cabbages resonant as kettledrums when thumped. Tammy says they're looking for one more enterprise, a small orchard perhaps, to round out their operation. More than any other farm I've visited in Princeton, the Walkers' seems to me to exemplify the practices and ideals that Bill Norris has in mind.

But a guided tour through George's pig house tells a decidedly different tale. George Walker keeps a hundred sows. He farrows ten weekly, and holds as near as he can to a ten-pig-per-litter average. He has ten farrowing pens, all full, all the time. The barn is plainly overcrowded, but George says he can't cut back. "If we were paying five percent of ninety thousand we wouldn't have to have a ten-sow farrowing room," he says. "But we're not. We're looking at better than three hundred thousand now." He allows that he doesn't much like the total confinement system either—one of his sows died during labor in last week's heat—but it's the only way he can manage that many animals alone. He is more generous than many of the project's farmers in his assessment of Control Data, but he faults the company for having poured in so much cash. A beginning farmer would not normally start with a quarter-million-dollar investment. George recalls having gone to the Farmers Home Administration in search of an operating loan. He was turned down flat, he says, on the grounds that no twenty-three-year-old first-time farmer should have a hundred sows.

George has had to hit the ground running. He has no time to explore different production techniques, or to look into alternative marketing plans, or to do much of anything other than crank out feeder pigs as fast as he possibly can. Listening to him, I realize that his is a depressingly familiar refrain: the lament of the farmer caught on the agricultural treadmill, compelled by his debt service to push his farm's resources past their limits. I'd come to Princeton with high hopes of hearing a new tune, but here instead was the familiar swan song of modern agriculture, sung in a minor key. The Walkers are good and good-hearted farmers, and I wish them all the success in the world, but somewhere along the way to their farm the Princeton project has gone badly astray. It has bought into precisely the sort of high-volume, mass-production-oriented agricultural philosophy to which it was supposedly an alternative.

On top of a two-hundred-foot tower alongside the Walkers' house, Control Data has installed a ten-kilowatt Jacobs wind turbine. The turbine and tower together cost the company approximately thirty thousand dollars, on which the Walkers are paying five percent annually, and which, George says, he could have come up with a few other ways to spend. On the way out to my car I stop to look at the windmill, idling along in a light evening breeze. It seems a grand ornament, like the statues that adorn the hoods of luxury automobiles. Watching the propeller spin, it occurs to me that Control Data's approach to small farms is a lot like Detroit's approach to small cars. The intent was never to make something genuinely small, but rather to produce scaled-down versions of large originals. So the subcompacts roll off the line loaded with opera windows and landau roofs, power seat adjustments, automatic transmissions, and air-conditioning. They are oddly proportioned freaks, like the knee-high horses favored as house pets by a decadent French royalty. It's hardly surprising that consumers are staying away in droves. So it is with the Control Data–style small farms. Instead of starting small and growing, they seem to have begun big and shrunk. They are advertised as bold new models, but they're not new models at all. They're only recast versions of the old one, squeezed into smaller containers.

9

REMODELING THE FARM

Eastbound on Interstate 70, just west of Willard, Kansas, nodding cross-country travelers drone past a billboard-sized homemade proclamation posted on a low bluff beside the highway: ONE KANSAS FARMER, the sign says, FEEDS 78 AMERICANS. The equation's sum has been painted onto its own individual shingle, like the hamburger box-score on a McDonald's marquee, to facilitate regular upward revisions of the total. For as long as anyone can remember, the number of Americans fed by a single Kansas farmer, like the number of hamburgers sold by McDonald's, has been steadily rising. The belief that this trend will continue indefinitely is a postulate of our national folklore. Growing suspicion that it won't, or more accurately that it can't, has spawned a host of troublesome questions, and prominent among the questioners is a native Kansan named Wes Jackson.

"Do you know about the gift of denial?" Jackson inquires. We have just loaded into the box of his battered red Chevy pickup its only spare tire, fully deflated, and we are about to drive into town, seven miles distant, to have the tire repaired. "I've got the gift of denial," he says. "I'll *never* have a flat on the way to town." This seems fortunate in view of the fact that even if a spare tire was available, the truck's jack has long since disappeared. The gift of denial, Wes Jackson goes on to explain, is what allows us our credulous faith in the endurance of the American food system. We ignore the warning signals of agricultural trouble ahead the same way we ignore the oil light lit up on our dashboard, convinced by the gift of denial that what we know *can* happen can nonetheless never happen to *us*. Wes Jackson calls our attention to the flashing lights. He has looked hard at the future of American agriculture, and he does not like what he sees. "It takes eight thousand pounds of fossil water to produce one pound of feedlot beef," he will typically warn. "Water sucked up from aquifers many, many times faster than the aquifers can be replenished. That's indefensible. We obviously can't go on doing that forever." It is characteristic of the man that having said this, he will pause a measured moment while his rueful grin blooms, then add, "But we're surer than hell going to try!"

It might be argued that the most valuable product of agriculture as it is conventionally practiced across most of the United States is a thriving crop of articulate critics. Of these, it's safe to say that there is no one whose criticism is as thorough—or as profoundly radical—as is Wes Jackson's. If Bill Norris has a vision of old wine in new bottles, Wes Jackson is looking for new wine. "Most of the analyses of the problems *in* agriculture do not deal with the problem *of* agriculture," Jackson writes in the preface to his 1980 book, *New Roots for Agriculture*. "This book calls essentially all till agriculture, almost from the beginning, into question, not because sustainable till agriculture can't be practiced, but because it isn't and hasn't been, except in small pockets scattered over the globe. So destructive has the agricultural revolution been that, geologically speaking, it surely stands as the most significant and explosive event ever to appear on the face of the earth."

Jackson's thesis is deceptively spare: the problem of agriculture, he says, is agriculture itself. He singles out for particular reproach two of the most firmly entrenched canons of conventional agriculture: tillage of the soil and annual grain crops. Jackson claims we'd be better off without either. Both, he says, are inherently destructive and wasteful, and are especially so when poorly or excessively used. They are poorly and excessively used more often than not, because the economics of contemporary farming force most farmers to consider production first and everything else second. The consequences of such skewed priorities are well documented: groundwater depletion, topsoil erosion, air and water pollution, not to mention the human and financial costs. "If we select corn as the symbol of our agriculture," Jackson has written, "we can say without exaggeration that corn, as a technological product, has reduced more options for future generations than the automobile." Our excessive dependence on tillage of annual grain crops, in Jackson's view, is the logical outgrowth of an agriculture modeled on hunting (or as he would more likely put it, on industry). Gathering, he argues, might make a better model. An agriculture modeled on gathering would reap the surplus from a healthy perennial stand without diminishing its ability to sustain itself.

What's needed, then, is a new model for agriculture, and to that role Jackson nominates the Great Plains prairie: a durable, diverse, mostly perennial mix of grasses and legumes. Until the relatively recent arrival (by geologic standards) of modern agriculture, the prairie had endured several centuries as a stable perennial polyculture, self-sustaining and productive. The Great Plains prairie is all but gone now, displaced by fragile monocultures of wheat, corn, or soybeans. It is this triumvirate, in one form or another, with which that solitary Kansas farmer feeds fourscore of the rest of us. We've turned the prairie upside down for bread, breakfast cereal, and, by way of a feedlot, for hamburgers. We have as a consequence come to lean heavily for our sustenance on those few annual feed grains, crops which, as Wes Jackson points out, in turn rely on us for their very survival. Whereas the prairie got along better when we weren't around, without our constant intervention on their behalf, corn, wheat, and soybeans as we know them today would quickly die out—clear evolutionary losers. From the perspective of the prairie, the highway billboard's boast must be seen as ill-advised bravado.

A hundred miles due west of that sign, on 188 acres alongside the Smoky Hill River in Salina, Kansas, Wes Jackson champions the prairie's perspective. Here, in 1976, Jackson and his wife Dana founded The Land Institute, "a nonprofit educational research organization . . . devoted to a search for sustainable alternatives in agriculture, energy, shelter, and waste management," where he now conducts a far-reaching investigation of potential replacements for corn, wheat, and soybeans. He does not propose to tinker with conventional agriculture in hopes that it might be improved. He proposes, instead, an entirely new agriculture. By establishing study plots of naturally occurring perennial plants and applying to them conventional research techniques—testing for yield, uniformity, and hardiness, then seeking improvements by crossing and back-crossing the genes of promising candidates—Jackson hopes eventually to assemble a sophisticated medley of seed-bearing grasses and legumes, combining perennialism with high yield in new grain crops that can be grown without annual tillage, and therefore without its allied drawbacks. What he's after is a sort of domesticated, superproductive wild meadow: a pasture that performs like a wheatfield. This is a concept without precedent in modern agricultural research. Wes Jackson, a trained plant geneticist and former university professor operating independently of the established agricultural research system, has set out to remodel the prairie. Since the publication of *New Roots for Agriculture*, Jackson's stock has steeply inclined among proponents of agricultural change. At the same time, while more traditional researchers insist that what Jackson has in mind is theoretically impossible, their rebuttals have seemed unusually subdued, as though they'd caught themselves wondering whether this guy might not be onto something.

The reformation according to Wes Jackson is rooted in topographical imperative. Of 316 million acres planted to America's top ten crops, 48 million, he says, are erosion-resistant flatlands. "That should be sufficient to produce more than enough food for direct human consumption, if only we'd cut out the cattle and hog welfare program." The other 268 million acres range from gently rolling to sharply corrugated, and all of them are prime prospects for conversion to perennial agriculture. Leaving aside for the moment the energy that would be saved by our not having to till and plant every year, erosion control is probably perennial agriculture's greatest promise. Tillage necessarily promotes erosion, and topsoil loss is arguably the most destructive side effect of conventional till agriculture. Even so-called low-till or no-till planting methods, though they minimize disturbance of the soil surface, still involve some sort of plowing that leaves the land relatively prone to erosion. Good sod, however, practically eliminates erosion. There is no topsoil lost from a hayfield. Sod retains rainfall, reducing the need for supplemental irrigation. Legumes fix essential nitrogen from the atmosphere, and deeply rooted plants like vetches draw nutrients up from the lower reaches of the soil profile, helping to keep soil fertility high without intensive—and expensive—chemical inputs. On sloping terrain, given the present rate of erosion, replacing corn, wheat, and soybeans with some kind of perennial grain crop would seem to be not just logical but urgent. The problem is that no such crop exists. Our major feed grains are without exception annuals. It remains for Wes Jackson to demonstrate the feasibility of something categorically dismissed by most plant geneticists: high-yield perennial grains.

The author of *New Roots for Agriculture* cuts a commanding, Brobdingnagian figure. Wes Jackson fills small rooms. He is a haberdasher's waking nightmare: thick-chested, broad-shouldered, and tall, with uncommonly long arms. He favors bib overalls, into which he seems to have been dropped from a height, like a fireman into his boots. An unruly thatch of chestnut hair falls insistently across his brow. When he laughs—and he laughs often—his big head lolls back to reveal an array of prominently splayed incisors. His laughter pours out in a rolling, infectious torrent, which should in no way be construed as abridging the seriousness of his purpose. "Somebody once asked me how I can laugh and carry on as much as I do," he recalls, "and I said to her, why, if I couldn't laugh I think I'd about have to give up."

Jackson matches his sense of humor with a rhetorical style borrowed from the revival-tent Baptists. He speaks in a potent, slightly nasal midlands drawl, salting his monologues with one-liners and Biblical references, and he sometimes comes across as equal parts country preacher and stand-up comedian. He has suggested with a more or less straight face that all Future Farmers of America, upon entering agricultural school, should be required to enroll in a course devoted exclusively to Goethe's *Faust.* "That way," Wes says, "when they go off to sign their herbicide contracts, or buy their new four-wheel-drive tractors, they'll at least understand the Faustian bargain they're making." Pressed to explain for the public at large exactly what it is he's trying to do, Wes Jackson will deliver what he calls his standard speech: "Herbaceous Perennial Seed-Bearing Polycultures as a Contribution to the Solution of All Marital Problems and an End to Nuclear War." Once, prior to an appearance at the New Alchemy Institute, Jackson received a telephone call from the Institute's then director, John Todd, who wanted to know the title of Wes's talk. Wes told him. There was a brief silence on the line, then Todd is reported to have asked, "Will you need a slide projector?"

"You cannot have a sustainable agriculture with conventional crops," Wes rules. We are standing at his kitchen table, armed with sharp knives and cutting boards, stripping sweet corn from the cob for freezing. Corn, of course, is a conventional crop—an annual, yet—but Wes displays no qualms about sustaining himself with it. He ingests two or three ears from every steaming colander that Dana deposits before us. The corn comes from Dana's garden, and is perhaps exempted from his fiat by virtue of having been grown in polyculture among dozens of other vegetable varieties, and on a small scale. "I make a distinction between the patch and the field," Wes says. It is possible to make almost any agriculture sustainable at the patch level, because the attention paid by the farmer to the process of farming on that scale is so very great. This helps to explain why the agriculture of China, practiced almost exclusively at the patch level, is still producing food after eons of intensive cultivation. When a farmer expands from patch level to the realm of a field or fields, his concentration unavoidably thins out. He begins of necessity to rely more on tools and technology and less on intuitive knowledge and intimacy. The character of his farming thus begins to change. If the Chinese vegetable patch represents one polar extreme, Central Valley carrot production exemplifies the other. "The central dichotomy, as I see it, is energy-intensive versus information-intensive," Wes says, poaching a mouthful from my pile of cut kernels. Chinese agriculture is information-intensive. "American agriculture used to be information-intensive, but it became energy-intensive. Now we're going to have to make it information-intensive again. There are two kinds of information involved, too—cultural information and biological information. But just look at the biology! If you took the information contained in the DNA chain for a modern cornfield and typed it all out, you might fill a shelf of books. The DNA from a prairie would fill all the libraries in the world."

Wes Jackson, I have decided, is information-intensive.

For the better part of an hour now, Wes, Dana, and I have been freezing corn and talking. We cover the usual topics: the fate of the earth, the relative merits of watermelon varieties, paradigm shift, the responsibility of individuals to society, whether freezing or canning is better for corn, whether cities, in the long run, are thermodynamically feasible. Wes seems unable to talk for long without slipping off onto tangents. He will interrupt himself while discoursing on one subject to pick up the thread of an entirely different discussion, dropped hours or even days earlier. He has been known to resurrect his previous line of thought in midsentence. We got talking one afternoon about the temperature in New York City during July and August, and how the heat lingered into the summer night. New York was a huge thermal mass, Wes determined, all that concrete and brick: the city as solar collector. He wondered then why that mass did not moderate winter temperatures in the city, especially since the colder and heavier air overhead then ought to serve as an insulating blanket, preventing the warm air from rising from the buildings. He poked at this problem for a few minutes until he got bored, then moved on to other things. Two days later we went for a late-evening dip in an abandoned and flooded sand pit on the Smoky Hill River across from the Jacksons' house. We were floating there in silence when Wes's voice boomed suddenly out of the darkness. "It's the solar angle," he exclaimed. "That's got to be it. The angle of the sun gets lower during the winter, so the thermal mass can't heat up as much." Then silence again, and splashing.

Wes Jackson is Kansas born and bred. He grew up near Topeka and attended Kansas Wesleyan University at Salina. He received a master's degree in botany from the University of Kansas, taught high school science for a couple of years, then took a three-year teaching assignment at his alma mater. He left in 1964 to get his Ph.D. in plant genetics from North Carolina State but returned afterward to teach again at Kansas Wesleyan. "That was the era of relevance," he recalls, and he says that he "became an environmentalist," then, altering the curriculum of his introductory biology courses to reflect current events and concerns. And it was then, too, that his unorthodox view of agriculture began to incubate. He realized, as he puts it now, that the thrust of modern agricultural science represented an attempt to understand and manipulate agriculture as if it were a separate and self-contained entity, wholly distinct from the biological world around it, and he was becoming increasingly persuaded that agriculture could only really be understood in context, as one part of a larger ecological whole.

While in the midst of his second stint at Kansas Wesleyan, Jackson, still in his thirties, was offered a full professorship with tenure at California State University in Sacramento. The position was a professional plum, and Wes took it. He lasted three years before coming back to Kansas. The job wasn't so bad, he says, but he deeply missed the plains. He and Dana had three children by then, and the longer they lived in Sacramento, the less they liked the idea of raising the kids there. The upshot was that in 1974 Wes took a year's unpaid leave of absence. "We honestly didn't know what would happen," Dana remembers. "We came back here and lived for a year, mostly on our savings and what we could grow in the garden, trying to decide what we were going to do next." One year stretched into two, and finally they faced a choice: either return to Sacramento or forfeit Wes's tenure at Cal State.

"We decided to stay," Dana says. "Somewhere in the back of our minds we'd always wanted to have our own school, and a friend here offered to underwrite the cost of getting one started." Before leaving for California the Jacksons had bought and built a house on a piece of land outside Salina. Now they would build their school there as well. What they had in mind then was a sort of living laboratory where college undergraduates could come for a semester or two to explore various ways of approaching the environment. The agricultural aspects were not yet so prominent at that point, and the Institute embraced a more general notion of "environmental education." This sounds fairly amorphous, and it was. What gave it substance was what had drawn the Jacksons back to Kansas and kept them there: a devotion to the land.

Seven years on, The Land Institute is a remarkable place. Everyone connected with the Institute customarily refers to it simply as "The Land." Part school, part laboratory, part farm, and part research center, The Land is nothing if not diverse. Like the domesticated prairie of Wes Jackson's dreams it exists in a perpetual state of evolutionary flux, one dominant idea begetting another in seemingly natural succession. As Wes's hypotheses began to mature, the work of The Land turned more and more to testing and trying them out. Graduate students have slowly supplanted the original undergraduates. Semester-length sessions have given way to a full-year calendar, and the staff now includes a plant breeder and several research associates. To the Jacksons' original 28 acres, another 160 have been added, and where once there were single specimens in the field trials of wild perennial plants there are now thousands. The Land is still loosely structured, and probably always will be: a certain looseness of structure may be essential to Wes Jackson's work. What he is trying to do, after all, runs counter to everything sacred in conventional agriculture. He is using the methods of modern agricultural research, but he has no use whatever for its goals. "Some of the worst examples of what's wrong with modern agriculture are produced by people with advanced degrees in agronomy," he notes. The search for an herbaceous perennial seed-bearing polyculture will not be launched from Iowa State or Purdue, and for good reason. "The agricultural research establishment at the land grant institutions is under a great deal of pressure," Wes says. "They owe their livelihoods to the continuation of the present system."

To appreciate the magnitude of Wes Jackson's challenge to the conventional wisdom it may be useful to detour briefly east from Salina, through Kansas into the Corn Belt. Corn is the undisputed king crop of American agriculture: a humble native of indistinct origins catapulted to international stardom by the efforts of American farmers and scientists. "A grain of good seed corn, planted in good soil, will produce five hundred to eight hundred grains three or four months later," marvels Wheeler McMillen in *Feeding Multitudes*. Many grains are planted. The worldwide corn harvest now approaches 500 million metric tons annually. Nearly half of that total is produced in the United States, and eighty percent of this country's crop is grown in the five Corn Belt states.

In late summer, when the corn is tall, corn country highways crossing apparently infinite fields are bracketed by two impenetrable green walls. Spur roads sometimes peel off the main route into veritable forests of corn, where cul-de-sac parking areas have been carved from the field. These are seed-company demonstration plots, marked with signs bearing the company's logo and a numerical code—3780, 3541—denoting the particular hybrid strains on display. Here farmers pull over for a look at the latest from the corn breeders' laboratories. Probably no other plant on earth has been given the sustained attention that corn has received from agricultural science, and the results have been spectacular: consistently improved yields per acre, better resistance to diseases and pests, specialized hybrids high in certain starches, in amylose, in lysine protein. McMillen quotes the florid testimonial of Richard Oglesby, a nineteenth-century governor of Illinois: "Aye, the corn, the royal corn," Oglesby rhapsodized, "within whose yellow kernels there is of health and strength for all the nations. The corn triumphant! That with the aid of man hath made victorious procession across the tufted plain and laid the foundation for the social excellence that is and is to be. This glorious plant, transmitted by the alchemy of God, sustains the warrior in battle, the poet in song, and strengthens everywhere the thousand arms that work the purposes of life."

Though corn is far and away our most important feed grain, its dominance has come at considerable cost—not only in the toll corn takes on the soil where it's grown but in its effect on modern agricultural research. The much publicized technological revolution in agriculture can tend to be somewhat misleading. In point of fact, American agriculture has evolved as it has more than anything else out of deep-seated resistance to real change. For all the countless thousands of scientists who have devoted their careers to the improvement of corn, there aren't ten who have considered with any seriousness the possibility of an alternative—who have wondered whether there might not be something wrong with our dependence on corn (and, to a lesser degree, on wheat and soybeans). The truth is that we have got used to growing corn, wheat, and soybeans—so much so that a sort of intellectual rigor mortis has set in that prevents us from thinking of growing anything else.

Most of us, anyway.

"I see the agriculture of the future going through two stages in the next twenty to thirty years," Rodale's Dick Harwood predicts. "The ultimate answer, I think, is going to have to be the elimination of corn and soybeans. If we could do that, we could solve a lot of our problems. Thirty years from now we really should be heavily into perennials. It's a far more efficient nutrient-cycling system. We're already taking our cereals apart and reconstituting them, so what does anyone care if their protein comes from corn or soybeans, or from vetch or Eastern Gama Grass for that matter? Who cares where it comes from, so long as it bakes into bread?

"So I see us going through a transition, not because we want to but because we're going to be forced to by the cost—all the costs, really—of conventional agriculture. The first stage will be the transitional period, where we stabilize our conventional production systems somewhat by using the herbaceous perennials as nurse crops, your interplants and over-seeded legumes and whatnot. Then I think we'll go more and more toward direct use of the nurse crops themselves, and eventually to perennial cereals. Wes says fifty years, but I think we can hurry that up. With the new genetic engineering techniques becoming available, I can imagine making the change sooner, maybe in twenty or thirty years if we really put our minds to it. And some of Wes's stuff is yielding two thousand pounds to the acre right now, which is getting pretty close to being economical in a perennial crop. If you grazed it for a few weeks and then harvested two thousand pounds to the acre with minimal production costs, I'll bet that's going to beat hundred-bushel corn already."

"If you worry too much about the time frame," Wes says, "you become immobilized. You turn into a doom watcher." It is morning, cool while the sun is low, and I'm out for a walk with the farmer through his fields. By any traditional measure, they are exceedingly peculiar fields. They're neat enough, laid out in nice straight rows and regularly looked after, but no corn, wheat, or soybeans are anywhere in sight. Instead there are weeds: lovingly tended weeds, to be sure, the healthiest-looking weeds you'd ever hope to see, but definitely weeds. Here are four thousand accessions of the six key native grasses, planted so as to find which ones show the highest potential for increased seed production. Here is an acre or more of Illinois bundleflower—roadside pioneer par excellence—basking in carefully cultivated splendor. Fields like these take some getting used to. If you can picture a stand of blue-ribbon corn growing voluntarily and unattended on the slope of a railroad embankment, you begin to have some idea of how unusual Wes Jackson's fields are.

"We're just starting to look at the biology," Jackson says, "trying to find out if high yield and perennialism are compatible. We're told flat out that they're not, that flowering plants can't do it." What they are theoretically incapable of is producing a substantial seed crop and still saving enough energy to survive. Plants have available only a finite supply of energy, and plant physiology dictates that making seeds and roots demands more energy than making leaves and stems. So if you breed for high yield in a perennial plant, traditionalists say, you're working to the detriment of the rest of the plant, especially its roots. In effect, you're selecting for annualism. To achieve perennialism, high yield must be sacrificed, and perennialism must in turn be forsaken for high yield.

Wes doesn't think so. He points out that conventional crop research restricts itself to the study of single species grown in monoculture (the cornfield), while he is primarily interested in polycultures: complex and interdependent plant communities in which succession is a crucial factor (the prairie). He will concede the unlikelihood of high-yield perennial monocultures, but in polyculture he perceives real promise. "Monocultures require our constant attention just to survive," he remarks. "Diversity succeeds. Look at what happens in a wheatfield after cutting."

"C'mon in here," Wes commands, striking out cross-country through a tangled herbaceous mass still dripping from a pre-dawn rain. "I've got something in here I want to show you." He points. Do I see that perennial bundleflower over there? I do not, but say I do. Like the proud mother who can pick out her son among all the cadets in a drill corps parade, Wes Jackson sees distinctions among weeds that elude the uninitiated. The bundleflower, he explains, is weed-dominant. The purple prairie clover nearby is not. While the bundleflower is thriving, the prairie clover is being choked to death by unwelcome invaders. In a successional polyculture, Wes tells me, the bundleflower might serve to pave the way—"like Saint John the Baptist!"—for a nitrogen-fixing legume like the prairie clover. What's more, he says, since native perennial plants have no known economic importance, nobody has ever studied their seed yields to find out how well they can actually do. On this score he savors small victories. Late yesterday afternoon, Marty Bender, a principal researcher at The Land, emerged sweat-soaked and dust-covered from the threshing shed to report that a sample of curly dock—a distant cousin to domestic buckwheat, harvested wild from the Cheyenne Bottoms in south-central Kansas—had a seed yield that extrapolated out to better than five thousand pounds per acre. Wheat, by comparison, at thirty bushels to the acre and sixty pounds to the bushel, might weigh in with eighteen hundred pounds per acre. "Of course it isn't edible," Wes admits, "but we're arrogant enough to think that we can breed for that. First we have to prove that perennialism and high yield aren't mutually exclusive. Then we can go shopping."

A good deal of Wes Jackson's shopping, when that time comes, will likely be done in the Herbary, a network of beds and walkways uphill from The Land's classroom building, where some three hundred varieties of native plants are reared in pampered privilege. Curly dock grows in the Herbary. So do prairie dock and intermediate wheatgrass, little bluestem, catclaw sensitive brier, soapweed, wholeleaf rosinweed, and hoary vervain. Wes Jackson's wild plants have superior names. The anonymous numbered hybrids purveyed by DeKalb and Pioneer Hi-Bred pale by comparison. Dense gayfeather. Thickspike gayfeather. Rough, smooth, and scaly gayfeathers. The Herbary is a storehouse of ecological capital. Goat's rue, plains coreopsis, sicklepod milk vetch. Asparagus and goldenrod. "I can foresee a time when someone developing a domestic prairie might want an early vetch, or a certain sort of tall Lespedeza," Jackson says. Roundheaded Lespedeza, prostrate Lespedeza, Stueve's Lespedeza, Japanese Lespedeza, and *Lespedeza daurica.* "I think of this as the kind of place that's going to keep suggesting possibilities." Hoary thick trefoil, panicled tick trefoil, woolly gaura and winebark. "Some of these plants might go into a mix in very light concentrations, for instance, because they're hosts for beneficial insects." Green sprangletop, light poppy mallow, white snakeroot, royal catchfly, bee balm, and black-eyed Susan.

Jackson acknowledges that most of these plants will probably have no part at all to play in his remodeled prairie. Standing in the Herbary at dusk, fending off ravenous mosquitoes, he contemplates the astonishing, tumescent, tubular purple bloom of a thickspike gayfeather. "Aw, I'm just keeping that one around because it's bew-tee-ful," he drawls. "It's not much good for anything else."

He keeps it around, one also suspects, because he is congenitally addicted to diversity. He expects one day to have a thousand plants represented in the Herbary. Because he is a long way from knowing with any degree of certainty which of those will prove indispensable to his plans and which immaterial, he is loath to relinquish any options. Jackson's love of complexity underlies his quarrel with conventional agriculture. The whole of modern agriculture's development, he accuses, has been aimed at limiting rather than expanding our options. "It's Baconian reductionism to the nth degree"—reducing the number of crops grown, the number of varieties within each crop, and the number of decisions a farmer makes during their growing.

The goal of modern agricultural research has been simplicity at any cost. For the purposes of removing weeds from a field, herbicides are no more effective than mechanical means, but they are a lot simpler. The chemical farmer merely has to spray his ground in the spring with a delayed-release, preemergence weedicide, and he's done his weeding for the season. A few very big fields are simpler to manage than dozens of smaller ones. One cash crop is simpler than mixed production. "Dana makes more agronomic decisions in our large family vegetable garden than most of my farmer neighbors do on six hundred acres of wheat and alfalfa," Wes says. Reductionism, in the form of cash crops like wheat, corn, and soybeans, is what has enabled farmers to farm thousands of acres, but it has also made them—and us—economically and biologically vulnerable. A simplistic system is far more susceptible to disruption than a complex one. "One of the virtues of a polyculture," Wes suggests, removing a mosquito from his forehead, "is that it presents insects with mathematical problems. In a polyculture a bug has to expend energy just finding what it wants to eat—energy that in a monoculture would be used strictly for eating and reproducing, increasing the swarm." The Herbary's mosquitoes seem to have these problems pretty well solved.

Some of the Herbary's constituents show more potential than others. Gama grass, for example, is a high-protein perennial relative of king corn. "It's an ice-cream grass for cattle," Wes comments. "Cows love it, which is why you see so little of it in pastures." You see plenty of it at The Land. To the left of the Herbary proper is a large plot of the stuff, four hundred accessions of *Tripsacum dactyloides* growing together in healthy profusion. The individual accessions are identified by numbered stakes, but it is impossible for an amateur to tell them apart. The patch is thick and luxuriant. Gama grass responds well to attention. It features exuberant foliage ("Look at that biomass!" Wes hoots)—clusters of narrow, cornlike leaves surrounding multiple stems, capped by heavy seed heads which when immature look vaguely reptilian, hard, and scaly, but unfold at maturity into feathery tassels. "Useful properties in some of the accessions are shatter resistance, male sterility, ninety percent seed fill, no seed dormancy, pollen and stigma exposed at the same time, high biomass production, and a large reproductive to vegetative ratio," a handy notice posted beside the plot discloses. By crossing gama grass with common annual corn and *teosinte*, a Mexican perennial closely related to corn, Jackson hopes to create a hardy and high-yield perennial corn analogue.

He has similar high hopes for sunflowers, marrying low-yield wild perennials to high-yield domestic annuals with an eye toward finding a happy and oil-laden medium. Perennial wheat, he says, is a distinct possibility, as is perennial rye. Wild senna, the object of much excitement and attention because of its extremely high seed yields, has no known use. "We're just looking for a high-yield perennial," Wes repeats. "At this point we really don't much care if it's useful to humans or not. We can work on that later."

The Land's program of horticultural matchmaking is carried out largely by resident plant breeder Walter Pickett, a slight, pallid man who patrols his test plots with Petri dishes and vials, leaving paper tape telltales on the plants he has visited. To accomplish the honeybee's legitimate business Pickett uses a delicate sable watercolor brush, shaking the pollen from one plant onto a saucer, then transferring it to the pistils of another with the soft tip of his Grumbacher No. 190. When he is out collecting seed, Walter wears a custom-made apron consisting entirely of tiny pockets. From every pouch on his front, a Kraft-paper envelope protrudes. They rustle as he moves, like the plumage of some exotic fowl.

"I've been emasculating sorghum," Walter said to me once when I asked what he was up to. He talks optimistically about crossing sugarcane with sorghum and Johnson grass—a weed whose perennial hardiness is all too well known to farmers—to make a winter-hardy, high-biomass, high-sugar-content crop for distillation into fuel alcohol. Sorghum, perennial but not hardy, might also be matched with Johnson grass—hardy, perennial, and noxious—to produce a perennial feed grain. One evening on the way home from a swim, circumnavigating the lush and weedy margins of a newly plowed field, Wes reflects on this possibility and reveals what for conventional farmers might seem a slightly alarming ambition. "One day we'll see this whole field in Johnson grass," he predicts, "or a Johnson grass–sorghum cross."

Wes Jackson is himself as complex and diverse as the prairie he so passionately praises. A self-proclaimed neo-Luddite, he is leery of technology's glittering allure. The Luddites, Wes opines, were not unwise in their approach to new technology—"putting their foot down on it first, then letting up slowly. I think there's a case for keeping our foot on computers awhile longer." But he is also a trained scientist, and is as such a technologist of sorts. He is, according to his close friend Wendell Berry, whose son Den spent a semester at The Land, "an example of a thoroughly informed, technically competent, practical intelligence working by the measure of high ecological and cultural standards—a specialist practitioner whose questions and criteria are not specialized." There is a paradoxical quality to this work: the technology of modern agricultural research put to the task of transforming American agriculture so as to lessen agriculture's dependence on technology. Jackson makes a point of distinguishing cleverness from wisdom. "Until we agree on a common environmental covenant," he says, "we'll still try to get by on cleverness, but we're too damned clever for our own good. What we are eventually going to have to admit is that we will never survive without wisdom. You don't stop topsoil erosion with the same cleverness that you use to build 747s. Building 747s and going to the moon are the consequence of big government and big business, and big business and big government are the direct consequence—and the cause as well—of the unsettling of America."

Straddling several worlds, Wes Jackson is a Kansan at heart, and Kansas keeps him honest. He is as comfortable trading practical jokes with his buddies out back of the Vickers station in Salina as he is with the "eco-stars," as he calls them, who gather for meetings of the Lindisfarne Association, William Irwin Thompson's free-ranging group of thinkers. Jackson imagines a "sunshine farm," where draft horses and photo-voltaic cells will work in tandem. "The idea that a horse is low technology and a tractor is high ought to be turned around. The horse is many times more technically sophisticated than the machine." Like Wendell Berry, Wes finds his agricultural heroes among the old order Amish. "The best models for a sustainable till agriculture in this country are the Amish," he says. "What American agriculture got convinced of, beginning in, say, 1946, was that a farmer should be a businessman. What the Amish said was that farming was the highest calling of the Lord. Now we find that those who made economics their god are the ones in the worst trouble, while those who put economics second—the Amish—have been making the best economic decisions."

Blessed with a farm boy's talent for improvisation, Wes is a masterful scrounger. Though he earned his Ph.D. in plant genetics, he has accumulated more than enough credits for a second doctorate, in creative salvage. A partial inventory of but one of The Land's many storage sheds would put a pack rat to shame. Wes once purchased two hundred sliding glass patio doors at an extremely favorable price, certain he'd sooner or later put them all to good use. Dana stakes the tomatoes in her garden with aluminum sills and jambs. Wes built the Jacksons' home in one summer, starting from scratch and drawing the plans on a Big Chief tablet as he went along. He later built the classroom building at The Land in much the same manner, this time assisted by family and friends—and when it promptly burned down he built it again.

The Land Institute operates on a shoestring, but the shoestring is black. Income accrues through student tuition fees, individual donations, and a smattering of foundation and corporate grants. One grant, from Rodale Press, made possible the purchase of a badly needed laboratory quality microscope. Expenses are kept tightly reined. Last winter, when more than $100,000 was needed on short notice for the acquisition of the new quarter section adjacent to the Jacksons' original land, Wes raised the money in just under two months. "He did it all on the phone," Dana recalls. "We had to put in a new line." What Wes liked best about that endeavor was the fact that most of the donors, even some of the larger ones, did not recognize one another's names. He had found the requisite funds without having to round up the usual suspects.

Wes seasons his conversations with "paradigm shifts" and "holistic understandings," but he is at root a staunch moralist, an enlightened Christian, and conservative in the best sense of the word. He is by no means a paragon of organic orthodoxy. He cools his home with fans and the fans are powered by windmills, but he has a weakness for jelly doughnuts, and he says he wearies of "long-haired, weenie-armed flower punks" who come round expecting adherence to their own rigid dogma. He wearies, it sometimes seems, simply of being Wes Jackson. "My problem," he complains as he tilts toward horizontal in a well used, tweed-upholstered La-Z-Boy, "is that I've got too many things to think about. I can't think about them all at once." Then he unexpectedly brightens, reminded of a favorite character from Monty Python's Flying Circus, the British comedy troupe, and drops his voice in a halting, psychotic impersonation. "Oh," he groans, "my brain hurts."

Beyond the classroom building and the Jacksons' low-slung, earth-sheltered house; past the windmills and the solar water heater; past the cow barn, the threshing shed, and the galvanized granaries that Wes picked up for a song, a small placard is set at the edge of an uproariously fecund strip of pasture.

"PRAIRIE ESTABLISHMENT," the headline reads. "In May of 1981 one-tenth of an acre was disced, and student Ed Newman planted thirty-seven species of prairie plants. The grass seed consisted of six dominant species: big bluestem, indian grass, little bluestem, switchgrass, side oats grama, and Canada wild rye. Some of the legumes were leadplant, wild blue indigo, Atlantic wild indigo, purple prairie clover, white prairie clover, Illinois bundleflower, and catclaw sensitive brier. Some of the composites were compass plant, black sampson, Kansas gayfeather, sawtooth sunflower, prairie coneflower, and stiff sunflower. Weeds were mowed once before prairie seedlings emerged." The most remarkable thing about this text is the last sentence. Farmers here would have difficulty distinguishing the rightful inhabitants of the Prairie Establishment from the weeds that were mowed to ease their passage. What his sodbuster forebears labored long to eliminate, Wes Jackson has diligently set out to restore.

The Prairie Establishment is just now ringing with the metallic rasp of thousands of thumb-sized grasshoppers simultaneously having lunch. They are skipping past the perennial plants, Wes insists, to nibble on "those nasty annuals." He plucks a stem of foxtail and plugs it into the side of his mouth. "You know what?" he asks, wading into chest-high switchgrass and Illinois bundle-flower. "We just might be the craziest sons-of-bitches there ever were. I have dreams sometimes of winding up like Lysenko or Lamarck." He chews vigorously at his cud, pondering the possibility, and then rejects it. "What I firmly believe," he finally announces, "is that if we can get high yields from a perennial cross for three years running, perennialism will be to agriculture what penicillin has been to medicine."

10

A THOUSAND TALENTS

May 3, 1981

Dear Tevere,

We turned the cows out on pasture for the first time today—the grass is just tall enough to wave in the breeze, that's how we gauge when to do it—and they went crazy. We opened the gate to the barnyard and they charged out with their tails up like flags, udders jouncing, bucking and hopping. They'd settle into a silly sort of rockinghorse canter, then put their noses down for a bite and suddenly remember: whee! it's spring! this is grass! and up the heels would go again. Not much milk tonight, I'm afraid. They'll spend more time running and checking fences than they will eating.

We've bought a farm, in Starksboro, north of Middlebury, twenty miles south of Burlington. The farm lies right in the village, but the land runs in a mile long strip back from the main drag, so the back forty's quite pretty and wild. Big old house, handily divisible in two, in fairly good shape; old barn in *rough* shape; two creeks; a sugarbush that's ninety-nine percent inaccessible; and forty-five to sixty (unsurveyed) acres of *fantastic* tillable land.

Hank and Cecilia moved over on April 1, have put up a greenhouse for their two thousand tomato plants plus assorted extras, plowed their ten acres, spread manure (ours) on it, planted strawberries, potatoes, onions, etc. We won't move over until May 15, when the cows can stay out all the time. The barn needs a lot of work before we can put them in it, and we have enough to do already: installing a whole new milking system in the milk shed, picking up trash, jacking up the barn, putting in a new hay seeding, building a new mow dryer, plumbing, wiring, painting, fencing, you name it—all of which *has* to be done before we move the cows over. We hope to get most of our first cut hay in by June 1, and we're going to try to get as many subsequent cuttings as possible, as much of it as possible barn dried. We've had to buy hay this year, usually of poorish quality as that's all that's sold, and we've been feeding a lot of grain. But grain costs are *high*, and with milk price supports weakening and our mortgage payments looming to boot, we can't afford to feed as much grain as we have been. So we'll have to put in fantastic forage to compensate for the grain cutback.

Finally I begin to feel like a real farmer, talking about all this as very immediately related to whether or not we can make our payments and keep the place, and how much there is left over for us to live on.

All very exciting. Come visit anytime.

Elizabeth

In September 1982, on a balmy afternoon caught in the cusp between seasons, I drive north through the hills of western Vermont. To my right the Green Mountains rise, partitioning the state lengthwise. To my left are Lake Champlain and the flat, fertile Champlain Valley—"Breadbasket of the Revolution"—and beyond them the great Adirondack massif, peaks banked like dark thunderheads on the western horizon. Traveling north, I pass from late summer into early fall. The leaves of oaks and maples are just turning, taking on a first hint of their autumn colors, and crystalline sunlight washes low and oblique over the fields at dusk. Northing I go through the fading day, through the fading season, through Rutland and Pittsford and Brandon, into Addison County, through Middlebury and New Haven and Bristol, to the village of Starksboro. To Lewis Creek Farm, Starksboro, Vermont 05487. Turn left across from the Post Office. It is a year since my last visit. There are lights on in the milk room.

"You're here," Elizabeth hollers when I poke my head into the barn. She is crossing from one rank of cows to another, her arms full of milking machines and hoses, a milking stool strapped to her behind. "You just missed the latest fight of the day."

I retreat to the milk room to pull on my boots. It's warm there, and humid, imbued with a characteristic sticky sweet aroma, like the smell of infant formula heating on the stove in a small kitchen. The room throbs with the compressor's dull roar. Milk surging into the bulk tank makes a soft, rhythmic, shushing sound—the sound of the sea lapping at a sandy beach. The swinging door to the barn claps open and Elizabeth jogs in, rinses something in the big work sink, and bangs out again. "Hello," she offers on her way through. "How'd you like to get hay down for the heifers?"

I go out and around to the mow, push several bales back through the hayhole, then jump down after them and distribute the fodder among calves and young heifers tied to a rail along the barn's east wall. Elizabeth and Philip are running late, only about halfway through milking. The barn is bright, cool, and noisy. There are thirty-odd cows assembled inside, giving up their milk. There is a radio playing; the cows listen to "All Things Considered" while their udders empty. They eat as they're being milked, inhaling messy mouthfuls of grass and alfalfa. When they've cleaned their own plates they steal from their neighbors. A cow at milking is a study in cyclical symmetry, synchronous consumption, and production on display. They defecate often and explosively, dropping ample deposits of loose, sloppy manure—summer pasture manure—into and around the gutter that extends the length of the stall row behind them. Now and again one raises her voice in mild protest over the indignities to which she is being asked to submit. "Mmmmmmuuuhhhhh," Ulita complains as Phil attaches the milking machine to her teats. "Oh, shut up," says Phil.

Milking in a stanchion barn is a kind of ritual dance, a ballet scored for thirty cows, four milking machines, and two milkers. The cows remain stationary while the milkers move in jig time around them. Phil and Elizabeth are everywhere in the room at once, removing a milking machine from one animal and fitting it onto another, snapping a hose off the overhead pipeline above one stall and clipping it on again elsewhere, now stooping to resecure a madly hissing slipped inflation, now squatting, supported by their milking stools, to provide a cow's ablutions: dipping her teats in disinfectant, washing and drying her udder, massaging each quarter until their owner lets down her milk, stripping a thin quick stream into the test cup, then attaching the machine and moving on. The cow, connected thus to one end of the American food system, masticates contentedly. Her milk is drawn out of her by suction, automatically, through soft rubber inflations into a plastic hose, into a stainless steel pipeline, into a refrigerated bulk tank, and eventually into the insulated tanker truck that calls at the farm on alternate days to transport milk to the local cooperative creamery. And thence into quart cartons or gallon jugs—or, as is true for most of the milk from the cows of Lewis Creek Farm, into the manufacture of vast quantities of mozzarella cheese, and onto America's pizzas.

"I don't like the look of Utica's mastitis. It doesn't seem to me to be getting any better at all."

"Have you done Annie yet?"

"I think I'll give the vet a call again tonight."

"Did the dry cows ever get fed?"

From the close of World War Two onward, the census of American farms dwindled annually. Average farm size nearly doubled as the size of the farm population was cut in half. In 1981, for the first time in decades, this decline was reversed. The number of farms counted that year was higher than the total for the year before. Not higher by much, but higher. There were eight thousand more working farms in the United States in 1981 than there had been in 1980.

One of these was Lewis Creek Farm. In the spring of 1981 title to the old Smith place on Lewis Creek in Starksboro passed into the hands of four young farmers: Hank and Cecilia Bissell, Elizabeth St. John and Philip Gerard. The four had formed a limited partnership for the purpose of buying a farm, and they'd spent the better part of a year searching for one to buy. They looked at a lot of farms. Some were too worn out to warrant serious consideration. Some were unsuited to one or the other of the partners' dual enterprises: dairying and vegetable farming. Some were simply too expensive. One otherwise promising candidate, endowed with decent enough cropland and a state-of-the-art dairy setup, was reluctantly vetoed on esthetic grounds. It was located just up the hill from a housing development.

They found what they wanted at last in Starksboro: a down-at-the-heels, run-of-the-mill Vermont dairy farm, hard-used over the years and somewhat the worse for wear. The farmhouse was huge and drafty, set back only slightly from the road, vaguely Victorian in style and sporting a wraparound roofed porch—the sort of porch on which, in winter, you might expect to see a pair of freshly laundered long johns hung out to dry and frozen stiff on the line. The attached ells and sheds were swaybacked, sagging, generally porous. A derelict and decapitated cement silo stood, or more precisely leaned, against the barn, and the barn itself had long since left its better days behind. The haymow up top wasn't too bad, though the floor and floor beams wanted some attention. The milking barn below was a disaster. The last farmer to rent it had departed some years before, and he'd evidently departed in a hurry. Of one hundred and fifty total acres offered for sale, sixty were densely wooded and so steep that even cutting the timber from them presented a formidable logistical challenge. The home pasture was bumpy and rough, grown over in weeds and scrub, showing the telltale signs of years of overgrazing and under-fertilization. Though the asking price for the property was not exorbitant, its drawbacks seemed so numerous that on first inspection the partners passed it by. Later, when they returned for a second look, they were struck by the farm's principal asset: a forty-five-acre piece of fine, level bottomland west of Lewis Creek. Better vegetable ground would be hard to find in that part of the state—or better feed and forage ground, for that matter. So Lewis Creek Farm took its place among the eight thousand.

The new owners were unusual in several respects, not the least being their determination to get into agriculture at a time when so many of their counterparts already farming were searching for some way to get out. None of the four had grown up on a farm, as most young farmers do, but they could not be considered neophytes. Hank Bissell, vegetable grower, is an architect's son. Elizabeth St. John, herdswoman, descends from a long line of secondary school headmasters. Three of the four got their first taste of farming from Putney School, a prep school in southern Vermont, whose students, when they are not academically occupied, supply the labor pool for a small, diversified farm and large-scale vegetable garden. Hank and Elizabeth are Putney alumni, and Phil spent a year there. Putney School sends quite a few of its graduates on to Princeton, Harvard, and Yale. It sent Hank Bissell on to the forests and fields of Vermont, to log over rough terrain with a team of draft horses, make maple sugar, and raise organic vegetables for market. Elizabeth St. John matriculated at the Sterling Institute, a sort of agricultural version of Outward Bound, and then enrolled for three years in the school of general agriculture at the University of Vermont. Philip Gerard, dairyman, was raised in an upper-middle-class family in suburban Westchester County, New York. By the time he moved his cows down to Starksboro from a rented farm in East Charlotte, Vermont, he had been working on dairy farms more or less full time for eight years.

Getting a new farm off the ground these days is no simple task. The U.S.D.A. estimates the cost of just outfitting a modest dairy operation—never mind buying the land in the first place—at close to a quarter of a million dollars, roughly twice what the partners have invested, all told, in Lewis Creek Farm. Economics, of course, are part of what initially prompted the partnership: neither couple could afford to buy and equip a farm alone. Working in tandem, moreover, meant that they could share not only their standing debt but their experience and expertise as well. Because their two enterprises were more complementary than competitive, having different but largely compatible needs, it seemed reasonable to superimpose two farms on one location. It was not to be one common farm—about that all concerned were adamant. What they had in mind was two quite independent efforts coordinated in a mutually supportive operation on the same place: a partnership but definitely not a commune. When the couples went looking for financing, they went separately, and this separation has been deliberately maintained. The partnership's paperwork is specific and labyrinthine. When Phil and Elizabeth want vegetables for supper, they buy them from Hank and Cecilia. When the Bissells want milk, they pay for it by the gallon. During the summer of 1982 the two farms jointly employed a hired hand. Caroline Herter worked three days a week for each, and took her meals for the day with whichever pair she was then assisting. Sometimes, in the evening, Hank would climb the stairs to Philip and Elizabeth's apartment to ask, "Could we have Caroline tomorrow, if we give her to you an extra day next week?" On the budget for Lewis Creek Farm, Caroline Herter appeared as a line item.

The partnership offers an elegant answer to the aspiring farmer's archetypal dilemma: how to get started on a farm without going broke in the process. What may be more significant, however, is the challenge it poses to the conventional American definition of what a farm *is*. In Europe and Asia, where very small farms are still the rule rather than the exception, farmers customarily reside in town and travel out to work in their fields every morning. They enjoy the efficiencies and social benefits of a close-knit village community while keeping their agricultural lands open and contiguous. The physical pattern of rural settlement overseas implies cooperation: the farmers' houses are clustered together and surrounded by their collective fields. In this country, by unhappy contrast, we have a rural settlement pattern that is implicitly divisive. Rather than build our farmhouses in compact towns at the interstices of our fields, we build them instead as far apart as possible, isolating each house at the center of its own individual holding. The legacy of the frontier, and some would also say of the combative Puritan approach to nature, is an American agricultural ideal of the farm as a fortress. This is less true in New England, where old-style farm villages got a foothold early on, than in the Midwest and West, which were settled by pioneers staking their homestead claims. In the popular imagination the modern American farmer has come to be regarded—and to an extent still regards himself—as a paragon of independence, ruler over his own land and free to do with it whatever he pleases. It does not often occur to him, as it naturally would to many European farmers, that he and his neighbors might enter into common ownership of costly equipment they all occasionally need. What in some societies is seen as productive interdependence is in ours more often seen merely as dependence. If you have any doubt about how deeply this trait is ingrained in our national consciousness, you would do well to visit a typical suburban street on the morning after a snowfall, where you will find two or three dozen proud and fiercely independent homeowners wrestling their own private snowblowers up and down the sidewalks out front of their own private homes. As a culture, we're not too keen on cooperation.

In our agriculture (and elsewhere) we have paid dearly for this aversion. The notion of two farms working the same land in partnership makes a great deal of sense. The cost of capitalizing each operation could be substantially reduced, since start-up expenses could be split and many major implements could do double duty, but there are other advantages. An often-heard complaint about organic production methods, for instance, is that too much of a farm's valuable cropland is planted to less profitable legumes, which must be kept in the crop rotation to sustain soil fertility. But with a dairying and vegetable-farming partnership, that legume hay could be put to good use feeding cows, while the cows' manure, composted, would supply fertilizer for nutrient-hungry vegetable crops. With prime farmland an increasingly scarce commodity, and with what little there is priced beyond the reach of most new farmers, joint ventures like Lewis Creek Farm's would seem a welcome and sensible alternative. So it is all the more discouraging to note the reception that such plans—or, indeed, any plans—for new small farms receive from those who are in a position to arbitrate our agricultural future. When Lewis Creek's partners sought financing from the Federal Land Bank, an institution whose sole chartered purpose is the distribution of mortgages to farmers, they were refused on the grounds that they were underequipped, undercapitalized, and underestimating their projected living expenses. "Underestimating!" Elizabeth fumes. "We were actually inflating our real costs because we were afraid they wouldn't believe us." Furthermore, it was suggested, there was no way that Hank Bissell could make money raising truck crops in Vermont. Hank had by then been making money at it for several years already, on borrowed and rented land. In his second season at Lewis Creek Farm, with eleven acres under cultivation and without benefit of a Federal Land Bank mortgage, he made approximately two thousand dollars an acre.

For the purchase of Lewis Creek Farm each partner chipped in 25 percent of a cash down payment amounting to just less than half of the negotiated sales price of the property. Ila and Leroy Smith, the farm's former owners, retired and living up the road, agreed to take back a mortgage on the balance. The farm is encumbered with a twenty-five-year mortgage at 12½ percent interest—one percentage point more expensive than a Land Bank loan would have been, but cheaper than the rates offered by commercial banks, and from the Smiths' point of view, about equal to what they could have earned at the time from investments in money market mutual funds. The terms of the note stipulate that the seller will hold the mortgage for five years, at which point the partners must refinance and pay off their debt to the Smiths in a single balloon payment. In effect, Lewis Creek Farm was given five years to prove itself.

"This heifer is definitely off her feed. Any ideas?"

"If the calves are still running temperatures in the morning, let's give them all another shot of combiotic, but first let's wait to see what happens overnight."

"Did you change the grazing yet?"

"No. Damn, I forgot. I guess I'd better do that before we let them out, hadn't I?"

Phil leaves Elizabeth with the last of the milking and takes me along to the lower pasture, on the far side of Lewis Creek, where from May till October the cows spend their time between milkings. In an effort to make the best use of their standing forage, Phil and Elizabeth have this year begun an intensive strip-grazing program. In a strip-grazing system, livestock are allowed to graze only in strictly defined areas, and they are moved onto new ground as often as once a day. Left to their own devices, cows in open pasture are surprisingly finicky eaters. They take what they like best and avoid plants they consider less palatable. This is what gives permanent pastures their hummocky, tufted appearance. Confined, cows do a far more thorough job, and moving them regularly guarantees that they will always be eating new growth, the highest quality feed. Strip-grazing enables a farmer to double or triple the feed value of his pastureland, reducing his reliance on baled hay and bought grain.

Strip-grazing can trim a farmer's feed bills and make the farm more self-reliant, but as is so often the case, it also demands more management. The condition of a strip-grazed pasture must be constantly monitored. If the grass is too tall when the cows are let out on it, they'll trample it flat and waste more than they eat. If it's too short, they'll go hungry and their milk production will decline. Carefully practiced, the technique can be incredibly productive. Some north-country dairymen can reportedly sustain their animals on strip-grazed standing forage seven months out of the year.

Ten years ago, strip-grazing was not technically feasible. There was no practical or economical means of changing the livestock's grazing zone as frequently as was necessary. What makes the system possible now is a remarkable product of agricultural technology—and a striking example of the kind of benevolent technological innovation that's so distressingly rare in American farming. Instead of having to string conventional heavy-gauge wire on fixed posts, Philip divides his pasture into paddocks with New Zealand fencing, an entirely new sort of electric fence named after its country of origin. The new fencing uses thin, flexible polypropylene line into which has been woven a single stainless steel strand. Strung on light stakes, it is electrified by a specially designed transformer that delivers its charge in intermittent bursts too brief to melt the plastic twine—or to short out the fence on weeds or branches. One worker with an armload of stakes and a reel of the line can enclose an acre in under an hour. It takes Philip and me twenty minutes to pull up the stakes surrounding the closely cropped strip where the cows have most recently grazed and move them to fence in a half-acre of lush, verdant alfalfa and clover. "It took me a while to get used to the idea of grazing this stuff," Phil admits. "It just looks too good to be grazed."

Phil Gerard is in his late twenties, tall, square-jawed, handsome in an offhand, slightly unkempt way. If he were not so powerfully built he might be described as loose-jointed. He is a film buff, and at the least indication of interest from anyone else he will drive into Burlington after evening chores to go to the movies. He is a voracious and indiscriminate reader (*Hoard's Dairyman*, *Newsweek*, the Alexandria novels of Lawrence Durrell). Elizabeth reports that Phil occasionally goes into the house to make a phone call, falls prey to the temptation of a book or magazine, and fails to emerge again for hours. During the years he spent apprenticing on dairy farms in northern New England, Phil was called "Doc," or "Professor," for his studious mien. His acquired knowledge of agriculture is voluminous, impressive not only for its breadth but for the degree to which it is grounded in experience. While he was still a student at a suburban public high school, Philip somehow got it into his head that he would one day become a farmer, and so he has. I have the strong sense that had he decided instead on a career in, say, space exploration, he would be strolling this evening not in his pasture but on the moon.

One night, as we washed the day's accumulated dishes, Philip explained the circumstances of his decision. After his initial exposure to farming at Putney, he'd spent the winter of 1972 working on a cattle ranch in Montana. "That was the year that hogs made their big jump in market price," he recalled, "and everyone was talking about how they should get into hogs. I remember thinking for the first time that it might be possible to make a living from farming. Actually, I thought I could make a killing. I figured I could get two acres somewhere and grow six hundred bushels of corn—I'd read in *Farm Journal* that you could grow three hundred bushels of corn to the acre—and then feed the corn to pigs. I think I had it worked out that I could make twenty thousand dollars on those two acres alone."

When we've finished the fencing Philip and I traverse the pasture to examine the progress of a field of corn he plans to chop for silage. Early this summer Lewis Creek rose past its banks and flooded much of the farm's prime land. Hank and Cecilia lost vegetable seedlings and nearly mature strawberry plants. Phil and Elizabeth's first-cultivation corn was under water for four days. There were brook trout swimming in the rows. The corn, a long-season variety to begin with, was badly set back, and it's still not ready for harvesting. Phil yanks an ear off its stalk and strips back the husk to reveal hard, yellow, neatly dented kernels. He breaks it in two to show off the kernels rooted deep, like molars, in a narrow, pithy cob. "This really is good corn," he says, half surprised. In another week or so it ought to be dry enough to chop, maybe sooner. He tosses the corn into the pasture, a prize for some lucky cow to come upon, and we turn to climb the long hill to the barn. The last glint of daylight has given way to darkness. Jumping the stream, I land on the other side in a patch of wild mint, and for a moment the rapidly cooling night around me fills with the sudden, sharp scent of menthol.

In the year following the nation's bicentennial, Wendell Berry published a volume of essays entitled *The Unsettling of America: Culture and Agriculture,* in which he reflected on the rise of modern industrialized agriculture and the decline of small family farms. The book is an eloquent and impassioned piece of writing: angry, accusatory, fiercely moral. In it Berry writes like a man with his back to the wall, granting no quarter and taking no prisoners. Indeed, he admits in his preface that his impetus for the work came with the realization "that my values were not only out of fashion, but under powerful attack. I saw that I was a member of a threatened minority. That is what set me off." The consolidation of small farms into large ones, the eradication of rural employment opportunities, the proliferation of strictly cash-crop rather than subsistence farms, and the resultant rise in influence, even in rural regions, of the cash economy—all these, Berry said, had led to what he termed the "unsettling" of America's farm communities, and had contributed to the creation of a concurrent cultural crisis. The villain of the piece, by the author's own assertion, was former secretary of agriculture Earl Butz.

The appearance of *The Unsettling of America* not only established Wendell Berry as the poet laureate of the new small farm movement; it cemented the public image of Earl Butz as industrial agriculture's chief promoter. In November 1977 Wendell Berry and Earl Butz met in a small auditorium at Manchester College in North Manchester, Indiana—thirty miles southwest of where Butz was born and raised, and a hundred and fifty miles due north of Berry's Kentucky home. The occasion was advertised as a debate on "The Crisis in American Agriculture." Butz began by denying that any crisis existed, and Berry talked more of values than crops and markets. "I have read *The Unsettling of America*," Earl Butz offered in his opening statement. "There are a few paragraphs in it with which I agree, not many. . . . We've learned to feed ourselves with a little manpower and a shirt-tail full of resources. Let's never forget that. I'm talking about modern, scientific, technological agriculture. It's a big business, to be sure. . . . Our challenge is not to turn the clock back. Our challenge is not to go back to more inefficient ways. Our challenge is *not* to put more people back on the land and therefore decrease the efficiency of American agriculture. Our challenge is to adapt to the changing situation in which we find ourselves."

On this last assertion at least, Earl Butz and Wendell Berry concurred. They surely did not agree on what form that adaptation ought to take, and they didn't agree about much else. "As I see it," said Berry, "the farmer standing in his field is not simply one component of a production machine. He stands where lots of cultural lines cross. The traditional farmer—that is, the farmer who first fed himself off his farm and then fed other people, who farmed with his family, who passed the land on down to people who knew it and had the best reasons to take care of it—that farmer stood at the convergence of traditional values, our values: independence, thrift, stewardship, private property, political liberties, family, marriage, parenthood, neighborhood—values that decline as that farmer is replaced by a technologist whose only standard is efficiency. . . . But these values are not just native to small farms; they're native to all small enterprises. And again by policy we've wiped these out—neighborhood grocers, little shoe shops. We have to drive forty miles now to get our shoes fixed. Maybe you're not supposed to get your shoes fixed anymore. Maybe you're supposed to throw them away. I try to get mine fixed."

What Earl Butz either did not or could not foresee was how fast the new agriculture he'd championed would become obsolete. The first wave of petroleum price hikes crashed onto America's shores midway through Butz's term, and except for an occasional leveling fluctuation oil and chemical prices have been rising ever since. So, too, in a tighter and more recessionary economy, has the cost of borrowed capital. The export market for American agricultural commodities seems to have wilted as quickly as it bloomed. According to a report in the August 30, 1982, issue of *Forbes* magazine, "The troubles of agriculture won't end if and when interest rates finally go down. Nor can they be solved by additional mechanization. All the glorious statistics about the productivity of U.S. agriculture, it seems, have become self-defeating. . . . There is no quick or easy way out—no more than for the sickness of the steel and auto industries or for the economic ills of the big cities. . . . At bottom the problem is very simple: American agriculture expanded because its efficiency, its high ratio of capital to labor, and the fertility and vastness of the American plains made it the logical supplier of food to the growing armies of the hungry millions. So the supply materialized but the effective demand never did."

In what must be the consummate irony for Earl Butz, who coined the repugnant concept of "food as a weapon," his own and subsequent administrations took that notion to heart and slapped embargoes on a variety of American commodities, with the result that foreign buyers learned to look elsewhere for more reliable supplies. An accompanying article in *Forbes* documents the success of the Japanese—once major consumers of American soybeans—at developing soybean production in Brazil following Richard Nixon's short-lived ban on bean exports, further undermining the position of the United States in world markets. Ten years after Earl Butz barnstormed through the Farm Belt proclaiming the dawn of an era of unlimited prosperity for the new American agriculture, the new agriculture itself is on the ropes.

But if Earl Butz's wishes have gone unfulfilled, so, unfortunately, have Wendell Berry's. In real terms, we are in worse shape now agriculturally than we were when Butz resigned; yet we are not much closer to adopting anything different. The failings of conventional agriculture are far clearer now than they were then, and the alternatives are better defined. But there has been no rush to begin making the changes that will be necessary for their realization, either within the agricultural sector or in society as a whole. We seem, in fact, to have fitted our blinders more tightly than ever. In early 1983 the Production Credit Associations of the United States, on the event of their fiftieth anniversary, released a report called *Agriculture 2000: A Look at the Future*. The document, prepared by the staff of the Battelle Memorial Institute, better known for their work in high technology research, includes these predictions:

> In thousands of agricultural research projects now under way, scientists are discovering new and better ways to grow crops. . . . Changes in marketing practices will be just as important as development of new technologies. Farmers must market omelettes instead of milk and eggs, ready-to-heat precooked chicken parts instead of whole chickens. . . . well-managed agribusiness firms will use a new mix of assets—more equipment, fewer buildings, more management dollars, better management systems, better paid employees, and more technically trained people. . . . Crop production will benefit from advanced seed treatment methods. Plant growth regulators are another avenue to higher crop yields, once their reliability is established. Salt-tolerant crop varieties are being developed for areas with saline soil and water. . . . More sophisticated tractors and engines are being designed. Some tractors will be steered by on-board sensors and computers guided by signals from buried wires. Advanced custom prescribed tillage systems and computer-controlled planting are also under development. Fruit and vegetable harvesting will become more mechanized, and future grain combines will transfer control responsibilities to the machine itself.

More than any other factor, what retards the transition to a more sustainable, more self-reliant, more regionally oriented and decentralized system of food and fiber production and distribution is apprehension over the enormous amount of additional labor that such a system would entail. This added requirement in itself would not seem a bad thing at a time when the national unemployment rate exceeds ten percent and when in some exceptionally distressed regions of the country fully a quarter of the citizens are without jobs. The problem is paying for it. The cost of food would probably have to go up. (There is some debate over whether it would have to go up very much, given the energy savings that would be realized through decentralization and decreased farm size, but almost everyone agrees that some increase would be inevitable.) The benefits of smaller-scale, more labor-intensive farming would be plentiful—from fuller employment to reduced environmental pollution—but even though Americans at present spend a smaller fraction of their incomes for food than anyone else on earth, they are in no hurry to pay more.

"Have you run across anybody who knows anything who's optimistic?" Wendell Berry inquires. I have stopped in Kentucky to spend a day with him at the end of a long trip through farm country, and I am submitting to an informal debriefing. Wendell Berry lives with his wife Tanya and their son Den in a neat white frame house overlooking the Kentucky River, on a piece of ground that escapes being vertical by only a few degrees. It is land well suited to sheep, which he raises there, and most capably worked with the draft horses that are his passion. "He'd like horses even if this was flat," Den says. I was greeted on my arrival by a gaggle of hissing geese. Den was sleeping in; Tanya was at church; and Wendell was in the woods, as is his wont on a Sunday morning, working at clearing. Over the past dozen or so years he has claimed back several acres of once badly eroded pasture from the scrub and trees.

The four of us eat lunch around a comfortable oak table in the Berrys' kitchen while I answer questions about my trip. Wendell is gracious, retiring, unfailingly polite. "A hill country drawl on the tongue of a smart man is a wonderful device," one observer wrote after listening to Berry lecture. "It gives him time to pick his words carefully; what he says comes out sounding relaxed, precise, and wise at the same time. Berry speaks with the pace of a farmer gazing over his land and spelling out to the hired hands what needs to be done, and in what order, to make the farm safe before danger comes, lacing into his instructions a few wry jokes to loosen them before the effort." We talk about the prospects for small family farms, and about the difference between hope and optimism. "I'm hopeful, I guess," Wendell says, "but I'm not optimistic."

After lunch we go out to the barn. The afternoon will be spent breaking two foals to the wagon. "Long yearlings," Wendell calls them—fifteen-month-old Belgians who have never pulled in harness before. "We'll see quite a bit of the country this way," he says. "I imagine we'll see some of it more than once."

We drive out at the rear of the barn, turn in a steeply sloped paddock, then meander along a narrow country road to the home of a friend some miles hence, where we reverse direction. We complete the circuit three times, once with each of the young horses working beside a seasoned mare, and once with the two fillies in harness together. "They're a ways yet from being a pair," Wendell concedes, "but don't they walk nicely?" He drives standing, reins looped over one wrist, legs splayed as if he were balanced on the pitching deck of a ship at sea. We pause now and again to converse with neighbors, taking on or discharging passengers. Powerboats sweep past on the river below, and the day evaporates under a high, hot sun. The horses settle down and acquit themselves well, and when we're done Wendell pronounces himself tickled to death.

Later, drinking cold water from the pump, Wendell returns to the subject of optimism. "The cause for pessimism comes out of realizing that civilizations have failed, in the past, because they've abused their land less than we've abused ours. The cause for optimism is that we know it's possible to do better. We can see that by looking at the Amish." It is in the old-order Amish and their horse-powered agriculture that Wendell Berry places his principal hope for the future. He sees in the Amish farms a model, a standard we might try to live up to as well as a repository of skills and knowledge that would otherwise be lost. "Working those horses today was more profound than anything in any of my books," he remarks. His fondness for horses is evident as he grooms and curries the fillies, speaking to them in the soft melodic and monosyllabic language that men use with animals, mostly vowels, but his interest extends beyond an indulgence of his own affections. For Wendell Berry the draft horse serves also as a symbol—as opposed to the three-hundred-horsepower, four-wheel-drive, air-conditioned, eight-track-taped tractors still coveted by farmers who can't afford them—of the agriculture we *should* have, and could have if we wanted it: an agriculture at once productive and adaptive, conserving of resources and human values, renewable, sustainable, thrifty, and dependent more on craft than on capital.

October 8, 1981

Dear Tevere,

It's been lack of time . . . that's kept me from answering your letter. . . . Any time taken from work at this point has to be paid for extremely dearly, in simple time lost, or lost powers of concentration (*you* go to bed at midnight, get up at five, shovel shit all morning, and then try to do fancy arithmetic!), or both. So although I am relaxing, I still find I can get literally sick to my stomach when I contemplate how much we have left to do, and how little time to do it in. The cows should be able to stay inside nights right now. Thirty to forty degrees and raining and windy is nothing a dairy cow ought to be out in, especially an old one. In all likelihood we won't have the barn done until November. Certainly we're already losing milk production. If we're lucky we won't wind up with any really sick cows, just lame feet from standing around in the cold and wet and deep mud, a few stiff legs and mild colds. But how they *hate* it! You have to beat them out of the barn after milking, into the rainy night. They stand around with their backs humped and won't even chew their cuds (and a ruminant who won't ruminate is in sad shape).

If we can dig up someone to hire, we will. Not having tried very hard yet, we haven't found anyone, but I'm not sanguine about our chances. Short term farmwork for low wages isn't exactly a high demand item. Left to do still: pour *a lot* of cement; weld up tie rails and dividers; put in water lines and bowls; install vacuum and milk lines, and a gutter cleaner, and pens and lights and fans; build a new grain bin and rebuild the end wall of the barn. And fall plow for next year's corn. And move hay from Charlotte for the heifers. And cut wood for the winter. And, and, and. . . . Chores take an awful long time, as you know. It would be great if we could find someone to help me with them, so Phil could work a full day on all the other stuff, and I could join him when the chores were done. As it is, we just get our momentum up, and then it seems it's instantly time for chores again. . . .

> Of course Phil wishes he were welding all the rails and dividers for the cows himself (we're hiring it done to speed things up). That kind of thing—doing things cheap for yourself, inventing clever methods of doing them, figuring it all out on your own and then scrounging up your own materials—is a very important part of farming for him. It makes him ashamed and unhappy and cross to see someone else doing it, and at a greater (visible) cost. But it's absolutely necessary at this point that we do anything we can to get the cows inside faster. . . .

This morning after chores Phil draws the unpleasant assignment of scattering quicklime over the carcass of a dead cow. One of their better animals, a high-producing Jersey, has committed a kind of bovine suicide. Or perhaps it would be ruled an accidental death. She was grazing in the upper pasture, north of the barn, foraging about for particularly tasty morsels, when she nibbled her way too close to the rim of a narrow gully and toppled off the precipice, backwards, breaking her neck and wedging herself inextricably into the tight spot below. It was several days before she was found. Elizabeth and Philip had consigned her to the coyotes, but a neighbor came by yesterday to report that the scavengers were not doing a very complete job. The decomposing corpse was rapidly ripening. Would Philip mind terribly seeing if he couldn't find some way to speed that process up?

I help him lift a hundred-pound sack of lime into the bucket of his tractor, and he drives off across the meadow, leaving me to go on with a job which has already consumed the greater part of one day. I am employed at a sort of coarse-grained agricultural archaeology. With pinch bar and pickax and heavy sledgehammer, I am attempting to unearth from beneath eight inches of old concrete two cast-iron corner wheels for an automatic gutter cleaner. A gutter cleaner is a wondrous machine: a chain-driven manure conveyor inset into a channel in the barn floor, it exponentially eases the perpetual necessity of mucking out the barn. Phil and Elizabeth still muck out by hand, having found neither the time nor the money to install a new gutter cleaner. Phil is slowly amassing the pieces he needs to put one in himself, and if he can get hold of these corner wheels he will be that much further along.

The wheels, however, will not give up without a fight. It seems there was once a gutter cleaner in the barn, but that at some point the previous tenant decided to change the configuration of the space, and as he no longer had any use for the gutter cleaner where it was, he simply filled up the gutters with cement. After many hours of pounding and chipping I have got down to the wheels themselves, frozen solidly in place, and it becomes apparent that the barn's former occupant, in his zeal to redecorate, declined even to run the system one last time before pouring concrete. I remove mummified cow manure from around the corner wheels. It takes a concerted and none too judicious application of cold chisels, penetrating oil, and pry bars to loosen and extract the wheels and the spindles and platters they turn on—all pitted and corroded, but still usable. Phil salvaged a gutter-cleaner drive mechanism when he renovated the barn—rusty but sound—and he says he knows someone who would be willing to let go of some chain for next to nothing. If he can locate a rebuilt motor he will have assembled the elements of a capital improvement worth several thousand dollars for a cash outlay of somewhat less than the cost of a single new corner wheel.

This is typical Lewis Creek Farm economics. ("The lifeblood of most small farms," says Penn State agricultural economist Patrick Madden, "depends on three things: off-farm employment, access to markets, and used equipment.") "You can't sell me anything," Hank Bissell claims. Philip and Elizabeth buy new only that which they absolutely cannot find any way to fabricate from cheap or free used parts—their new stainless-steel milking system being the most obvious of these exceptions, though even that contains a fair number of second-hand components. The roving equipment salesmen who go door to door in farm country do not profit much by calling here. At this farm the labor-to-capital investment ratio is unbalanced to the labor side so much as to practically eliminate the capital side. There are disadvantages to this approach, as all those present will readily admit. Philip, for instance, devoted six hours yesterday to trying to secure an inspection sticker for his venerable three-ton dump truck. (Fifties vintage, bought five years back for six hundred dollars and worth that much today, having in the interim hauled a few hundred thousand pounds of hay and livestock, sand and gravel and sawdust, lumber and sugar wood, and miscellaneous household cargoes.) "I've gotten to where I can see the sense in buying things new," Phil commented, his feet and ankles protruding from beneath the truck. "I feel as if I spent most of last year fixing old equipment, an occupation from which I receive no particular pleasure."

Acknowledged drawbacks duly taken into account, the fact remains that few convenient alternatives present themselves. Lewis Creek Farm could not exist without old and rebuilt equipment. Debt service on a full complement of new farm machinery would quickly break the partnership's financial back. Take tractors, for example. The farm gets by with two: Hank's ancient Farmall, in dire need of an engine overhaul ("You couldn't pull your hat off with it," says Phil), and Phil's more contemporary four-wheel-drive Long, with attached front-end loader. Phil has been weighing the possibility of selling the Long and replacing it with two used two-wheel-drive tractors, having discovered that he needs two tractors more often than he needs one tractor with four-wheel drive. If he proceeds with this plan, he will still have to have at least one machine with a front-loader on it, for manure handling and loading and unloading his bunker silo.

So what if the partners get fed up with their rickety and recalcitrant equipment and resolve to buy new? They might want to make a visit to their friendly local Massey-Ferguson dealer (the best-selling line of tractors in the world, third biggest seller in the United States, the only medium-sized farm tractors still manufactured in North America, and, Phil grants, "a very good tractor") for a look at what he's got on the lot. What they'd be shopping for would be three tractors in the fifty to seventy-five horsepower range, one of which would have to have a major attachment (the front-loader). For all three together they could anticipate paying somewhere between fifty and seventy-five thousand dollars, maybe more. At the same time they might understandably lust after pristine new implements as well. When Phil seeded rye into the rough meadow above Lewis Creek he used an antique ground-driven McCormick-Deering spade-planter, wooden-bodied, steel-wheeled, bought from a neighbor for twenty-five bucks. The machine was designed to be powered by horses, and when the neighbor converted to tractor power he sawed off the long wooden tongue and affixed a steel flange to the stub. To make silage, Phil calls on a restored one-row corn chopper (two hundred dollars at auction), and to improve the condition of his fields he fertilizes them from a used manure spreader (four hundred dollars) and stirs the fertilizer into the soil with a spike-toothed harrow (discarded as junk, free for the taking). Hank and Phil between them own probably a dozen operable tractor-drawn implements, for which they paid not more than five thousand dollars total, and whose replacement value at retail is, again, perhaps fifty thousand dollars. If they wanted to retire their yardful of second- (and third- and fourth-) hand farm equipment and buy new instead, it would cost them roughly as much as they paid for the farm to begin with.

One of the more remarkable things about Hank Bissell and Philip Gerard is that, not having had the advantage of an agricultural upbringing, they have nevertheless attained real mastery of that most valuable but most ineffable of the agricultural arts: undifferentiated handiness. There is a Japanese word for "farmer," I am told, that translates into English as "man of a hundred talents." It seems to me more like a thousand. The ability to make do with whatever comes to hand—a requisite for successful small-scale farming—seems to be something that cannot be learned but is, rather, a sort of genetically transferred gift, an innate ability, like telescopic vision or perfect pitch. Observing as Philip persuades his old corn chopper into serviceable shape, I am reminded of Sam Smith's altercation with his tractor, and of all the similar sad encounters I have witnessed between mechanical objects and mechanically disinclined people. Hank and Phil have overcome a potentially disabling handicap with grace and apparent ease—an accomplishment that I find nothing short of miraculous.

"I think we both realized that it was the only way we'd ever be able to get started farming," Hank tells me, and after a moment's reflection adds, "I think it's the only way *anyone* can get started." As he says this, Hank Bissell is up to his elbows in the chain-and-sprocket drive train of a battered one-row potato digger. I have come down to his and Cecilia's cropland to lend a hand with the carrot harvest.

"The carrots this year were a series of experiments," Hank says, "some of them profitable, and some not so profitable." First off, he explains, he bought pelletized seed instead of the less expensive raw seed. Pelletized seed is coated with a soluble glaze, making each individual seed a uniform size and shape. Raw carrot seed has the texture of beach sand, and cannot be mechanically planted with any degree of precision. Pelletized, the seeds drop out of the planter one at a time into a furrow, exactly spaced, eliminating any need for later thinning. Hank did not do much weeding in his carrots this year either, since he forsook his organic vows and sprayed. "I agonized over that," he allows, "but I finally decided to go with the herbicide. Nobody else seemed to care but me." He planted his carrots in hilled rows, using a potato hiller to form the ridges and a light roller to slightly flatten their summits. Because the rows were hilled, he can harvest this year's carrots with a potato digger—a distinct technological advance over the spading forks we used when I helped with his harvest last year. "We've put so little labor into this crop, it's ridiculous."

Hank grinds down the long row, the clattering potato digger in tow, churning up a variegated line of black and tan dirt, pale stones, crimson-orange carrots and emerald-green tops. Where the herbicide got a good set and there was no competition from weeds, the carrots are excellent: long, well-colored, tapering down from a broad-shouldered crown to a slender tip. Caroline Herter and I trail in Hank's wake, snapping the tops off and dropping the carrots into five-gallon plastic pails, then emptying the pails into feed sacks and lugging the sacks to the truck. Earlier, Hank had hatched a plan to circumvent one of these steps, the topping, by digging the carrots pretopped. His idea was to walk the row first with a weed-wacker, a lawn-trimming gadget that uses a length of monofilament fishing line spinning at high speed to mow down offending plants. He went up the street to borrow a weed-wacker from Ila and Leroy Smith, and he left instructions that if he hadn't returned in an hour we were to call up there after him. Leroy Smith has a well-deserved reputation as a marathon conversationalist. Visits with him have a way of becoming prolonged. Regular repetition of this pattern has produced a new verb, used, so far as I can tell, only at Lewis Creek Farm, and used there only in the passive. "If I'm not back in an hour, call," Hank had said. "I might get leroyed."

The weed-wacker, alas, was a failure. It left uncut two inches of carrot top that still had to be trimmed by hand. So we fall back on our original method. We have been picking carrots for nearly three hours when I look up at the end of a row to see Phil and Elizabeth's cows voluntarily climbing the lane toward the barn. I seem to have gotten leroyed myself. It's almost time for evening chores. I fill one final bucket, pour the contents into a feed sack, haul the full sack to the truck, then take my leave of the carrot patch and fall into step behind Toulouse, the dowager of the herd, an elderly Jersey named after the celebrated French artist because of her game leg. The cows wander into the barnyard and wait patiently to be let in, while inside the barn Phil and Elizabeth prepare anew for the familiar twice-daily routine.

The barn has been vastly improved since I was last here in late summer 1981, when the cows still had to be milked in small groups, ushered a few at a time into an improvised milking parlor, then escorted out again. Milking then was a frustratingly slow and laborious process. Now there is pipeline installed throughout and the cows can be milked at their stalls. With the notable exception of the missing gutter cleaner, in fact, most of what Phil and Elizabeth had hoped to have done in the barn is done: water lines and bowls, a weather-tight north wall, pens for the calves, steel pipe tie rails and stall dividers. Name plates are hung above each stall, giving its occupant's identity and lineage: Kali-Yuga's Noble Gloriana, for instance, by Kali-Yuga's Noble Diamond, out of Kali-Yuga's Glorious Mistress, or the somewhat less exotic Fescue, by Vermonter, out of Fatso. The barn in its new incarnation is well organized, freshly whitewashed, and a far superior place in which to work—or in the cows' case, to live. In the rebuilt north wall Phil has installed a salvaged casement window that must have done duty once in someone's house. One of its panes still bears an oval decal showing a helmeted fireman carrying a little girl to safety from a burning house. The legend reads: TOT FINDER. Elizabeth has crossed out the word TOT and written in HEIFER instead.

Milking is faster and pleasanter now, but it remains laborious and slow. Milking is the dairyman's albatross, the burden he bears in return for a regular and reliable income. Morning and evening of every day, seven days a week and fifty-two weeks a year, the cows must be milked. Phil and Elizabeth are in a quandary. The more time, money and effort they put into their dairy operation—either in the form of improvements to the physical plant, like the gutter-cleaner in the barn, or improved genetic quality in their herd, by artificial insemination of their best cows with semen from prize-winning champion registered bulls—the easier and more profitable the chore of milking will become. But that raises the difficult question of whether or not to continue milking. "It's the same old problem," Phil says. "If we're not going to keep milking indefinitely, or even for very long, how much should we invest in improvements that we won't be able to sell?" This seems to me to be representative of perhaps the most problematical aspect of farming: the constant mixing of long and short-term decisions. Agricultural decision-making involves a tentacled lattice of cause and effect that is almost impossibly complex. In farming, all long-term decisions necessarily have a short-term impact (as when a cash-grain farmer adopts an organic production system that idles some of his land, and so must forfeit a portion of his income). All short-term decisions also have a long-term impact (as when a cash-grain farmer plows down forty-year-old erosion-controlling windbreaks to increase the amount of corn he can grow in a year while the price on the export market is high). For a farmer, even the most basic decisions present a stiff intellectual challenge, obliging him to consider myriad possible ramifications stretching well into the future.

Neither Philip nor Elizabeth intends to go on milking cows forever, and in their rare idle moments they will speculate about alternatives. Elizabeth has proposed pick-your-own small fruits and berries. Philip mentions an orchard, the current crop of choice being plums, under-supplied and in demand locally. Cutting flowers are a possibility, or bedding plants, or specialty crops for direct sale. "Sugaring too, I suppose," Elizabeth says. "We'd likely try a bit of just about everything to get by." Minutes later, having thought on this, she somewhat defiantly amplifies: "But I'll be damned if I'll work in town for the privilege of living here. I want to find some way to make this place work, or else I'll go someplace else and do something different. I'll do relief milking for farmers around Starksboro, but I won't get a full-time off-farm job. I've always thought that my work and my life should be united. I mean, that's the point of all this, isn't it?"

"Plumbing," Philip explains from deep inside the cramped crawl space beneath the kitchen floor, "is a Latin word that means: uncomfortable position." Last night after supper, while we tucked into bowls of the season's first applesauce, a pipe burst, sending up a geyser of icy water. Philip's day begins with an attempt to splice a section of cast-off sap tubing into the sink's cold-water feed line, to serve as a temporary detour around the split section of copper pipe. Elizabeth is making breakfast—pancakes fortified with yesterday's oatmeal—and talking on the phone. She's trying to connect with the farm's veterinarian, in hopes of persuading him to stop by the barn this morning for a look at some bovine patients. It is Friday. Philip and Elizabeth have made tentative plans to leave this afternoon for Cape Cod, to spend the weekend at Phil's family's summer cottage in Wellfleet. If they go, it will be the first time in more than a year that the two of them have left the farm together for longer than twelve hours—the interval between milkings.

If they go. Their barn has begun to resemble an infirmary. Most of the calves have head colds. One of the Jersey heifers has gone completely off her feed and mopes about her stall looking miserable. Utica, a mammoth and until recently reliably durable Holstein, is battling her second consecutive bout of mastitis, contracted after she tore her teat on a strand of barbed wire. "Cows decide they can jump a fence," Phil says, "but when they get their front legs across they tend to forget about their hindquarters." The teat is swollen and pussy, and she has a 107°F. fever—near life-threatening, according to Elizabeth. "If she weren't such a tough old cow she might already be down." Phil and Elizabeth had intended to leave the herd in Caroline Herter's care, assisted at milking by a neighbor's young son who helps out often on the farm, but the mounting health problems seem to preclude that possibility. With the future of their vacation in jeopardy, Phil remembers an old friend in Burlington—once an aspiring dairyman, now in medical school—who might be persuaded to cow-sit for a couple of days. A flurry of phone calls ensues: to the vet, to the friend in Burlington, to Phil's folks, and the upshot is that the weekend away remains, if not a certainty, at least a possibility.

Farming, from the safe distance of a speculative daydream, exerts a certain romantic appeal. The romance abates considerably after a night spent sitting up with a dying calf. June frosts have a sobering effect as well, as do fields full of hay ruined by the rain, or tractor axles that snap during plowing. There is not much romance involved in the actual practice of farming at any level, and agriculture as practiced at Lewis Creek Farm—with no back-up capital and almost no margin for error—has as one of its predictable side effects a numbing, bone-crushing exhaustion. Two years into the partnership's five-year trial, the tension of continually living so close to the edge has begun to make itself felt.

The stress surfaces in odd ways: curt, clipped conversations where once there had been long talks; missed assignments and neglected details; domestic disorder of various sorts. Philip is prone to insomnia. Elizabeth bustles. She runs when she might walk, bangs pans when she might set them down gently, loses her temper. "Not much desire for anything," she wrote in one of her letters, "except not to be here—we've all played *that* game plenty lately: absent your heart and mind as far as possible from where your body's stuck." Isolation and frayed nerves have taken their toll, and the frustration is exacerbated by the inescapable sense that all small farmers must have, of being in an adversary relationship with the rest of conventional agriculture. "An occasional sunny day helps," Elizabeth wrote. "So does a sapwood fire in the kitchen stove." The partnership might help as well, but it's no panacea.

The vet arrives at eleven, steps into his jumpsuit and gum boots, slips on a fresh pair of disposable rubber gloves, and crouches low in Utica's broad shadow. He examines her wounded teat. Phil and Elizabeth stand by, anxious. "She's one of our best cows," Phil says. "She's never made less than nine hundred pounds of fat." (Later, when Elizabeth takes him to task for this slight exaggeration, Phil will defend himself by saying, "I always like to tell the vet how good a cow is, so that he'll stop to think of every possible remedy. Otherwise he may just look at the animal and decide she's not worth a lot of effort.") The doctor opens the teat and strips it clean, then bandages the infected area and prescribes an antibiotic to be given twice a day by injection. He briefly surveys the rheumy calves and says, "They'll live. I wouldn't worry too much about them if I were you." He considers the diffident young Jersey who's lost her appetite and diagnoses a probable case of hardware: a malady induced by the ingestion of nails, baling wire, or some other scrap of metal. The cure for hardware is a thumb-sized magnet dropped down the cow's throat, and extra bedding at the front of her stall, so that she will recline at a slight slope, the better to pass whatever is bothering her along through her stomachs to a less irritating position. "The darkest place in the world," wrote W. D. Hoard, a one-time Wisconsin governor and the founding editor of *Hoard's Dairyman*, "is the inside of a cow."

Starksboro's Baptists have lately installed an electronic carillon in the steeple of their church, and exactly at noon the taped bells ring out over the village. Phil and Elizabeth are now officially late, having passed their intended departure time. The vet has told them he can think of no particular reason why they should not go. There isn't much they could do if they stayed. Phil is reviewing the mechanics of the automatic milking system with Hank, so that he can stand in if the need arises. Elizabeth is making lists: for Caroline on the cows' dietary preferences (the menu for the dry cows in the upper pasture includes "one brook clean water"); for Morris, the medical-student friend, on the animals' prescriptions and symptoms to date; lists of everything from emergency telephone numbers to the accustomed mealtimes for Ben, the black Labrador, who will stay behind. Elizabeth is the sort of person who habitually underlines the key words and phrases in her notes. She underlines furiously today, in bold, decisive strokes, sometimes two or three deep.

At one o'clock Elizabeth is making an inventory of the milk-room medicine chest. Phil is welding a stack of half-inch nuts together on end to make a short length of threaded tubing, so as to render operable a portable bucket-milker in case the regular system fails for some reason. Both his and Elizabeth's conversations have degenerated into monologues made up of incomplete sentences that begin with the words *and if*.

"And if the calf's temperature goes over a hundred and three, you should probably call the vet again."

"And if the power goes out, you can milk with the bucket-milker run off the vacuum system on the truck."

And if the barn burns, call the fire department. And if the fire department doesn't respond, there is water in the brook and buckets in the shed. And if the buckets aren't in the shed, there are pots in the kitchen cupboard. And if the brook runs dry . . . I place a five-dollar bet with Hank that Phil and Elizabeth will call back to the farm at least twice before they reach Cape Cod, to add another *and if*.

Two o'clock comes and goes, and then three, and at a quarter to four Phil and Elizabeth finally pull out of the driveway and turn right onto Route 116, hoping to get to the bank before it closes so that they can deposit their milk check and withdraw enough cash to pay for the gas and tolls. Hank has been washing and bagging carrots in the shed. He emerges to wave good-bye, peels off his plastic apron, and sits down beside Cecilia on the porch. They sit quietly in the old glider as the car disappears into the distance, then Hank puts his feet up on one arm of the swing and lays his head in Cecilia's lap. "This is my vacation," he says. "I think I'll take it right here."

December 27, 1982

Dear Tevere,

We sold our cows. They left December 15th. I'd have written to tell you earlier, but the last two months have been so busy and tense, I haven't written to anyone at all.

You knew we'd always planned to sell the herd sometime—neither of us relished the idea of waking up one morning fifty years old, not knowing where our lives had gone to. In fact, last August, Phil brought up the idea of selling the cows next spring. He said he was approaching terminal dairy burn-out, couldn't get up the will or the energy to do a good job with them anymore, and couldn't stand doing a bad job. The idea upset me very much. I don't accept change (good *or* bad) easily, and I also couldn't stand the thought of parting with my *friends*. After we'd discussed the pros and cons for some time, though, and I'd had a chance to picture life without them (and how peachy keen that would, of course, be) I decided that it would probably be a good idea, especially if Phil was otherwise going to collapse.

So we called a cattle broker, in early November, just to find out what cows were going for, and to get some advice on what would be the best way to sell a small mixed herd. We were only sounding out the idea, and had no intention of going any further at that point. He said that cows were down, and that a mixed herd was very hard to sell, especially a small one. Generally fairly discouraging.

Then he called back a week later, to say that he'd found someone who was *looking* for a small mixed herd to buy right away. We had a week to think it over and decide whether we'd be willing to sell now, if the guy *did* want them. If we hadn't thought earlier about selling them next spring, it would have been a lot harder to think under that pressure. As it was, we said sure, come on up and have a look at them.

We brushed them and made the barn all pretty and waited with our hearts in our mouths. He liked them as soon as he saw them, was impressed with their records and how well cared for they looked, and how honest we were in describing each one. In fact he said before he left that he wanted them, and at our price (which we thought was a fair one for both sides, but which was also higher than we would have gotten at an auction—which was, in fact, better than most people have been able to get, according to the broker, by two or three hundred dollars each).

A lot of other reasons have come up, since we first talked to the broker, for our wanting to sell the herd. We turned out to be *very* short on feed—more than four thousand dollars worth. It's been a bad year for a lot of crops, and it would have been hard for us to find more to buy. We'd have run out by mid-February at the latest. As you probably know, the milk market is also doing badly now. Secretary Block assessed fifty cents per hundredweight starting in December and promises to take out another fifty cents in April if the milk surplus doesn't drop by then. It won't. Everyone will only make *more* milk, in order to keep up with their payments, and the bigger farms which can more easily add on more cows will do so, while the smaller dairies will have a harder time staying in business at all. We netted about $250.00 last year—almost all of our income went back into the farm, or into our nominal living expenses ($250.00 doesn't do much for a savings account. I guess you'd have to consider the farm as our account, and the herd. Not too stable). Anyway, the new milk assessments would have meant plus or minus four thousand dollars less income for us next year, and given last year's profits compared with how much feed we'd need to buy, you can see that would have squeezed us pretty hard.

We also didn't consider our herd a particularly good one to build on. Upgrading it through breeding looked unbearably slow; selling out and starting again (??? maybe? someday?) with fewer, more expensive cows, seemed like a better and faster route. It makes an enormous difference to be milking cows with better genetic potential for milk production.

So for a variety of reasons, we went ahead with the deal. We miss them. They were such personalities, such fun and interesting and friendly creatures. I know a lot of them better than I know any of my human friends (and like some of them a lot more than I like some humans). But overall it seems like a good thing. We've kept the heifers and calves, twenty-seven of them, and Toulouse, because he didn't want her and we didn't have the heart to ship her, as we did some others. We'll raise all these and sell them as bred heifers or ready-to-breed heifers next fall. (We are not planning to start again *that* soon.) This winter we'll both try to find at least part-time work, to help pay the bills. The interest on what we got from selling the herd will pay the rest. We've invested that money rather than paying the mortgage right off, partly because we want to be able to start some new venture with it sometime, and partly because we're not sure whether we'll be staying here or not past next summer. . . . It's hard to know where to begin to tackle the whole business, there are so many ramifications and variables, and at the moment it's almost impossible to see beyond the here and now.

To be a farmer is to be of necessity an optimist. Agriculture is at root an anticipatory enterprise, demanding of its practitioners an ability to look beyond the present into an uncertain future and see opportunities in the offing. A farmer plants seeds and looks forward to harvest, harvests and looks forward to selling his crop, sells and looks forward to the next year, when he hopes his situation might improve. "You can't farm one year at a time," Phil Gerard said to me one afternoon in his upper pasture, kicking contemplatively at a clump of thistles. "This field has been in permanent pasture for I don't know how many years. It's good ground, though. I think I'm going to turn it over next spring and seed it." No matter how mournfully a farmer may lament his immediate circumstances, he will hold out for himself the prospect of better times to come, the proverbial carrot dangled before the mule. Optimism, as much as sun, soil, and water, is an essential ingredient of agriculture.

It is impossible nowadays to spend very much time on America's small family farms without wondering if that crucial emotional resource is not eroding as surely as the topsoil from sidehill fields. At one Nebraska farm where I called, the owners had for some time been waging a protracted war with mounting debt and incipient insolvency. After the farmer had showed me around his place he excused himself to go back to work and sent me into the kitchen to meet his wife. She made me welcome, filled a Mason jar with iced tea for me to drink, then asked what my book was about. "The survival of small farms," I told her, and she chuckled. "It ought to be a mighty short book," she said.

It seems certain now that conventional large-scale agriculture, with its abject dependence on fossil fuel energy, its capital-intensive industrial technologies, and its devotion to high-volume, standardized mass production, cannot continue indefinitely to reign supreme in an economic and biological environment where adaptability, efficiency, and conservation are ever more important assets. We are entering a period of transition. Big agriculture is headed for eventual extinction because, like the dinosaurs of a previous transitional era, it is thermodynamically maladapted to existence in a changing world. Already some innovative if fairly specialized small farms have found niches in the marketplace that have been left overlooked or looked over and left by agribusiness, and by serving those markets have survived and even prospered. Unfortunately, for the overwhelming majority of small farms the suggestion that they will someday be uniquely well positioned to benefit from large-scale agriculture's inevitable dissolution must be tempered by the realization that someday may not come soon enough.

"In the short run I see a worsening situation," says veteran farm writer Gene Logsdon. "If we would just let the collapse happen, we might actually be better off. I think we might come into an age then that's far better in many ways than the one we're living through the end of now. We're all trying so hard to convince ourselves that the collapse won't happen, but it will. We can't keep it from happening. It's not a question anymore of whether the system will fail; it's a question of when."

As defenders of conventional agriculture square off against advocates of agricultural change in their ongoing and often acrimonious debate, Gene Logsdon allies himself unequivocally with the forces of reform. But he brings to the confrontation the perspective of a man who has fought on both sides. Over the past several years, as a regular columnist for Rodale's *New Farm* and the author of a shelf-full of Rodale Press books, Logsdon has become closely identified with the reformists' cause; but for nearly a decade from 1964 until 1973—during the glory years of the new industrial agriculture's ascendance—Gene Logsdon was a staff editor at *Farm Journal*, the closest thing conventional agriculture has to a house organ. He remembers his change of heart occurring slowly—not as a revelation so much as an incremental loss of faith.

Then as now, *Farm Journal* favored a style of reporting agricultural news that tended toward applause rather than analysis. The magazine was larded with flattering profiles of up-and-coming model farmers, which Logsdon refers to now as "Young Tiger" stories: testimonials to the American way in which Farmer Bob and his pretty wife Betty raise their family and build their farm up from nothing to a multimillion-dollar business before they turn forty, thanks to hard labor, allegiance to God and country, and the munificence of modern agricultural technology.

Logsdon wrote dozens of Young Tiger stories during his years at *Farm Journal*, and after a while it dawned on him that he had stopped believing what he was writing. The fabric of the myth had begun to unravel. At one farm whose attributes he'd been assigned to extol, he got up in the middle of the night to go to the bathroom and stumbled upon the Young Tiger awake at three in the morning, sitting in a straight chair, unable to sleep, nursing a caustic stomach ulcer. At another, the Young Tiger's wife told him that her husband was so tense sometimes that he couldn't keep his dinner down.

I drove out to Ohio to visit Gene Logsdon because I was curious about how someone who'd managed the switch from *Farm Journal* to *The New Farm* might view the future. "I expect we'll see a significant increase in very small, garden-scale farms," he said, "but I think there will always be big farms as well, and that's probably not such a bad solution. Moving back to twenty acres in the middle of the country is just *not* the answer for most people. I grew up milking cows and making hay, and let me tell you, do I remember when the first baling machine came along! What a wonderful thing that was! If you had come to me then and said that I shouldn't buy a baler because one day it was going to help big farmers put small farmers out of business, I would have laughed you right out of the field."

Most of the more credible blueprints for small farm survival, Logsdon points out, are predicated on the perpetuation of some form of large-scale agriculture to supply society's basic food and fiber needs, and to leave unfilled the niches into which adaptive and enterprising small-scale farmers may insinuate themselves. Like Sam Smith, Logsdon worries about what good those few small farms would do in the event of a more comprehensive food system failure—a possibility he refuses to dismiss. Gene Logsdon is stocky and bald, a gentle, sturdily built fellow whose broad grin and ready laugh belie the fact that he is also gravely worried. "I am surprised that you find anything genuinely encouraging in so-called alternative farming," he had written to me a few months before we met. "I find less and less, to tell the truth, but then I do not find much encouraging about anything except strawberries and maybe playing softball. We are an island here, surrounded by huge machines spitting violence and gaseous humors on the land, and opposing them I still see mostly rhetoric." Logsdon has lost a lot of his farmer's optimism. His extended forecast includes ecological as well as economic collapse, and violent social trauma. "I don't know any other way to predict the future than by looking at history," he says, "and throughout history those who have had the land have never let it go to those who didn't have it without violence."

Logsdon carried this line of reasoning to its logical conclusion in a column for *The New Farm*. "We're not going to begin to understand solutions to farm problems until we stop calling them farm problems," he wrote. "What ails farmers, ails all society." He takes up the theme again as we stroll over his farm, on a roundabout errand to the corn patch for past-prime sweet corn to feed his chickens. "When you ask what the problem with agriculture is, you're really asking what the problem is with human nature. The root of the problem is that we're all frail, dumb, greedy sons-of-bitches. We don't have an agricultural problem. We have an economical problem. Everybody's standing around waiting, as if we didn't know how to farm right, but we do! We do know how to farm properly, but we don't know how to make it make money. I've set myself up here as a spokesman for natural and organic farming, and yet I have to admit that much of what I see going on around me in conventional agriculture is absolutely necessary to farming in this economy."

He pulls a rusted corn knife from the ground at the edge of the field and walks down the row, chopping. He gathers a bundle of stalks and we shuck the ears from them, filling two big buckets. "Whatever we don't get, the coons will," he remarks. "And I hate feeding coons. They've got thousands of acres of corn around here to eat besides mine." He tosses the husks and stalks into the pasture, fodder for his cows and saddle horses, and we proceed to the chicken house with the birds' supper. The Logsdon farm is compact and diverse. Gene earns his income as a writer, but in a very real way he makes his living here. He has two cows for milking, fattens their calves for freezer beef, and sells surplus milk to his neighbors. His hens provide eggs and an occasional stew, and they share the coop with a small flock of broilers. The family keeps sheep as well, and markets their wool and extra lambs; raises a few pigs for slaughter; and tends both a large vegetable garden and a small orchard. Logsdon recently wrote a book on organic orcharding, and he says he's determined not to spray. "I'll find trees that bear well enough without spray, or I won't have fruit." He has rescued plum and apple whips from fencerows buried deep in the woods, and planted them out in his orchard on the chance that they might bear better, unsprayed, than common domestic varieties. He chooses to keep his own place rigorously organic, he tells me, as a matter of personal preference, but his quarrel with agricultural chemicals stems from larger concerns. "It may turn out that herbicides aren't so much of a problem ecologically," he suggests. "What's most wrong with herbicides is that they allow one man to farm five thousand acres and force out five other men who might have made their livings on five hundred."

Gene Logsdon is the only writer I have ever met who sponsors a summer league softball team, like an automobile dealership or a dry cleaner's. His squad is called the Country Rovers, after his column's byline, and they take the field in natty blue, white, and gold uniforms. Logsdon is their manager, relief pitcher, and utility outfielder. I sat in the bleachers one evening and watched as the Rovers hung on to a one-run lead and squeaked by their opponents, 8 to 7. After beer and pizza with some of the players, Gene and I sat up late into the night talking.

"You want to know what the problem is?" he asked rhetorically, sometime past midnight. "The problem is interest on capital. That's what it all comes down to. The standard measure of everything in American culture is profit. Anything that's done in this country now lives or dies on whether or not it will pay for a few CD's. I've tried to think of how it might be if money didn't earn interest," he confided, "and you know, I can't do it. I can't think it through. I just can't hardly imagine what that would be like."

The problem of interest on capital, Logsdon wearily acknowledges, is just too big of a problem—too complicated, too amorphous, too paradoxical. It is, as such, very much like the problem of reforming conventional American agriculture—a problem that for all practical purposes defies imposed solutions. Before we gave up trying and turned in for the night, Logsdon tendered a last horrifying anecdote. He has an acquaintance, he told me, a farm management consultant, who reports that a few of his more desperate clients have come to him openly discussing the possibility of suicide as a potential option—as if it were no more than some sort of clever legal maneuver.

"The small landholders are the most precious part of a state," Thomas Jefferson wrote in 1785. "Cultivators of the earth are the most valuable citizens. They are the most vigorous, the most independent, the most virtuous, and they are tied to their country, and wedded to its liberty and interests by the most lasting bonds." Jefferson in his time worried about the fate of the nation's small farmers, and his worries then were not dissimilar to Gene Logsdon's today. The next morning, Gene took me touring through the Ohio countryside to look at some of what makes him so worried, and to look, too, at something in which he finds reason for hope.

"We've passed four family farms already, and none of the four any longer supports a family," he said soon after we started out, driving south on a blacktopped county highway through a succession of flat, open fields. "All gone in my lifetime. They were all complete little self-contained units, all of them fully livestocked, each with its own small woodlot—all bulldozed over now for corn and soybeans." He took me past his own family's old home place, past what little remains of the woods where he played as a child, past newly planted groves of ranch-style suburban houses, indicating one by one the spots where working farms had stood. "This is what makes me sad," he said, "all of these places that used to be."

A few miles farther on, next to a fine-looking hayfield, he pulled his truck over into a rutted lane and parked. "Let's just walk out into this clover," he said. "I do believe that this is the finest stand of clover I've ever stood in." The field had been planted to winter wheat and harvested in July. Afterward, the farmer had broadcast clover and lightly disked it in. "And he's not an organic farmer, either. He's just a damn fine farmer, is all." A month later the stand was already eight inches tall, a thick and vibrant leguminous broadloom. Standing in its midst, Logsdon's existential gloom seemed momentarily to lift, as though a shaft of sunlight had cut through a coastal fog. "This is what makes me happy," he declared. "I've seen completely eroded farms brought back to pretty good shape in eight or ten years. So I suppose there's no cause for panic yet . . . at least not for *absolute* panic."

FURTHER READING

The Unsettling of America: Culture and Agriculture
Wendell Berry
Sierra Club Books, 1977

A thorough, thoughtful, and passionate indictment of modern agriculture's methods and goals, by a poet and part-time farmer who has emerged as the small farm's most eloquent advocate. *The Unsettling of America* is especially important for its investigation of the effects changing agricultural technologies have had on rural society in particular, and on American culture in general.

The Gift of Good Land
Wendell Berry
North Point Press, 1981

A wide-ranging collection of essays, most written in the years after *The Unsettling of America* appeared, many of them first published in Rodale's *New Farm*. The contents move easily from the practical to the philosophic, from private musings to public polemics. All of the pieces collected here are eminently readable. Some of the best are reports from the fields: on the admirable organization of Amish farms, on sheep and scythes and, most poignantly, on one young man's determined attempt to create a farm for himself on a piece of strip-mined land.

A Time to Choose: Summary Report on the Structure of Agriculture
United States Department of Agriculture
Susan E. Sechler, Project Coordinator
U.S. Government Printing Office, 1981

The crowning achievement and parting shot of former Secretary of Agriculture Bob Bergland, three years in the making and released on the eve of his departure from office. *A Time to Choose* reveals the findings of a no-holds-barred study of the inequities inherent in the structure of modern American agriculture. The research is extensive, the analysis rigorous, and the conclusions frightening. The choice implied in the title is between a broad-based system of small family farms, and a monolithic system dominated and controlled by a handful of corporations. The time for choosing is now. The report, theoretically available from the Department of Agriculture, has been almost impossible to obtain since the Reagan administration came to power.

The American Farm: A Photographic History
Maisie Conrat and Richard Conrat
Houghton Mifflin, 1977

Extraordinary historical photographs, accompanied by an incisive text, recalling the American agricultural scene of the mid-nineteenth century—a previous period of enormous upheaval and change. The pictures give us a glimpse into how the typically small, self-reliant farm of that day functioned, how it felt, while at the same time showing the tradition under siege by the first major advances in mechanization.

The American Cropland Crisis
W. Wendell Fletcher and Charles E. Little
American Land Forum, 1982

A clear, informative, well-written study of a crucial resource under attack from all sides. Fletcher and Little concentrate on the impact of development: urbanization, industrial sprawl, suburban housing, and so forth. Significantly, the authors look beneath the obvious transformation of pastures into parking lots and assess the subtler implications of reshaping a once rural region's demographic character. Case studies examine the differing situations of various communities, and the variety of responses undertaken.

Hard Tomatoes, Hard Times
Jim Hightower
Schenkman Press, 1972

The report of the Agribusiness Accountability Project's inquiry into the land grant college complex, this study is ten years old, and, sadly, at least as pertinent today as when it was first released. The Hightower report documents the deliberate expropriation by big agribusiness of what should be the family farmer's most valuable resource: the land grant agricultural research and extension system. That system's intent, almost from its inception, has not been to help the small farmer to compete more efficiently, but to eliminate small farms in the name of efficiency. This is sobering stuff. In many respects, it is the story of how we got into the mess we're in.

New Roots for Agriculture
Wes Jackson
Friends of the Earth, 1980

A rarity among analyses of our agricultural difficulties, *New Roots for Agriculture* suggests a possible partial solution. Wes Jackson is a plant geneticist who argues that much of the trouble with contemporary agriculture may be traced to its dependence on monocultural production of a few annual crops. Such a dependence is costly on every level, dangerous, wasteful, and destructive. A better course might be to emulate nature, designing perennial polycultures—like the Great Plains prairie—which might one day be made to yield as well as more conventional plantings. Jackson is deeply committed to this concept. His book is a progress report on the ongoing effort.

Three Farms: Making Milk, Meat and Money from the American Soil
Mark Kramer
Atlantic–Little, Brown, 1980

Kramer set out to tell the tale of American agriculture in transition, beginning with an uncommonly well-run family dairy farm near his home in western Massachusetts, then moving across country, through a hard-pressed Iowa hog farm, and on, finally, to a vast and utterly disorganized California corporate vegetable-growing operation. The author is an excellent reporter, with an eye for telling detail and a fine ear for dialogue. He is a very engaging writer. He is also a compassionate observer whose book raises a simple and troublesome question: how is it that skilled people, dedicated workers who are good at their jobs, and whose goods are in obvious demand, can no longer survive in our economy? That his book leaves this question mostly unanswered testifies both to the issue's complexity and to Kramer's admirable avoidance of pat rhetoric.

Feeding Multitudes: A History of How Farmers Made America Rich
Wheeler McMillen
The Interstate Printers and Publishers, Inc., 1981

The long-time editor of *Farm Journal* has compiled an exhaustive and adulatory account of modern agriculture's countless triumphs, and at the same time, unwittingly, of many of its failings. McMillen presents the evidence category-by-category, and he offers a wealth of quirky detail. One feature is a time-line listing great moments in American agriculture from colonial times up to the present. It provides a startling and unambiguous testament to conventional agriculture's priorities, and as such sheds considerable light on where we went astray.

Radical Agriculture
Richard Merrill, ed.
Harper and Row, 1976

Essays and position papers, some of them slightly dated now, by an assortment of authors who have in common mostly their desire to redirect American agricultural development. The arguments and proposals are diverse and of uneven quality. A few dwell on specific agricultural alternatives; others take up economics, sociology, and politics. Together they provide a good overview of our agricultural dilemma.

The Protection of Farmland: A Reference Guidebook for State and Local Governments
National Agricultural Lands Study
Robert E. Coughlin and John C. Keene, Senior Authors and Editors
U.S. Government Printing Office, 1981

Of the many important publications to come out of the multi-agency National Agricultural Lands Study, this is perhaps the most pertinent and pragmatic. It serves as a sort of cookbook for communities confronted with the loss of their nearby agricultural lands. With ample background information, detailed case studies, and extensive and careful instructions, it manages to offer hope and ammunition to those attempting to stem the tide, without understating the enormity of their struggle.

Farmland or Wasteland: A Time to Choose
R. Neil Sampson
Rodale Press, 1981

If development pressure constitutes one threat to America's continued agricultural productivity, misuse of the land still being farmed poses another, possibly more serious. Neil Sampson here takes a hard look at the implications of our abuse of limited resources. He is particularly concerned with topsoil erosion and irrigation, pointing out that if current practices in some of our most important agricultural areas continue unabated, we will very soon have exhausted our supplies of soil and water both. Sampson's book is well written and comprehensive. His findings and forecast are not encouraging.

The Myth of the Family Farm: Agribusiness Dominance of U.S. Agriculture
Ingolf Vogeler
Westview Press, 1981

Ingolf Vogeler assails one of the sturdiest fantasies of the American political culture: the belief that small family farms form the backbone of our agricultural economy. Politicians invariably insist that agricultural appropriations and legislation are intended to serve family farms. Vogeler shows just the opposite to be true, and he documents the sad consequences of that fact. He sorts out our true allegiances from our professed devotions, and in so doing charts the path of power and influence along which decisions are actually made.

INDEX

Index